Cuttings

Anne Underwood Grant

A DELL BOOK

Published by Dell Publishing
a division of
Random House, Inc.
1540 Broadway
New York, New York 10036

ISBN: 0-440-22553-1

Book design by Kathryn Parise

Printed in the United States of America

Published simultaneously in Canada

July 1999

10 9 8 7 6 5 4 3 2 1

OPM

HIGH PRAISE FOR
THE SYDNEY TEAGUE MYSTERY SERIES

SMOKE SCREEN

"Compelling . . . Grant's plot is both unique and timely. She writes now with the comfort of a seasoned author who truly knows and loves her characters, while retaining the freshness of a newcomer."

—*Times-News* (Hendersonville, N.C.)

"Sydney is engaging and brainy. . . . *Smoke Screen* is a cracking second."

—Mystery Lovers Bookshop

MULTIPLE LISTING

"A terrific debut! Sydney Allen Teague may be a single mom flawed by her past, but she takes control of her present with strengths that should make for interesting reading in the future."

—Margaret Maron, author of *Killer Market*

"A super ending tops off this series debut."

—*Publishers Weekly*

"*Multiple Listing* is packed with attitude. . . . Call it the Kay Scarpetta Effect, after Patricia Cornwell's character, but Sydney is a woman born to lead."

—*The Herald* (S.C.)

"Anne Grant's words pack a wallop!"

—Elizabeth Daniels Squire, author of
Is There a Dead Man in the House?

DELL BOOKS BY
ANNE UNDERWOOD GRANT

Multiple Listing
Smoke Screen
Cuttings

For Lynne Pou

ACKNOWLEDGMENTS

As usual, I've been delving into somebody else's business and have needed guides to walk me through. I want to thank the following people, without whom this book never would have flowered: Sergeant Rick Sanders of the Charlotte–Mecklenburg Police Department; Seana Corbeil and Ted Lewis of the Charlotte Convention Center; Garrett Rhyne of Rhyne Floral Supply for the contacts and the glue-gun lessons; Buff Moore of Todd's Flowers; Greg Damron of Floral Trends; Harold Blackburn of Hill's Floral Products; and, in no way least, David, Cecil, and the rest of the gang at Elizabeth House Flowers, especially the original Peg.

1

Joel Fineman had put such artistry into his casket spray that seeing him slumped upon it dead like this was a shame as well as a shock. He had fallen dead center, where his once erect calla lilies "pulled the mourners' eyes upward toward the heavens."

Those last are Joel's words, not mine. My name's Sydney Teague and I own a small ad agency called Allen Teague in Charlotte, North Carolina. "Small" is an overstatement in the case of Allen Teague. It's just an art director named Hart, an administrative assistant named Sally, and a salesman whose name changes regularly. And me, of course. I do whatever those three don't do.

Fineman wasn't my client, but I admire a good show and good design wherever I can find them. Joel Fineman always delivered on both. When he died, Joel was competing against two other designers in a Sympathy Competition. Floral designers are among the most competitive people I know.

This competition was one of the scores of events

happening during a three-day period in the middle of March at the first annual FloraGlobal Show, which had taken over the Charlotte Convention Center, all 850,000 square feet of it. Florists, growers, manufacturers, and international suppliers were all here in some form—as sponsors, as exhibitors, as event presenters, or as working florists, primed to learn something and make lists of things they covet. It was being sponsored by a new organization called United Floral Associates Symposiums, or UFAS. The acronym is pronounced with emphasis on the "U" and it sounds like the long "u" found in, well, "you." Allen Teague had two long-term floral clients, and we'd been hired by UFAS as well to create all the printed material for the show; design and build their show booth; and place the trade ads that had been running for the eighteen months leading up to it. How the crackerjack marketing crew with the Charlotte Convention and Visitors Bureau snagged this group I'll never know, but I was grateful they had. UFAS had chosen Charlotte first, then come looking for a local agency with floral experience and found only us. That's the kind of competition I like.

The Convention Center is so big that an exhibiting company can get lost in the sheer volume of its competition. That's where Allen Teague really could make a difference. We were helping showgoers notice our clients. Not UFAS. Their work was complete before the show began except for a few PR photo ops I promised to set up. I mean our floral clients who had products to sell. To that end, we were taking some pretty drastic measures. What Allen Teague lacks in size, we make up for in creativity. I value creativity above all else.

That's why I felt I had to resurrect those smashed calla lilies once the emergency personnel had removed Joel's body. Joel Fineman had been the dean of funeral arrangements, the only floral designer I knew who dared to bring a personal vision to what, for most florists, was perfunctory work: casket drapes and floral tributes. For Joel to die like this, in the middle of his motif narrative, would have horrified him. Dying, of course, was bad enough. But to destroy his floral creation, while losing his life, would have been unpardonable to Joel's way of thinking. A part of me thinks the same way, so even though Joel Fineman wasn't my client, I took it upon myself to try to upright his callas and return order to his creation.

The hundred or so florists who'd been watching, along with the design panel judges, had left the room as soon as the convention nurse announced she couldn't find a pulse. The two other panelists had remained, as had Peg Corbeil, a floral designer who happened to be my client.

The callas were a mess. Joel wasn't that big a man, but dead weight holds back nothing in a fall. Many of the flowers had broken just above the picks Joel had attached with wire to help insert the callas into the floral foam. The essence of Joel's design, its upward symmetry, was in jeopardy.

After the two EMTs rolled the gurney out the door, I mounted the stage and began frantically straightening stems only to have each one flop over again immediately. The two formerly competing panel designers stared at me. My actions must have confused the hell out of them because they both resumed their places behind their caskets and commenced to stare at me—as if I were going to continue on in Joel's stead.

Out of frustration, I glared at them both and said, "What are you two looking at? And what are you still doing on the stage, huh?" I pointed toward the door. "Don't you get that the competition's off?" I shook my head to shame them, then watched them begin to gather their belongings from the edge of the stage.

"What are you doing, Sydney?" Peg said as he joined me where Joel had stood only moments before. "You're crying. I didn't think you even knew Joel."

I hadn't known I was crying, but now I touched my cheeks and found them wet. "I hardly did," I said, "but I knew his reputation. This disarray would have really bothered him. He was a perfectionist."

Peg nodded, and without any more questions began to survey the ailing arrangement. "Here," he said as he held a calla stem before me. "Unwrap the wire as much as you can without losing its connection with the pick." He straightened the wire, then carefully rewrapped it in a lazy serpentine fashion up and around the bent portion of the stem. "*Voilà!* Unbroken. As if it never happened."

I nodded and did as he showed me to each broken stem.

"Only it did happen," I said as I felt new tears heating up behind my eyes.

"Now, now, Syd. Let me do some of those lilies." He took the one I was working on out of my hands and began to unwrap its wire. His fingers, though large and long, were nimble. Peg was tall enough for me, at five eight, to look up to, and his broad shoulders belied his artistic skills. He could have been an athlete if his interests had been different.

I fumbled in my blazer pocket for a tissue but couldn't find one. Peg pulled the perfectly starched cotton handkerchief from his sport coat's lapel and handed it to me.

"It's too nice, Peg. I'll ruin it. Then what will you do?"

"Twenty more just like it in my booth. You don't think the starch holds all day, do you? We designers plan for everything." His profile showed new flecks of gray on his thick wiry sideburns. His hair was even thicker than mine and so black that it sometimes looked blue.

I dabbed the handkerchief at my eyelids to dissipate the sting. I watched the two panelists walk across the room, open the door, then pause to look back at us. If I read them correctly, one still looked confused, the other angry.

"I'm sorry," I said to them both. "I shouldn't have yelled at y'all. Really. I'm very sorry." The confused one nodded. I took the nod as acceptance of my apology. The other one, the angry one, turned and left. I heard the door close as I was handing the handkerchief back to Peg. I sighed.

"He was winning the panel, don't you think, Peg? Joel's description of his work was far superior to the other two."

Peg nodded. "Sometimes all those flowery words make a difference with the judges. Sometimes they don't. Depends on the judges. Of course, Joel was one of the few sympathy designers who tried to work in some meaning as well as the ample expense they're known for."

I jabbed him with my elbow. "Don't be catty, Peg. From what I've seen, all of you make as much as you can off your arrangements."

"Most of us don't make our clients feel guilty if they don't go for our tops-of-the-line though."

"No, you don't." I smiled in his direction. "You just let them know their taste is poor." We both laughed, although my laugh was heartier. "Two basic human emotions to sell into, Peg," I continued. "Guilt and inferiority. Most of what we buy is a shield against one or the other."

Joel Fineman's presentation had truly been inspirational. He'd been the third and final panelist to explain the casket creation before him. The other two had sounded alike to me. They'd said nothing more than what each flower represented: the iris, faith; palm leaves, victory over death; a deep crimson rose, mourning. While their casket drapes were pleasing and their explanations logical, there was nothing special about either. Then Joel stepped onto the stage. A slight man, five six at most, beginning to stoop a bit at sixty-five, he opened his mouth and the velvet, melodious tone of his voice drew everyone's eyes to him.

"We are born into this world and crawl at best in the overall possibilities of the universe," he'd begun. As he said these words he'd stroked the variegated ivy—the variety with white margins, not yellow. Joel had placed the ivy so artistically within its thin strips of foam that it looked as if it had grown there from seed. Above the ivy, actually seeming to float there, was stemmed gypsophilia, or baby's breath, a flower more accustomed to the gaiety of weddings than the somber tone of funerals. When he spoke of death, he also referred to the gypsophilia and its flighty freedom from the "earthbound limits" of the ivy. He was building the drama little by little. "All of a sudden," he'd said, "we can see beyond the mind's eye. We can fly; we can float; we can see God's plan in the universe." And, indeed, the gypsophilia looked like clouds where angels might perch to view this life from a whole new light.

At this point in his talk, he was soaring. His plaid jacket came unbuttoned as he reached his arms around the arrangement to signify the world one's beloved has just left. His face had become flushed. He'd loosened his tie. I thought he'd done it for effect, the way preachers of certain denominations do, when they begin to look disheveled. He'd staggered back from the casket then, as if the emotion had been too strong for even him.

I was thoroughly enjoying the drama of it all. I admired his creativity, both in the design itself and in bringing it to life for all of us. As a finale, he looked from face to face in the audience, engaging us one by one in his big question. The question was: "Once we see it all, from all sides, everywhere, what do we choose to do?" He must have asked this question three or four times as he stared at us. The buildup was quite effective because by the time he whispered "You choose to soar!" the white callas that rose out of the midst of the gypsophilia seemed to be angels themselves beelining for heaven. Until that moment, I'd thought the other two caskets fine looking examples of floral design. At that moment, however, they looked merely decorous. Joel's work was organic, was life and death and the struggle in between, all played out on the three-foot-by-eight-foot box before him. Joel made death almost desirable.

He went on to explain how shape, texture, and movement release our primordial yearning for God, then began to describe the mourners' cathartic response to that release. That's when he fell over. None of us registered at first that he hadn't planned that too. Not even the ninety-five percent of those in the room who, as working florists, were there for a few tips. The florists knew instinctively that he wouldn't purposefully break his callas, but his spell over all of us wouldn't break easily. Thirty seconds went by before a woman in the front row said, "What's wrong?"

"There," Peg said as he carefully replaced the last stem he'd been able to salvage. "How's that?"

He couldn't see the calla that still lay crippled at my end of the casket. "Fine," I said, "except this one." I reached down into the gypsophilia and gripped the calla by its pick. When I pulled it out, a balled-up piece of paper came with it and tumbled to the floor.

"What's that?" Peg asked.

"I don't know." I handed Peg the calla, then bent down and retrieved the paper that was no bigger than a small index card. The card was wadded like a hastily crumpled piece of scrap one tosses into the trash basket at least twenty times daily. I held each side of it with thumb and forefinger, pulling it open as one would an antique miniature accordion.

A drop of water had smeared the first word, but still I could tell it was "When." The rest were perfectly legible, although their meaning was less than clear:

When Words Are Not Enough

I repeated the phrase to myself. Typical sympathy sentiment though it was, what was it doing all wadded up inside Joel's competition arrangement? Had it fallen out of his lapel pocket when he toppled into the callas?

I stepped down from the stage to get some distance from the arrangement. It was perfect again.

"It looks wonderful, Peg," I said from my place in the audience. "You've made it soar again. Joel would thank you."

A grin spread across his elfish, pretty features. He cocked his elbow, bringing the back of his hand up next to his face. He spread all four of his fingers wide, displaying his trademark stump where a middle finger should be. "Don't let it be said Peg Corbeil can't give the bird." His grin spread as wide as his fingers.

"You're a smart-ass, Peg. A silly, kind-hearted smart-ass." I grabbed my pocketbook from where I'd been sitting. "Let's get out of here and get some lunch, okay? I'm starving now that this ordeal's over."

He bounded off the stage with the resiliency of a twelve-year-old, although he was thirty-five if he was a day. Peg seemed emotionally untouched by Joel's death and I found that odd. I knew they'd been lovers eight or ten years ago. At least that's what someone had told me because Peg had never mentioned it. I didn't think it was my place to bring it up now, but the mother in me yearned to comfort him if it was true, to tell him it's okay to cry, to tell him I know how old loves own places in our hearts always. But he acted so unconnected to the man who died that I wondered if what I'd heard was exaggerated gossip instead of truth. In this town—Charlotte, North Carolina—people exaggerate the truth, too, so not much of anything is pure.

2

Hart Johnson is Allen Teague's art director and has been continuously since graduating from the local branch of the university. He's a mere twenty-nine years old, but he acts older than I do most of the time. I decided a long time ago that Hart has no interest at all in sex. Not with women or with men. Gay men find the artist in Hart very attractive, though. His delicate features, long, thin hands, and lithe way of walking have given false signals to more than one horny homosexual. Hart is shocked and upset whenever someone hits on him. In fact, he'd been concerned about working this show because the overriding majority of male florists are gay. In Hart's defense, he would have been just as wary if females were to come after him with the same verve as gay men have shown. It's not a prejudicial reaction on Hart's part. No, not at all. It's just a simple aversion to sex.

We found him in the booth of our other floral client, Garrett Floral Supply. Garrett manufactures glue guns, pick machines, floral ribbons, and straw wreaths, along with a host of smaller items that come and go according to trend and industry whim. The company's been in business since the dawn of man, or so it seems sometimes to me. The owner is one of the most cantankerous people I know and very hard to please as a client. For instance, Rhyne Garrett got it into his head that he wanted a "living" booth at this show. His idea of "living" was to place poor Hart inside it and have him actually painting the foam core walls and demonstrating the company products throughout the run of the show.

"I am not an exhibitionist, and I shouldn't have to do it," Hart had complained.

"No, you are not and, no, you shouldn't," I had agreed.

"How am I supposed to demonstrate his products?" Hart had asked me.

"I don't know," I'd said honestly. "Glue-gun tips? Straw wreath–decorating know-how?"

"I am not Martha Stewart."

"No, you are not, although the money would be nice."

But it was a good idea for grabbing passersby, and we both knew it. Poor Hart's tenure as showgoer bait was well under way at this point in the show.

As Peg and I approached the Garrett booth, I warned him not to pick on Hart. "He really can't stand it when you put your hands on him, so please don't do it."

He glared at me for a second, then turned his eyes toward the ceiling. "What's the big deal, Syd? You both need to lighten up."

We were snaking our way through two layers of observers. They all appeared spellbound by my Michelangelo with marker, oils, and pastels. "Just promise me, Peg. Otherwise, Hart won't want to go to lunch with us." He looked away.

I briefly examined the faux wall Hart was building and

could see that he'd already decorated a straw wreath and hung it in 3-D relief against its drawn counterpart. My hunger was overwhelming me now. We slipped inside the twenty-by-twenty-foot booth.

"What was on the piece of paper?" Peg asked without a trace of his momentary anger.

"Joel's paper?" I'd almost forgotten the crinkled card. "Nothing really. Trash." We were waiting for Hart to clean up as best he could without a water source. The old familiar small of turpentine stung my nose as Hart poured it liberally onto an old white T-shirt and wiped his hands and lower arms with it.

"Just trash? He must have been sick before the competition began." Peg was watching Hart with obvious pleasure while he talked to me.

"Why do you say that?" I asked.

Peg smiled widely, looked at me, then lowered his brows. "Joel Fineman would never use a casket spray as a trash can. A casket was Joel's canvas. It was art. And today's was for competition."

"Actually, it did say something, just not something meaningful. It said 'When Words Are Not Enough.' "

Peg looked deep in thought. "Is that all?"

I nodded.

"How trite," he said, and shook his head.

"I guess so." I hated to admit how hungry I'd become in those last thirty minutes.

"Something's not right there," Peg said, and bobbed his head in a conversation with himself. "Joel Fineman could be a lot of things, but trite's not one of them. If he wrote those words, he was sick then too."

"Who's sick?" Hart asked me as he stood at my side, eager to leave the booth. He looked hopeful that he might catch something and go home. I noticed he had not looked at Peg, almost as if he didn't realize Peg was standing on the other side of me.

"Joel Fineman," I said, "the great sympathy designer. He just fell over dead in the middle of the casket design panel."

Two large, vividly made-up women bumped up against Hart as we left the booth. One turned to him and gushed over his artistic talent. "I just love performance art," she said, turning to me. I nudged Hart past her nimbly as I smiled at both women; then the three of us walked through the crowd as quickly as we could.

"Talk about performance art!" Peg came to a sudden halt just as we were making our way beside the last of the show booths. I followed his eyes to the front of the oversized FloraGlobal booth where a small crowd had gathered.

3

I was particularly proud of this booth, which was roughly double the size of the largest of the others. One of the perks, for UFAS, of being the show owner. From a distance of twenty feet or more, as we were now, the front panels looked like simulated wood. That illusion was Hart's particular genius at work. If we were to move five feet closer, we'd begin to see that what looked like rough-hewn board-and-batten siding was actually newspaper and magazine ads, glued onto thin plywood and sealed with a sepia-stained varnish. I'd conducted the research to find the ads, a hundred years' worth of floral hype from archived newspapers and old standards like *Colliers* and *The Saturday Evening Post* to newer magazines like *Modern Bride*, *Florists' Review*, and *American Funeral Director*. Since UFAS as an organization and FloraGlobal as a trade show were so new, Allen Teague's job had been to make them look old. We have the opposite problem with companies that are, in fact, quite old. The Garrett company falls into that category.

Another advantage of show ownership was the height of these panels. Every other booth was enclosed by six-foot-high dark green curtains in the rear and sides and waist-high curtains on the front, all of which were unceremoniously attached to metal poles that crisscrossed above whole sections of the giant exhibit hall. Hart's foam core drawings along the side of the Garrett booth were an effort to personalize this antiseptic arrangement. The FloraGlobal booth, besides having double the area of all the others, had taller "walls" as well. Our ad-laden plywood panels rose ten feet all the way around. The overall effect of this facade was rustic storefront. The booths of all other exhibitors looked like booths. The entrance to the storefront was a six-foot-wide "door" opening and three-foot-by-three-foot sections cut out on either side to look like windows. Hanging from the window cutouts were lightweight cardboard windows boxes filled to overflowing with dried everlastings and silk greenery.

It was in front of one of these window boxes that Peg's eyes were transfixed. There stood two human cartoons, a bumblebee and a ladybug, pushing and shoving and calling each other names. The bee was a six-foot-tall black woman wearing spiked heels, black tights, a yellow-and-black-striped bodysuit that was fashioned of a fabric with the texture of cotton candy, a bonnet that fit like a bathing cap with two parallel antennae, and delicate wire-rimmed gauze wings on her back.

She seemed to have the advantage over the poor ladybug, who, for starters, was almost a foot shorter and a hundred pounds heavier and whose costume bore no resemblance to clothes. The poor bug's arms were constricted by straps, which held the undersides of a mounding black-spotted orange shell. Although the shell looked to be made out of light vinyl-coated Styrofoam, it was exorbitantly huge in comparison to the poor human who was wearing it. It spanned the whole body from the bend at the back of the knees to above the shoulders. The ladybug wore an orange bathing cap and orange tights covering the arms as well as the legs. The matching orange body suit would have been much more flattering had it been loose and fluffy like the one worn by the bee because the poor ladybug was truly obese. Whereas the bumblebee had one distinct hump at the chest line, the ladybug had rolls of fat, bulging from every inch of that body suit. Even among all those rolls, however, one thing was very apparent. The most obvious bulge of all was the one between the ladybug's legs. This bug was clearly a man. In spite of what normally would be a gender advantage, the ladybug was getting his shell whipped. The bee kept pushing him, and he wasn't fighting back. The assembled crowd was jeering and egging the two on.

I was stunned. Having these two insects at the show had been my idea. They weren't supposed to be here at the same time, though. At least not on the show's first day. We were trying to choose a cute UFAS mascot, one that could be used to identify a UFAS product or show. My idea was to build some excitement for the idea. A voting box sat inside those FloraGlobal antiqued walls where showgoers were supposed to drop their ballots during the run of this inaugural show.

I hadn't auditioned either insect. UFAS had done it themselves, thank God. Still, I could guess who'd be held responsible for this mess unfolding. The prospect made me fighting mad.

"What are those two creatures?" Hart said, then forgot to close his mouth.

"Hold this," I said as I shoved my pocketbook into

Hart's stomach. I ran to the scene, pushing aside by-standers to get through. The poor ladybug was lying in his shell, helpless to stand up, arms and legs flailing aimlessly, his more than chubby orange body rocking back and forth as rhythmically as a newborn in a bedside cradle. He looked like a flipped turtle. The bumblebee stood over him. Each time he rocked toward her, she drove her black vinyl heels into his belly.

"You fat, conniving fag," she screamed for fifty or more showgoers to hear. "I was here first. You take your damn pumpkin body outside and wait your turn. You hear me, fat boy?"

The bee was right about taking turns, although she didn't have to correct the ladybug so viciously. They weren't supposed to share the spotlight until they'd both had time to work the crowd solo.

The ladybug whimpered. He couldn't bring his hands together enough even to protect himself.

I reached the bumblebee just as she was poised to stomp on the ladybug again. "Stop it!" I yelled, and tried to grab her by a shoulder but was thwarted by one of her wings. "Stop it, please. You're hurting him!"

The bee turned toward me abruptly. I leaned back, afraid that I'd be the next victim of her sting. But the expression on her face was one of bewilderment and . . . oddly . . . hurt. Her right hand shot quickly to her left shoulder in search of her wing, which was now doubled over in the middle of her back.

"My wing," she said breathlessly. "You've hurt my wing."

That's when the ladybug chopped her in the calf with the side of his hand and brought her down. I jumped back for fear of joining the heap myself.

Just as a couple of showgoers were bending over these two sorry excuses for humanity, I saw a Charlotte–Mecklenburg policeman work his way through the crowd and take control of the wobbly situation. I recognized him as Jeep Ford, head of Special Security and a good friend of my friend, homicide detective Tom Thurgood. Jeep was close to retiring. His arthritic limp reminded me.

"Everyone move on," he said, then nodded toward me in recognition. I saw a slight smile on his face. I suppose the scene was humorous even to a policeman.

I helped the bee stand first and then the ladybug. The bee's wing was hanging down the middle of her back now.

"Where is it? Where's my wing?"

I pointed to her back. "Don't worry. You can't see it, but it's there." I smiled reassuringly.

She looked doubtful and glared at the ladybug.

"You heard me," Jeep was saying to the crowd. "Move on now." They began to disburse, but not as quickly as my UFAS clients would have liked.

I turned to Jeep and whispered loudly, "Can't you take them inside the booth?"

He nodded, then pulled his stick out and held it up in front of both insects. The haughty bumblebee threw back her shoulders as she extended her chin. She took three long strides toward the panel opening. As she passed me she glared. "I'll have your hide, girl, if this fucked-up wing keeps me from getting this gig."

"I'm going in next," Jeep said to the tattered ladybug. "I want you to follow me, you hear?"

And follow he did. Quite pitifully, I might add. The bee's heel had done its number on the bug's orange tights and bodysuit, creating stocking-like runs in several directions. Tears of pain and anger still clung to his bulbous cheeks.

Hart miraculously appeared beside me, Peg at his elbow. "This place is insane," he said.

"Where were you two during that? I could have ended up on the floor with the both of them."

"And been stung to death," Peg said between guffaws.

I retrieved my pocketbook from Hart and headed toward the Convention Center exit. I knew I'd have to deal with the mascot debacle after lunch, and it wouldn't be pleasant. On days like today, I wondered what had ever attracted me to agency work.

Behind me, Hart said, "Sydney, if you'd hired the Charlotte Hornet like I suggested, that never would have happened."

I was walking ahead of them both.

"Nice insect, that Hugo," I heard Peg say to Hart. "The mascot for the Charlotte Hornets, right?"

Hart was nodding. "Already trained too. He's a gymnast."

I knew Hart was going into all this detail for my benefit. I tried not to let on he was getting to me. "UFAS needs their own insect," I said with false serenity. "Hugo belongs to the basketball team." I stopped and turned to fact Hart, his face no more than a foot from my own. "Dammit, Hart, we've already discussed this."

He shrugged. "Don't think the competition idea's working out too well, that's all."

"I didn't audition these two," I said. I looked into his pale blue eyes expecting to feel anger and instead felt the tightness begin to seep out of my shoulder muscles. "God, what a morning," I said, and let out a sigh and then a weak conciliatory smile.

Hart stared evenly at me. He gave a slight nod as he said, "Fineman."

Peg had eased his arm around Hart's shoulder, probably thinking Hart was distracted enough not to notice.

"You can say that again about this morning." Peg quickly jumped into animated detail about poor Joel's demise. I walked briskly in front of him. I opened one of the doors leading to the Stonewall Street landing.

I looked back at Hart's expression as I pushed the door wide enough for all three of us to go through. What I saw was horror. Absolute and total horror. Come on, Hart, I almost said. Don't let Peg get to you.

But Hart's eyes weren't connecting with mine; they were straight ahead. And his horror was not because of Peg. I turned again to the landing and the steep steps that spilled down to the street and there I saw the focus of Hart's fear. At least fifty people—angry, pious people— were marching up and down those steep steps. All were carrying placards with some version of "God hates homo- sexuality" boldly written on them. They saw us, and two or three dropped out of formation to jeer at Peg and Hart up close.

I recognized one of them: a short, wide man with a beak nose, riddled with purplish-red veins. I knew him only as Curtis, a sometimes visitor to my Saturday night Alcoholics Anonymous group. He lowered his sign to a horizontal position and, using it almost like a jousting tool, lunged at both Peg and Hart. "The Lord will slay thee," he exhorted. Hart jumped back. Peg shielded him, keeping his arms firmly about Hart's shoulders. The sign Curtis carried said STAY AWAY FROM MY CHILDREN! I was staring at it when he recognized me. He pulled back, but only a bit. I think he was embarrassed that another alco- holic had caught him in a lie. I knew Curtis didn't have any children. And he knew I knew. I could see it in his blood- shot eyes.

I heard someone yell what sounded like a camera di- rection and looked to the street to see the van belonging to WBTV, Charlotte's CBS affiliate. A young female reporter was indeed directing a man with a camera to pull back from us and get the entire marching group again.

Hart wouldn't take his eyes off the ground. I knew he was mortified. Peg was doing just the opposite, defiantly, even arrogantly, staring into that sea of hatred. I grabbed Hart's hand, held it firmly, and led the three of us down the steps, past the van and away from that horrendous scene. We were almost to my Trooper when a woman in the group called out, "Stay away, you floral fags!"

"Good Lord," I said once I'd closed the car door. "What was that all about?"

"Gay hatred. What else?" Peg said it with boredom in his voice.

"But this is a floral industry trade show, not a Gay Pride convention," I said.

"Some of us were on the local TV last night. We're starting a gay florists' network. We went on to promote it."

"Were you on television, Peg?" I hadn't been watching.

"Yeah. I warned the other guys Charlotte wasn't the place for us to take our stand. They insisted." He nodded in the direction of the homophobes. "These distinguished members of society must have watched the nightly news."

Hart hadn't said a word since we'd left the confines of the Convention Center. He hates commotion of any kind and this commotion was major.

Peg was right about Charlotte. The town used to work so hard at its progressive image, used to be so politically correct in all its visible goings-on. Now, though, some of the far right wing was raising its head with a vengeance. More and more protests like this were showing up. Some of the right-wingers were even getting themselves elected. And they were particularly determined to quash what they saw as a growing gay movement in Charlotte. Poor

Peg. He must have had to deal with this kind of despicable behavior more than once.

"Floral fag," Peg repeated. He slid closer to Hart, leaving me feeling like a chauffeur. "I like that one. It has a nice ring: 'floral fag.' Almost like something you could buy at a show like this."

I held onto the rearview mirror to adjust it and saw Peg's expression when I did. He was smiling at Hart, an open, inviting smile. I tilted the mirror a little more so I could see Hart's face too. He was cutting his eyes at Peg with clear disdain. No way the recipient of that stare could misunderstand it.

"Where to, gentlemen?" I said, with mild emphasis on the "gentle."

We all confessed a need for something hearty. The temperature had fallen from forty-five to thirty-five during the morning, and none of us was wearing an overcoat. What had begun as a beautiful spring morning, complete with dew on the daffodils, was becoming something else. Peg suggested Mangione's over on East Boulevard where my office is.

I backed up beside the curb, then turned the steering wheel and put the Trooper in drive to pull onto Stonewall Street. I heard a horn honk and instinctively put my foot back on the brake. The coroner's van moved slowly past us. We all three stared as it eased alongside the Trooper, then in front of it and on down the road.

And I, for one, was thinking as it did: Poor Joel. He's really not soaring at all.

4

Mangione's has been a Charlotte fixture for twenty-five years. It has the reputation, at least among those of us who frequent it, of offering authentic Italian food, the kind that might be served in someone's home in Palermo on a Sunday afternoon or in a good New Jersey restaurant any day of the week. I like it, too, because there's nothing too cute about its decor. No Chianti bottles dripping with candle wax. No red-and-white-checkered tablecloths either. Just comfortable chairs at sturdy rectangular tables draped in starched white linen with soft cotton napkins. And, of course, there's Roberto Mangione himself.

Roberto greets me as if I'm a visitor in his home. He seems to be waiting just for me. He is a splendidly impeccable man, usually adorned in an Armani suit worn over a dress shirt with a thread count higher than my mortgage. Roberto Mangione is from Sicily, and even now, thirty years after coming to Charlotte by way of New Jersey, he will tell you he fled his homeland for love of the girl neither his family nor hers wanted him to marry.

"In Sicily," Roberto always says, "you do as the parents wish or you leave the country."

"Welcome back, Sydney. But where is your Tomasino?" Roberto pulled a chair out for me while Hart and Peg seated themselves.

"Can't I come here as just plain Sydney as I always did before you met Tom Thurgood?" I was teasing him, but only partially. Even out of the mouth of a man whose notion of Nirvana is being owned by his wife, the possessive pronoun is not my favorite part of speech.

Roberto smiled widely, nodded at the grinning Peg, and winked at Hart, who didn't see him. In fact, Hart had already picked up the menu.

"Did Tom and you eat here last night?" Hart asked with studied indifference, his face behind the long, laminated piece of printed card stock.

Roberto answered before I could. "And the two children."

"It was so good, Roberto," I said, "that I couldn't stay away."

"Your Tomasino. He is a lovely man. I am glad you have found him."

To tell the truth, I was too. In just about anyone's book, Tom Thurgood was a great find. Six and a half feet tall, good-looking in an angular, Irish sort of way with green eyes, deep auburn hair, and a long, thin face that squared off at the last second in a perfectly horizontal chin line. I hadn't been looking for a Tom Thurgood; nor he, someone like me. Except on the tennis court. For that most hallowed slot in his life, I do believe Tom had been consciously looking for a partner. Particularly a female partner. Tom Thurgood dearly loves mixed doubles.

That's why we'd eaten at Mangione's the night before. We were mapping out our drive to Savannah this weekend to play in the town's St. Patrick's Day Invitational Tournament. I'd promised Tom that if any United States Tennis Association sanctioned tournament committee was fool enough to seed us number one, I'd play in that tournament with him. Damn if those desperate people down in Savannah hadn't come through.

Roberto took our orders himself. Peg and Hart both ordered Mangione's specialty, osso buco, a fine veal shank. I asked for the veal scallopini and a side salad, exactly what I'd ordered last night.

After Roberto left, taking with him Hart's menu, Hart had no choice but to be with Peg and me. "When are you leaving for Savannah?" he asked me.

"As soon as the show's over on Friday, thank God. Don't worry. I'm not running out on you and Sally until I'm sure our laborers are going to show up. I figure it'll take us a couple of hours after it closes at noon to make sure our responsibilities are being met. Besides, the kids won't get home from school until three-thirty. Then we can leave." I was actually getting excited about the trip as I talked about leaving.

Hart smiled. "So, you're finally looking forward to it."

I nodded, fully realizing it myself for the first time.

When our meals arrived, we ate in silence, a tense and very full silence. It broke only when Roberto stopped by the table again, as is his habit, to ask if we were pleased with our selections.

"Exquisite shank, Roberto," Peg said. He held up the "peg" hand and made an "O," one finger off center.

Roberto leaned closer to Peg. "What trick have you performed to hide your finger?"

Peg straightened his four fingers to show Roberto there wasn't any trick. "No trick," he said. "No finger," he added cheerfully.

Roberto stepped back, holding his own hand over his mouth. He spoke through his fingers. "Oh, forgive me. Please, Mr. Corbeil, I did not mean to draw attention. I did not know."

I watched Peg smile. To "draw attention" was exactly what Peg used that missing finger for. "Roberto, let me tell you a story," Peg began. I settled back for this story he loved to tell. I knew Roberto would see he'd done the opposite of embarrassing Peg. He would see that Peg's missing finger was Peg's Purple Heart. What he was about to hear was no less a warrior story than David's recounting the undoing of Goliath—at least in Peg's sculpted mind.

Peg's given name is Theodore, but while Peg was young his anxious father called him Butch—hopefully, I am sure. When Theodore, Butch, Peg was in junior high, which was not long after I was in junior high, some educational requirements fell along gender lines. As the State of North Carolina had mandated it, Butch was toiling away in shop class, miserable and envious of the girls across the hall who were decorating cookies.

"It was Easter," I interjected. "The cookies were pastel, shaped like rabbits and chickens."

Peg straightened up dramatically, swiveled his head in my direction, and let me know without a word that my interruption displeased him terribly. All mock, of course. Peg dances around seriousness but never lands on it.

Roberto stood beside my chair, across from Peg. His stance was respectful, almost military in the attention he was giving. I eased back into the chair. I wondered how Roberto was going to take this.

While the girls were making exquisite cookies, the boys were making drab mailboxes, Peg explained. "Nothing like the gorgeous mailboxes you can buy today. No interesting shapes, no faux birdhouses, not even curved tops." He raised just one eyebrow and dropped the corners of his mouth down into his chin as he leaned toward a rapt Roberto. "In those days, Roberto, my dear man, one was not allowed to follow one's heart. I may as well have been in Sicily for the choices given me as a young man."

Roberto was nodding. He thought he understood and could identify with Peg. Poor man. He was trying so hard.

Hart yawned. He'd heard this story before, although not as many times as I had.

"You see, Roberto," Peg continued, "I wanted to take home ec. I told them the infernal buzzing of the saws gave me a headache." He paused.

I peered up at Roberto to see how he was taking the story so far. His expression hadn't changed: The man was rapt. I dabbed my mouth with my napkin, picked up my fork, and pushed half a black olive around on my salad plate until hooking it with a lone prong and bringing it to my mouth. Settle back, Sydney.

Peg breathed deeply, an exaggerated breath, and continued: "They told me they wouldn't authorize such an unseemly request, but if my father would, they would go along. My sainted mother died when I was but an infant." He sighed long and loud, while looking into Roberto's eyes. "So, I went to my father and begged him to authorize my transfer. I said, 'Dad, I love everything the girls do. I want to make those cookies. When they sewed aprons, I wanted to join them then; but you wouldn't let me.'

"My father said, 'It wasn't good for you, Butch.'

"So, just to spite him, I told him I made clothes all the time. I told him I used my mother's old sewing machine and had ten finished aprons in my bedroom closet if he wanted to see them. Part of that was the truth. Only the number was an exaggeration. I had two aprons, not ten.

"I guess I should have known he wouldn't be proud. It wasn't something he encouraged 'Butch' to do, but still I didn't expect him to go off the deep end the way he did."

"So he didn't let you?" Roberto had been pulled in.

"Ha! Not my macho father. Not only did he not let me, but he also told me what he really thought of his pretty, motherless boy. He screamed at me. He said, 'No son of mine's going to be a fairy. You will stop all this crap at once.' My father retrieved my mother's sewing machine from under the kitchen counter and carried it out the back door and threw it into one of the large garbage containers. I walked to the kitchen window and watched him. Father continued on into our backyard and trampled my tulips and daffodils. I could hear him from where I stood in the kitchen. He kept saying, 'I will not allow it.'"

Peg rubbed the valley between his fingers with the forefinger from his other hand. "I left the kitchen and went to bed early that night. I finally had a word for what I was, and, as ugly as Father tried to make it sound, I thought 'fairy' was a lovely word. I told myself he'd change his mind in the morning, and our lives would return to routine."

"Did he?" Roberto asked, then instinctively glanced toward the door at the sound of customers entering.

Peg sighed, then looked into and held Roberto's eyes. "He had calmed down by the following morning, but he hadn't changed his mind. If anything, he was more resolute in his desire to mold me into a carbon copy of himself. What he did that morning at breakfast was to apologize for not being a better role model for me. He promised to change. He said we'd play basketball together down at the Y. He'd teach me what real carpentry was all about. We'd build a doghouse together."

Peg was shaking his head back and forth slowly.

This was the longest version of this story I'd ever heard.

"We didn't even have a dog," Peg continued, "but Father said we'd get one. 'We'll hunt together,' he said. 'We'll get us a big black Lab, train him to do our bidding, then go out during dove season, and I'll teach you to shoot like a man.' " Peg shook his head at the memory. "It was pretty clear to me it was going to take something really big and dramatic to get me out of shop." He then propped his elbow on the table with his shortchanged hand front and center.

Roberto nodded at the couple who had entered the room. He smiled at them the way he always smiles at me—as if he'd been waiting just for them.

Peg didn't notice either the couple or Roberto's waning attention. He was transfixed by his own hand. "I knew what had to be done," he said. "I went to shop without protest that day. I was holding a one-by-two, running it through the table saw at different angles to create some decorative trim for my mailbox. I decided I would teach my father to leave me be; I would teach all of them. I might not ever get to make aprons and cookies, I knew, but I'd be damned if I'd spend another minute in shop.

"So, I ran my finger directly into the running blade."

5

"Your finger? *Directly* into the oncoming blade? Oh, no, Mr. Corbeil!" Roberto's voice was barely above a whisper.

I could tell from his bright eyes that Peg was thrilled with Roberto's reaction.

Peg nodded. "That fall I'd seen a boy have his finger sewn back on after losing it in shop. They'd been able to do that because he'd cut it off so cleanly. I went for the biggest mess I could imagine when I cut mine off 'cause I didn't want to take that chance."

Roberto gasped, of course. "No! Don't tell me you did this to yourself on purpose." He held both hands about a foot from his head on either side as if measuring for a newer, larger head. Then he clasped a hand over each ear, then let his hands slide down his neck, then onto his shoulders and finally to his sides.

Roberto's demonstrated horror greatly pleased Peg. It was, after all, the result he'd been after. "Why, yes. Of course I did it to myself." Peg was still staring at the hand. "It is my badge of honor." He then smiled coyly at Roberto. "So you see, Mr. Mangione, I am never embarrassed about my hand. It has allowed me to be who I am."

"But such extremes," said Roberto as he shook his head. "What about your poor papa? How did he feel about what you did?"

I had this part memorized, so I said along with Peg: "He let me do what I wanted to do."

"Surely, your papa is proud now? You are the most respected floral designer in the world, Mr. Corbeil. How could he not be?"

Peg finally took his hand off display and laid it in his lap. "As for your assertion of my talent, it is totally dependent on whom you ask. My style is too bold for some. As for my father, however, there is no question. He is long dead. Within a year of my fingerectomy, he had a heart attack climbing a mountain much too steep for a man so out of shape as he was. I think he was trying to be man enough for the both of us."

Roberto looked at me sadly, then backed away from our table to belatedly greet the couple, who'd seated themselves.

Hart, Peg, and I returned to what was left of our meals.

Hart paused with a piece of veal on his fork. He looked at Peg for the first time since we'd been in the restaurant. "You shouldn't have done that," he said. "You made Roberto uncomfortable."

Now it was Peg who wouldn't look at Hart. He put his own fork down, tapped his forefinger on his salad plate, and sought my eyes. "What's wrong with your guy, Sydney? Where's his sense of humor?"

"Leave him alone, Peg," I said.

Hart wouldn't let go. "He didn't need to hear that story. Did telling it make you feel powerful, knowing how awkward it made Roberto feel?"

"What's the matter with you?" I said to Hart. "You too," I said, turning to Peg. "Why do you have to pick on each other? . . . Just stop it, please. Both of you." I put my hand over Hart's, and I looked pleadingly at Peg. "This day's been bad enough already. Just let it go. Think about poor Joel."

"I didn't really know him," Hart said.

"That sad fact," said Peg sarcastically, "doesn't make Joel Fineman any less dead."

Hart excused himself and went to the men's room.

Peg watched the bathroom door swing behind Hart, then turned his attention back to me and shrugged.

I shook my head. "Why do you do that? Why does angering Hart thrill you so?"

He heard the seriousness in my voice, saw it in my eyes. He chose to look away, a feigned expression of expectation in his eyes as he glanced at the front door. Finally, he looked down at the table and muttered, "I don't know. The challenge, I guess."

"Challenge?" I thought about it a moment. "Well, pick on somebody else, will you? You're really making him uncomfortable."

Peg nodded, still staring at the table surface. "His mother's still alive. Did you know that?"

"What are you talking about?"

He looked up at me. "Joel's. His mother's still alive," he repeated. "His father died just last year." He shook his head. "He should have lived a long life."

"I forgot how well you knew him, Peg," I said, rationalizing my tiny lie. "No history of heart disease?"

He stuck out his lower lip as if it could help him

remember, then pulled it back in and shook his head. "Nope. I would have known." He paused. "I guess I should call his mother in Atlanta. Damn, I hate to do that."

"Better coming from you than from some impersonal voice at the hospital or, worse, the medical examiner's office."

Peg was folding his napkin but stopped and looked into my eyes. "Medical examiner?"

"Well, I'd think so. No history of a medical problem. Just falling over in a public place like he did might trigger an autopsy."

"God, Mrs. Fineman's going to hate that too."

"Joel didn't live with anybody?" I asked. Maybe there was someone else who could break the news to Mrs. Fineman besides Peg.

"Not any longer. Joel may have been a great sympathy designer, but he was an old nag when he wasn't designing. He didn't even have a cat."

I watched Hart walk back from the men's room. Maybe I was imagining it, but his walk had a bit of a male swagger to it just then.

He stood behind his chair instead of sitting down. "Want me to call Sally or are we going by the office?"

"Go ahead and call her," I said. "We need to get back to the show as quickly as we can."

As Hart went to use Roberto's phone, Peg made one last crack about him. "Ah, the man takes charge," he said to me. Thankfully, Hart didn't hear that one.

"Dammit, Peg, I mean it. No more. Leave him alone."

He put both hands in the air and leaned back in his chair. "Okay, okay, okay," he said. "Change the subject. What do you think of the brave new floral world? You think UFAS considers this effort successful?"

"You don't?" I asked.

"Depends on what they expected, I guess. If they expected South American growers, hundreds of grocery store clerks and telephone order fulfillment companies, who specialize in acting as if they're your neighbor, then this brave new floral world here this week is made to order."

Peg and I'd had this discussion before, many times before. The floral industry was changing and had been, in fact, for the last thirty years. Technology had finally backfired on florists. For years it had done the opposite. Jet transport, refrigeration—those advances had been the florists' friends. Thirty years ago, who else had rare and exotic species? Nobody but florists.

In fact, twenty years ago florists had a lock on flowers. Nobody much gardened until the seventies. So flowers weren't to be found in backyards. You could get them only from your local florist, who, at that time, was one of the three or four most respected people in town.

To top off those golden years, products like Styrofoam and the florist's basic design tool, Oasis foam, were invented. That's when serious floral design was born. I'd been studying some of that early foam-based design in preparation for this show and the UFAS booth panels in particular. The designs were wonderfully tacky by today's standard, real fifties Americana. Right up there with Elvis and pink radios shaped like poodles. My favorites were the arrangements I'd seen in an old *Bride's* magazine from that era. Two bridesmaids were each carrying half a basket. They were posed with the bride and groom, each carrying half a heart.

Whenever we have a new design "toy," and foam was revolutionary in that respect, we are enamored of the toy to design's detriment. You can bet on it. Those fifties floral designers were a lot like those of us with computer design tools and no real design sense in using them. The results are sometimes laughable.

Things change. Everything since that time had conspired to dismantle the typical florist shop, to make one indistinguishable from the next. Today, upwards of ninety percent of grocery stores have floral departments. In sheer numbers, those floral departments almost equal the number of florists left in America. The technology that had allowed California growers to gain control of the American floral market now advanced beyond them. South American growers can deliver the world's finest flowers to a doorstep anywhere in the world in less than twenty-four hours. And Peg was right. You never know who is choosing and arranging your order when you pick up the phone these days. Design originality isn't part of what the masses get when they order, although everything Allen Teague does for our clients is to convince the public otherwise. Ordering flowers is now like ordering a Big Mac.

Unless you order from someone like Peg Corbeil. Peg was lucky enough to have a unique design talent, so unique that it set him apart. Like the top fashion designers, Peg had the wealthiest people in the South flying him to weddings and state affairs to create his special "art." Feeding off carefully cultivated snob appeal, Peg had done so well that he could buy and sell a few of the people who sought his services.

As his ad agency and public relations firm, we'd been trying for five years to find the right words to convey what set him apart. To date, I hadn't found those words. Instead, we resorted to the best photography we could find because the only words that mattered when selling Peg's talent were the simple headline I always used: IT'S A CORBEIL!

"Everything's becoming homogenized," I said to Peg. "You can't stop it."

"Soon, there'll be no place for the artist, Sydney." Self-pity had crept into his voice.

"Come on, Peg. The more alike everyone else becomes, the more a true artist stands out. Your success is the best example I know of that paradox at work."

"It can't last forever."

"What can't?"

"People wanting me. I'm a fad right now. Someone else will come along. Then where will I go? What will I do?" His artistic whine had a wistful lilt to it.

I folded my napkin and put it on the table. "You'll go where all fabulously wealthy fads go when they retire. Probably to one of several expensive homes wherever you want them in this homogenized world." He'd folded his hands on the table and was staring at them. I tapped the top of his hands lightly with my own hand so Peg would look up at me. "Hey," I said, "you're a hula hoop. You've got staying power."

He chuckled and nodded, but he didn't smile.

"I know you care about the industry, Peg," I said more seriously. "You can't save everybody. It's too big. Change just happens."

We both looked up as a smiling Hart returned to the table.

"Someone sent you flowers, Sydney. Sally's still on the phone. Go talk to her."

I must admit I was flattered. Even more, I was curious about who might have sent me flowers on this cold March day. Perhaps it was Tom Thurgood, priming me for the tournament this weekend. Or a happy client, grateful for an ad well received. By the time I'd reached Roberto's phone, I'd decided it was probably UFAS thanking us for our hard work on this show. And we had worked hard. I was thinking the gift of flowers from them was most appropriate.

"I haven't touched the card, Sydney. I swear I haven't," said an obviously lying Sally.

"Why don't you then? Go ahead and open it. Read it to me."

"Just a sec." Her voice dropped off as she held the phone between her shoulder and neck. "Here we go now. This doesn't make much sense. Not unless it's real personal. But they didn't put their name on it."

"Sally, just read it," I said as I watched Hart and Peg leaving tips on the table.

She said, " 'When words are not enough,' " then waited to hear if I had an explanation for such an odd, unsigned note.

Needless to say, I didn't. The words rang a bell with me, of course. I'd seen them on a crumpled piece of paper a mere hour and a half earlier.

"What does that mean?" Sally asked.

"I wish I knew," I said, feeling my voice catch in my throat.

6

The exhibit hall of the Charlotte Convention Center has thirty-foot ceilings. Toward the top of the most centrally located wall, a large window embeds itself like a poorly placed watercolor. It's the only evidence that someone "runs the show."

During FloraGlobal, UFAS executives populated this room. The room was actually part of the Center's entrance level, but to someone on the exhibit hall floor its window was an ominous sight, like the window of guards watching prisoners or psychiatrists watching patients in an overcrowded asylum. The window was reflective so you couldn't see inside it, even if you'd wanted to.

This room was my first stop after returning from lunch, and I'd been dreading it. I wondered whom UFAS had hired to cast those two insects. For a company and its products or services, mascots are more delicate matches than celebrity spokespersons. If the mascot is disliked, every bit of that dislike is directed back at the company. With a celebrity, most of the unhappiness is attributed to the celebrity and leaves with him. I'd already told UFAS as much and didn't want to play I-told-you-so. Neither one of these characters would do anything positive for UFAS. Tina Mauldin liked to place blame, though, so maybe the easiest way out for me was to just accept it. I didn't expect any more UFAS business after this show anyway.

Tina Mauldin was my UFAS contact, a six-foot-one-inch cheerleader for the latest in communication technology. By title, Tina was the UFAS public relations director, but by function she directed the wiring of gadgets. I judged Tina to be around thirty-five years old, ten years my junior, so our differing approaches to public relations didn't surprise me. I was raised on *Captain Midnight* technology, where a glass of Ovaltine could transport me to another planet. Tina Mauldin was post–*Star Trek* all the way.

"What are you doing?" I asked, hoping to learn something, in spite of what they say about old dogs. She sat in a sleek, ergonomically sculpted swivel chair as she flipped a series of switches on the mammoth control panel between her and the large glass window.

"Adjusting sound," she said in a clipped, efficient voice.

"What sound? Are you taping one of the presentations?" I walked carefully to a spot behind her chair so I could see the control board she was working. In addition to switches and buttons and a keyboard the length of an average desk, at least one-third of the board was taken up by a three-foot-by-three-foot block of tiny monitors, each flickering with a different image.

Behind us, four UFAS execs, all of whom I'd met at one time or another, were eating lunch at a round conference table. None of them looked up from their sandwiches. An impressively opulent floral arrangement sat in the middle of the table. It must have been a good two and a half feet in diameter at its drip line. The invisible vase was overflow-ing with Peruvian daffodils, birds-of-paradise, a mix of ze-bra grass and lily turf for drape, and a few dramatically placed anthuriums. A technician crouched in the far back corner of the crowded room seemed to be working on Tina's myriad cables. He didn't look up at me either.

"Those too," she said casually. She then added, "We're taping everything, Sydney."

"All the presentations?" I was impressed that she could do that from a central location.

"Everything," she said again as she swiveled to face me. "We have sound and cameras covering most of the ex-hibit space too."

I looked out her picture window at the sea of people and booths, then back at the busy rectangle of running video images in front of her. I knew her technology was ahead of my understanding, but all I could really see when I looked at the setup were dollar signs.

"I hope you're getting what you need," I said, attempt-ing to hide the magnitude of my awe.

She had a dry, sarcastic laugh that I'd rarely heard. When she laughed now, in fact, it worried me rather than pleased me. It wasn't a happy sound.

"I got the two buffoons going at each other," she fi-nally said. She sounded happy now.

"Do you have their understudies ready?" I asked, try-ing my best to sound light about the insect problem.

"They'll be okay," she said. I knew how wrong she was, but I wasn't in a position to give her any more advice. She wasn't, after all, asking for any. "The ladybug came in early," she continued. "They're not supposed to be on the floor together today."

"Did you hire those two yourself?" I asked as if the an-swer didn't matter one way or another.

"Aren't they funny?" she said instead of answering my question.

So, I didn't say what I would have to a longtime client, one who was used to my counsel and honesty. She really didn't want to hear my take on her choices: that she was entrusting her company's image to either a porn wannabe or a whimpering slob of a man more suited to peanut butter ads than flowers.

"Have a seat." She pushed a small metal chair in my direction.

I shook my head. "Wish I could. No time. Just checking in with y'all. Anything you need us to do?" I was relieved our bug talk hadn't gone further.

Tina removed the horn-rimmed glasses she usually wore as a hair band to hold back thin but unruly black hair. Her hair didn't need those glasses any more than her eyes did. They were strong and focused—her eyes, I mean. I would wager that her eyesight was just a smidgen off 20/20. Maybe she thought those glasses helped her image. Without them she was much more attractive. Probably not by geek standards, though.

"I was going to call you," she said. "Yes, I need you to handle the Fineman death."

Handle? I wondered what she meant by a word like "handle."

I didn't have to wait long to find out. She told me to hand-carry a news release to the *Observer* and the television stations in town. "Direct what they're saying in the media," she told me emphatically. "Can you have one of your people do that so you won't have to leave the show?" As soon as she'd spoken, she began to clean those thin lenses on her white tunic-length T-shirt.

"I was in the room, Tina. He just died." I paused a second, thinking those few words would be enough. Surely she must have heard some stupid rumor. Her expression, though, didn't change. I continued, "Nobody's going to turn his death into an indictment of your show. The poor man had either a heart attack or a stroke. That much was obvious to everyone."

"People hear the first three seconds of a newscast, Sydney," she said as if I were a student in her PR 101 class. "That's all they hear. And in the paper, they read only a headline. Surely you must know that." She stood and turned her long, lean back to me as she stared into the crowd through her window. "What do you think they'll say if we don't feed the story to them?"

I didn't answer her. Even if I'd wanted to, she didn't pause long enough for me to reply. The rhythm was becoming routine. I touched the metal chair in front of me lightly.

"The lead-ins to both will be 'Man Dies at Convention Center.'" She shook her head, her back still to me.

I was beginning to feel I had no business handling her company's public relations. As hard as I was trying, I had no idea what she was getting at. So I said, "People die all over the city every day. You don't have to worry about it. It's not newsworthy."

She finally turned to face me. "Make it news. That's your job." She put the horn-rims back over her eyes. "Let them know what a big name Fineman was in floral design. More importantly, make sure they say he died while demonstrating at the FloraGlobal Show and what we're all about. Then maybe we'll get 'World-Famous Designer Dies at FloraGlobal Show' instead of 'Man Dies at Convention Center' or, even worse, your scenario of no press at all."

I looked into her cold blue eyes and saw that she'd lost faith in me. If she'd been reading my eyes at that moment, too, and surely she was, she'd have seen that I'd lost the same thing in her. I couldn't just chalk it up to the differences between Ovaltine and electronic gadgetry.

"Okay," I said, and looked away. Then I turned and walked out of the room.

That Tina's request made me nauseous didn't mean I could refuse to carry it out. As much as I wanted to, I'd learned to take a stand only rarely and to be prepared to lose the client when I did. She wasn't asking me to rob a bank, only to spin a death into her good fortune. I sighed as I waited for the elevator to come up to the UFAS control room. When the door opened, I was truly shocked. There stood the whimpering ladybug, but he was whimpering no more. In fact, he looked determined, sure of himself, like a man with a job to do. Without his shell, he looked more comfortable, although still fairly idiotic: a fat man in an orange bodysuit. We both nodded awkwardly as we passed, each of us a reference of something we'd both just as soon forget. As the elevator door was sliding slowly to a close, I watched him walk into the UFAS room. He didn't even knock.

I didn't have much time to influence the night's news broadcast. It was close to three now, and anchors would alter their segments only if big, late-breaking news came in at this time of day. The newspaper was a different matter. They'd be building tomorrow's paper until late into the night.

Rhyne Garrett was in his booth, selling a big order of straw wreaths to a man with a French accent. Hart had progressed from his hands and knees to a stool. He was rendering a faux blueprint of a Garrett pick machine. Using a heavy-test fishing wire, he'd suspended a real pick machine from one of the steel poles that crisscrossed above each booth. He was staring at the swaying machine with the probing concentration of a portraitist seeking his subject's soul.

I brushed past him, breaking his concentration.

"Welcome back to the zoo," he said.

"The wall looks good, Hart."

"They think so too," he said, and nodded toward the small group of people assembled no more than five feet from him.

A few of his audience members chuckled when he said that. I wondered if they'd been bantering back and forth with Hart all day.

Rhyne Garrett's customer was signing a form for what I suspected to be a very large wreath order. Rhyne was obviously delighted but trying to hide his joy. I'd seen him suppress his own happiness before and had wondered where such an odd tendency came from. He was a big man in his late forties, maybe early fifties, normally not in any discernable mood, a practiced, steady tone to his voice. He wore lots of tweeds and, like Hart, would have probably been more comfortable in another century. I caught Rhyne's attention and mouthed silently my request to use his phone and fax. His response was so magnanimous, I knew for certain this wreath order was a big one. Until this moment Rhyne had been so proprietary about his booth that he hadn't even let me sit in one of his four director's chairs. In the midst of his big order, though, he said to me, "Whatever you need, Sydney. My booth is your booth." Amazing what a good sale will do for a person's love of mankind.

Once I got her on the phone, I had a hard time hearing Sally over the din. I gave her three short paragraphs for the release. I knew the important stuff by heart about FloraGlobal and UFAS and found a good bio of Joel Fine-

man off the show program, which I'd found sitting on a
Garrett table. I dictated it as I knew Tina wanted it, playing down the what and the where and singing the praises
of two whos—Joel and FloraGlobal—both of whom dan-
gled in my release like participles looking for something
to modify and coming up empty.

"That's a strange release," Sally said. "It almost sounds
like you're saying FloraGlobal is proud to announce this
man's death."

"I know," I said, embarrassed I couldn't hide the truth
any better than I had.

"Want to rewrite some of it?" she asked.

"No," I said. I could almost hear her head cock to the
side through the receiver as she tried to understand what I
myself could not. I was grateful I wasn't looking at her at
the time. I wasn't about to explain though. If I tried, she
would tell me how dumb and tasteless the whole thing
was, and I'd already been listening to the same condemna-
tion inside my own head. Instead, I told her to get Fineman's photograph from the program file since we were the
ones who'd put the program together. "Scan it and send it
with the release to the four affiliates. Note somewhere on
each release that a short videotape will probably follow.
But leave the part about the tape off the paper's."

She was silent for a couple of seconds, then said, "A
tape of Fineman's death?"

"Of course not," I said quickly. "Just a tape of show ac-
tivities. UFAS is trying to promote themselves with this."

I waited for her to protest, and she did. "God, Sydney.
Talk about bad taste."

"I agree" was all I said.

When she asked me where I planned to get such a tape,
I told her about Tina's multimillion-dollar setup. "If

UFAS doesn't have something we can use for PR out of what they've shot, then all this videotaping makes even less sense than I already think it does." Finally, I asked her to fax me two copies of the release here at Garrett's booth, one to give UFAS and one for me to take to the paper.

I didn't even hang up. Instead, I immediately called Tina up in the control booth. I looked up at her picture window as I listened to the rings. I couldn't see a thing through the high dark glass, not even a reflection of her horn-rimmed glasses. She never did answer the phone. Since I knew all too well how displeased Tina was with me and my inability to convert Joel's death to a positive UFAS story, I imagined her staring down at me, unwilling to communicate at all. As I hung up, I whispered my most sinister "bitch" into the receiver. Thank goodness Rhyne was still preoccupied by success.

In a way, though, I was relieved she didn't answer. As long as she didn't answer, I didn't have to ask anyone to run a show tape alongside what amounted to Joel's obituary notice. By not answering, Tina had given me the out I needed. I could legitimately say I'd tried.

I spent ten minutes each calling the four networks and telling them about the story I'd be sending them. While I was talking with the CBS anchor, I watched my copy of the release come through on the Garrett fax machine.

"We have some tape of the show, I think," the female anchor told me. "I saw it when I came in after lunch. People protesting something. Anything like that going on at the FloraGlobal thing?"

"Oh, God," I said. "No, don't use that tape with this. Those people are homophobes. They're out to make trouble, and if you run it, they'll get what they're looking for. Besides, it just won't work alongside Joel Fineman's truly great accomplishments."

The woman's voice lowered two octaves as she said, "I'll be the judge of what goes into my newscast."

I wasn't having a lot of luck helping Joel maintain his dignity in death. One negative response didn't mean I wasn't still trying, though. So I told the WBTV woman I thought I could find better videotape. I waited for her to respond . . . and waited some more. She still didn't answer. So I said it again and waited again. I finally figured it out: The damn woman had hung up on me.

By the clock on the wall in the lobby area of the Convention Center, it wasn't even three o'clock yet. Still, I needed to get to the newspaper as quickly as I could. I rushed across the carpet, a carpet awash in a color and pattern akin to an out-of-control forest fire. If I looked down while I walked this wildly psychedelic carpet, I truly got seasick, a dizzy, nauseous, stumbling feeling. Today, I looked straight at my destination: the doors leading out to Stonewall Street.

The protestors, along with their signs and banners, were all sitting in loose groups of two and three on the sprawling steps. I didn't see Curtis.

Maybe they were silent because Jeep Ford was strolling among them. If he hadn't had on his uniform, most people would have thought him one of the protestors. He was plump for a uniformed officer, but nothing like the mascot postulate he'd rescued from the bee. He was in his late fifties and nearing retirement. Tom sure was going to miss him when he finally did hang up his uniform. Tom always said the amazing thing about Jeep was his temperament. Jeep showed none of the anger I sometimes see in the younger cops I'd met through Tom Thurgood. He was an easygoing kind of guy, the kind who seem willing to drive the carpool or wash the dishes without any fear of losing his image. Not to give the impression he was married because he wasn't. I noticed his limp again. Jeep's arthritis was exacerbated by his job, in fact had made his retirement inevitable.

He had totally engaged the homophobes, laughing at jokes, telling one of his own, if I could gauge by the laughter all around. He was keeping their interest away from the Convention Center doors, making them forget, if only for a while, why they had come here today. No wonder he headed up the police department's Special Security unit. Still, I was surprised to see him here. He and his team were usually reserved for presidential visits and big-shot athletes. Homophobes at a floral show didn't fit somehow.

The *Charlotte Observer* building is also on Stonewall Street, on the other side of Tryon. Even though I had only two short blocks to walk, I felt the raw cold seep down into my bones. Not only had the temperature continued to drop, but this accompanying dampness on top of it gave me an uneasy feeling. I hated even saying it to myself, but it felt like snow. Now that I wanted to go to Savannah, I was afraid the tournament might be called off. I consoled myself with the knowledge that most late-season storms, like this embryo was threatening to be, came up from Georgia, although usually from Atlanta and westward. Since Savannah is on the coast, it probably wouldn't get any snow. Just rain. However, the St. Patrick's Day Invitational was an outdoor tournament. "Oh, lovely," I said aloud as I opened the big brass *Observer* door and went inside looking for someone to do Tina's bidding.

1

Merilee Gillespie was the Lifestyle editor at *The Charlotte Observer* and had been ever since the same section was called the Women's Page back in the mid-fifties. For the same editor to reign over a section that had undergone the magnitude of changes those pages had was nothing less than remarkable. Her longevity was a testament to her willingness to alter appearance for the sake of her job. She pushed her own agenda for the sake of her sanity.

That's how Merilee told it anyway. "Sydney Allen," she said, having a penchant for women's maiden names as if none of us had ever married, "you can make your readers believe the content has changed if you change its type style or the banner for the page. A new look is synonymous with a new thought in most people's heads. You advertising robbers programmed people for thinking that way decades ago."

Merilee was a baffling combination of feminism and femininity. She would argue with anyone—and win—over her right to be feminine. And to have opinions and even lead others. In short, Merilee had a swaggering swish, with admirers and detractors of both sexes abounding. Her agenda was unknown to most Charlotteans because they didn't look for such things in a Lifestyle editor. I discovered it early on, though, when I noticed her promoting underdogs in her society column and withholding the names of those you'd expect—the ones flying high and up there a long time. I called her agenda "leveling"; she called it "promoting civility." No matter its name, this agenda had been operative here for close to forty years. And in a town like Charlotte, where perception is king and some people make nothing but money, pushing civility or leveling the lofty is no easy task.

I'd struck out with Gordon Seltzer over in the Business cubicle. Gordon had enough sense to know that Joel Fineman's death wasn't business news. My hat was off to him on that one. I hadn't expected a favor from him but felt obligated to try. I did expect a favor from Merilee, though. The two of us, helping each other out, had probably been Charlotte's first "good old girls." Over the years, we'd both gone out of our ways to give each other a forum.

In spite of our history, Merilee had a good laugh at my request to report on the death as a social event. "Sydney, I know it's your job to get as much coverage for this show as you can, but don't you think we'd be stretching it a bit to give space to the man's death? What interest does it have for my readers?"

Her eyes twinkled as she goaded me. Merilee's at least eighty years old. Then again, she's always seemed eighty to me. It's the makeup, I think, that throws off my perception. She's of the school of circular rouge. She puts it in the hollow of her cheeks with less defined pink streaks moving from those circles to under the outside margins of each eye. Her eyes are a medium-deep ocean color, which isn't to say they're blue. The ocean I visit along the North and South Carolina coasts isn't blue at all; nor is it green. If you took out the pollution and the seaweed and the circulating sand, I suppose it would be. When the sun hits the surf, particularly at the crest of a wave, this color twinkles, just as Merilee's eyes were twinkling now.

"You're giving daily coverage to FloraGlobal already," I said. "Joel Fineman deserves a special story. No one could touch him in the sympathy category."

She chuckled. "But I don't think my readers are interested in the sympathy category, Sydney. Now, if someone like your client, Corbeil, had died, I'd do a story on *his* death."

We stared at each other. She was waiting, I knew, for me to give her an angle to make it work. I couldn't think of one.

"UFAS is a bit demanding of you, don't you think?" Merilee sipped from her always present glass of iced tea, then patted her vivid pink lips with a handkerchief she'd miraculously pulled from inside her blouse.

"It's my job."

She looked again at the release I'd given her. While she was rereading it, a young man with a pouch strapped to his back approached us with an envelope. As he handed it to Merilee, I recognized him as a bicycle courier we use to deliver contracts and material around town.

She thanked him and opened the envelope. As she pulled out the photograph of Joel that Sally had sent, she nodded to me. "Is this Fineman?" she asked.

I nodded in return. "I wish you could have seen him this morning, Merilee," I said. "He transformed his casket into an exquisite symbol. I've never seen anything like it."

All of a sudden, she seemed mildly interested. "What kind of symbol? A symbol of what?"

I thought for a few seconds. "I'd say the culmination of life."

She drew her penciled brows together. "Come again, Sydney," she said, but not sarcastically.

I took a deep breath and exhaled it. Explaining a casket design narrative and what made Joel's exceptional wasn't an easy conversational topic. But I tried. I told Merilee as much as I could remember about how the casket looked with the draping ivy, the baby's breath, and the calla lilies shooting up out of it all. Then I shared as much as I could remember about Joel's narrative itself and how mesmerized the whole audience was, so spellbound, in fact, that his very collapse didn't register with us for a minute.

"I'd say he was quite a performer, wouldn't you?"

"It seemed genuine," I said.

"Genuine performances are performances still," she said.

I nodded but watched her carefully. I couldn't decipher her thoughts behind those words.

"Sounds to me like the man made death desirable, or, if not desirable, at least attractive."

"You could say that," I said. "The first time I've seen anyone give meaning to the box we spend eternity in."

She sipped her tea again while her fingers punched the buttons on her phone set. While it rang through her intercom, she subconsciously fiddled with the chunky gold choker around her neck.

I heard a man answer.

At the sound of his voice, Merilee's hand instinctively patted her tight beige and silver permanent, and the corners of her mouth turned upward in flirtatious curls. I smiled as I watched her. Having those female instincts so alive at her age—whatever age that actually was—gave Merilee an edge in the social biz. Men liked to tell her things.

"I've been thinking about you, dear," she said. As she listened to him talk she winked at me and swiveled in her chair. If she'd been walking, the movement would have been a sashay. "I'm still trying to help you. That's why I called." She pushed an envelope in my direction while she listened to him some more. "I'm going to write you up tomorrow and run it this weekend. I just want to make sure you'll be home for a phone interview tomorrow. Say around noon?" She bobbed her head to the rhythm of his conversation. "Yes, dear. Yes, dear. You betcha. Gotta run now."

After she'd hung up, she pushed the large brown envelope even closer to me. "Take a look," she said. "See if you don't think it'll work." Then she leaned back and opened her middle desk drawer, where she found another envelope of the same size and color.

I didn't speak as I opened first one envelope and then the other. The first one held color photographs of totems. I'd heard that totems were fast becoming the "in" yard art for those who could afford it. Hiring a sculptor to carve the symbols of your life into a tree carried just the right kind of snob appeal in a place like Charlotte. I didn't know what this had to do with Joel. The other envelope held black-and-white glossies of topiary bushes in cemetery settings. The topiary was, in itself, exquisite; but I couldn't imagine who the topiarist's market might be. Certainly not a cemetery, not here in Charlotte anyway, where most of the graveyards are restricted to flat space, a small tube of flowers the only verticality allowed. I find that restriction boring as well as depressing, but many in Charlotte are in love with covenants and restrictions, no matter what is being restricted. Once I asked a friend of mine, a restriction enthusiast, why. His response was so immediate and direct that I didn't dare ask him to elaborate. His answer was simply "No surprises. You can count on it." Well, I can count on a Big Mac too, but I wouldn't want to live or die at McDonald's.

I held the two sets of envelopes in my lap and looked up at Merilee. "I don't understand the connection with Joel," I said.

"Oh, Sydney, Sydney." She licked her full lips and leaned forward, touching a photograph from each envelope. "These boys, the ones who do the totems and the topiary. They're two boys I'd like to help. I've been holding the totems for six months already, and I honestly didn't believe I'd ever been able to do an article on either one of them." She patted me on the knee.

"Thanks to you, I'm going to turn the three of them, your Fineman included, into a story. 'Deathstyle.' How does that sound? Think 'Deathstyle' is too much for the Lifestyle pages? Too morbid, too hokey, too what?"

I sat there a full minute before answering her. What would Joel have thought of something like this? I wondered. I really didn't know the answer because I suddenly realized, to my own surprise, I hadn't known Joel Fineman, the man, at all.

I looked at her tentatively. "Would you be able to work in mention of FloraGlobal? I'm doing this at the request of the UFAS PR director."

"Certainly," she said, her hand up around that gold choker again.

I smiled at Merilee. "You really like to shake things up, don't you?"

Her eyes twinkled. "I like to help these young people with new ideas," she said. "Somebody has to." Then she rubbed her hands together, her bracelets tinkling as she did. "Besides, I do like to rattle Old Charlotte a bit. My boss will get lots of complaints, and that's good for business."

"To an extent, I suppose it is," I said. "I'm sure you can go too far, though, can't you?" I stood to leave.

She stood with me. "Not on a story like this, I don't think."

She walked with me to the door of the newsroom, a city block by small-town measurements. At each workstation we passed, she stopped for a moment to introduce or reintroduce me to its inhabitant. Every one of them, I noticed, was working from a computer screen, even Charlie Pane in Sports. Last time I'd seen him here, he'd been a holdout.

Ollie Smith's station was closest to the exit. He's one of two *Observer* crime reporters and a man I've known for over ten years on the tennis court. He's a roly-poly kind of guy who makes his points with a grab bag of slices, chops, and questionable line calls. Ollie was putting on a heavy wool jacket and turning off his terminal.

"You'll need that jacket," I said. "It feels like snow out there."

Ollie was surprised to see me. "I hear you and Thurgood are heading down to Savannah for the St. Patrick's Day Tournament. Checked the weather down there?" He laughed. I wondered if he'd heard a forecast.

"Savannah's almost in Florida," I said.

"Keep telling yourself that," he said. He continued to gather his possessions off his desk: his wallet, a notebook, a pair of glasses that he slipped into a case and then into an inside pocket of his jacket. "I'm going to see Thurgood in a minute. I'll tell him I saw you."

All three of us continued to the door. "Come back to see me soon, Sydney," Merilee said. "I'll call you about the article. And don't worry. I'll mention FloraGlobal."

I thanked her as the double glass doors closed behind Ollie and me, leaving us alone. As we waited for the elevator to arrive, Ollie turned to look at me. "What did Merilee mean about FloraGlobal? You involved in that show?"

I nodded. "We're handling the PR for a couple of people."

"For the show itself?"

"Yeah, that too. That's why I was here."

"You've got some more work, I'm afraid."

The elevator arrived and the two of us walked inside. No one else was on it.

"What do you mean?" I asked when he didn't explain.

"That's where I'm headed," he said. "There's been a murder." He watched me for a reaction.

"A murder? Who told you something like that?" The elevator wasn't moving very quickly, but my stomach was behaving like it was.

"Picked it up on my scanner. Tom Thurgood's over there right now."

Perhaps the medical examiner had decided Joel's death was suspicious. If what Peg said about Joel's health being fine was true, then maybe the medical examiner thought it was worth investigating. Maybe someone had poisoned Joel. I knew, though, that poisons couldn't be determined so quickly. Somebody was jumping the gun to be calling it a murder at this point. It didn't sound like Tom.

Our elevator arrived at ground level and the two of us got out.

"I don't think they've proved anything yet," I said. "Toxicology reports take longer than a couple of hours to come back. It only happened late this morning."

Ollie's much shorter than my five eight, and he makes a big display of the difference on the tennis court by cocking his head sideways and peering up at me as if I'm a particularly high mountain to climb. He acts out like this only when I've hit a winning shot that he or his partner can't return. Best I can tell, it's a look of befuddlement. This was the look he gave me now.

"Since when does a stabbing warrant a toxicology report? You trying to throw me off?"

If one of us had been thrown by that exchange, it was surely I. When the large *Observer* door closed behind us, Ollie took off trotting in the direction of the Convention Center. "Hold up, Ollie," I screamed more than once, but he didn't slow down. He was acting as if I was another reporter about to scoop his story. Or maybe he thought I could suppress such news through some power invested by UFAS. Whatever his reasoning, Ollie was thirty yards ahead of me on his way to the scene of the crime. I was blessed with legs both longer and stronger than little Ollie Smith's, though, so once I turned it on, I was inside the Center before him.

8

Inside the building, I saw no sign of a crime scene. No hush had fallen over the boisterous crowd. No yellow tape had cordoned off a section of the large exhibit hall. To be certain of it, I walked the entire floor. I even opened the door to the room where Joel Fineman had died and interrupted a decorative-ribbon demonstration.

Yet a crime lab van had been parked on the sidewalk at the Stonewall Street entrance. And Ollie had heard it on his scanner. So where was the crime? And where was Tom Thurgood? As much as I hate to admit it, I was wishing I'd held back and followed Ollie, who obviously knew where he was going. Sometimes winning a race yields no spoils.

The only remaining possibility was Joel's booth. I knew he had one because I'd seen his name twice in the program, once for the design panel and a second time as a show participant.

I ran into Peg, who said he was bored and leaving for the day. I asked him if he'd heard anything about the police investigating Joel's death. He'd been moving toward the doors, but he stopped. Peg wasn't easily shaken, but he was when I asked him that question. "How can that be?" he said. "What do they suspect?"

"I've heard he was stabbed," I said.

At first Peg laughed. Slowly, however, the sound stopped, and then even the breath to drive it. He looked ashen. "But, Sydney, we'd have known that. There wasn't any blood."

"Someone could have used an ice pick," I said.

"And were they invisible, these people wielding ice picks?"

I shook my head. "Like I said, I just heard a rumor. I'm trying to confirm it. That's why I need your help."

When I asked, he said he'd gladly take me to Joel's booth. The booth turned out to be one of the smaller ones, a ten-by-ten, maybe slightly larger. The overhead fluorescent fixtures did nothing for Joel's work; in fact, in here the displays looked rather ordinary. The dry heat of the Center could wilt these arrangements in under a day. Three freestanding floral tributes took up much of the peripheral wall space, and a casket spray similar to the one he'd shown this morning was arranged on a florist's saddle on an antique wrought-iron "horse"—the kind that carpenters use. Pushed against a wall were a round table and two chairs. On the table was an exquisite all-white arrangement. White irises, freesia, campanula, daisies, and dianthus formed a perfect mound of traditional design.

"It's beautiful," I said to Peg, "but it doesn't look like Joel, does it?" I leaned over to smell the freesias.

Peg pulled out the plastic cardholder, which sported no card, from the center of the arrangement and put it in front of my eyes. "That's because he didn't design it. See this? Someone sent them to him. I'm surprised."

"Why?" I asked as I surveyed the rest of the surface contents of the table. I saw a couple of cups with old, cold coffee dregs and clumped nondairy creamer in one and the other still full and oily-looking like old coffee gets. A stack of papers lay in front of one chair, although I didn't stop to look at the content.

"Because Joel didn't have any friends, that's why. Who would send him flowers?" Peg bent down and retrieved a calla lily from one of the buckets beside the table. He handed it to me. "A lily for the fair lady," he said as he did.

I waved off his silliness, then looked down at the three buckets, each holding small numbers of the stems used this morning in Joel's presentation. "He put his design together right here? How could he? There's no room."

"He would have designed on the saddle." Peg pointed to another antique workhorse in the nearest corner. He leaned over a trash can beside the table and pulled out several light-green stem cuttings. "But he prepared the flowers while sitting here at the table."

"These must have been delivered after he'd finished," he said, gesturing toward the all-white display. "Knowing Joel, he'd probably finished designing by eight this morning so that's no surprise."

At the front of the booth, the area most likely to be seen by the showgoers, a large computer monitor was suspended to just above eye level. Since it was so easy to walk under, I hadn't noticed it when we entered the booth. I assumed it was just another business homepage like all the others flashing across screens in most of the other booths.

Once Peg and I were standing outside the booth again, I saw that it was more than that. The image was indeed a homepage but not for the customized sympathy designs Joel was known for. "Floral Tributes Online," the banner read. "Pay your respects with the click of your mouse. Ten designs for ten very special loved ones." The screen changed and a list appeared: "Loving Mother, Father the Protector, Cherished Child, the Hero, the Adventurer, the Thoughtful Friend, the Intellectual, the Spiritual Being, the Laughing Soul, and Beloved Pet."

"What is this?" I asked.

Peg stared as one thematic floral image after another filled the monitor. He shook his head. He truly looked sad. "Joel was selling out," he said. "He'd taken his gift and put it in a box."

"You mean he was selling his designs on the Web?"

"I heard he was going to. I don't know if this is actually up and running yet, but people were talking about it. He'd standardized some basic sympathy designs that he'd licensed to florists around the country. If you're in Peoria and your friend dies in Santa Fe, and let's say you're friend was a mountain climber, you just come to Joel's site, click on the Adventurer, key in your credit card number and you've done your duty to your dear friend." Peg's voice was full of disgust as he talked.

"Sounds like a specialized FTD setup," I said.

Peg nodded. "And it has them hopping mad, along with the other wire services. Nobody's tried to take a chunk of them like that before. They're afraid that if Joel can take a chunk out of the sympathy portion of their business, then who's to stop a grand wedding designer from ripping that portion of the business too? Thematic breakup of the wire monopolies."

"Wouldn't he have to get a bunch of florists to sign on with him?"

Peg nodded. "He had more than enough. All he was doing was licensing the designs and providing the link. He wasn't trying to force them into a two-way setup where most of the money would come to him." He looked back up at the screen. "And I heard he was linked into everything pertinent on the Web, every site that would let him anyway. The grief support groups, the commercial cancer pages, even links to obituary pages of newspapers online."

"I'm dumbfounded," I said. "I don't know whether this is really, really good or really, really bad."

"If we're voting," Peg said sarcastically, "put me in the column under 'really, really bad.' "

I sighed. "Don't worry. I doubt if his mother will carry it on. Did he have any employees?"

"None with brains."

"Did you call his mother?"

"Yes. She's not coming. Says she's too old to travel. Asked me if I'd send him to Atlanta. I told her I couldn't do that. She'd have to call a funeral home. All in all, it was a very mundane conversation. None of the hysterics I'd feared."

"If Homicide suspects foul play, though, she's not going to get his body from anyone for a while."

We had walked back into the vast aisle. Peg stopped and turned to face Joel's booth again. "But wouldn't there be some policemen in there if that were the case? Wouldn't they have wrapped his booth in that gaudy plastic yellow ribbon of theirs?"

"Maybe they haven't gotten this far in their investigation." Even as I said it, I knew it made no sense.

Peg knew it didn't either. He raised both brows while staring intently at me. "Well, Sydney darlin', I'd love to investigate further with you, but I've got a business to run that's suffering this week 'cause I'm here instead of there." He looked at his watch so dramatically that I might have believed he was seeing one for the first time. "It'll be five o'clock by the time I reach my car. I'll be glad when this whole FloraGlobal affair is over, and we can go back to work."

Hart and Rhyne Garrett would be leaving at five, too, if they hadn't already gone. I rushed to the Garrett booth specifically to ask Hart if Tom Thurgood had come by looking for me. Rhyne had left when I got there, but not Hart.

"Nope," Hart said when I asked him, although I hated to

in front of his adoring public. He was in the last stages of his finale for the day. This time he'd suspended an industrial glue gun from his fishing wire. He was dramatically curving the gun's trigger, both widening its angle and deepening the already dark blue hue as he did. With one magic swipe, the gun's dimensions shifted and popped into the realm of reality. The crowd of mostly older women all said "ahhhh."

At some earlier point in the demonstration, Hart had actually plugged the gun into an outlet, let it heat to its ungodly 600 degrees Fahrenheit, and zapped a blob of it onto the foam core wall. I'm sure he'd been going for what he'd achieved earlier in the day with his pick machine rendering. Beside that drawing, he'd taken an actual pick and attached it to a small bouquet of dried flowers, then afixed them both to the foam core. The effect was three-dimensional for the entire wall, not just the area with the actual flowers. But when he'd shot the wall with the hot glue, most of it had rapidly eaten the wall itself. So Hart had created an amoeba-shaped peephole and a large one at that.

Hart stood from his bent-over position, putting both of his hands into the small of his back and stretching backward before straightening up. As he did, the crowd of twenty cheered. I even heard one "Bravo" in the mix. He quickly grabbed his turpentine rag, rubbed both hands on it, then bowed obligingly to his audience, using the rag as a flourish. Miraculously, the throng of women dispersed.

I couldn't believe what I'd seen. His entire face, usually so delicate and pale, flushed magenta when our eyes locked.

"I'm through for the day," he said.

"So I see. So I see. What's the technical phrase? 'That's a wrap, ladies and gentlemen'?" I didn't dare laugh, but I couldn't suppress the smile. The truth is, though, I was more impressed than tickled, and I told him so.

"Rhyne's been impressed too," he said with unmistakable

satisfaction. "He says he's going to give us his new silk line to market. Weren't you telling me you wished he'd do that? Good profit for us?"

This was the first time I'd ever heard Hart mention the word "profit" in conjunction with our work. Usually he balks if even "deadline" is mentioned.

"Way to go. You sold him. Yes, it's good profit. And, yes, we'll be needing that business." I looked up at the UFAS window, and added, "The sooner the better."

He was watching me. "UFAS not too happy with us?"

"Not too."

"They liked their booth, didn't they?"

"Yes, they liked their booth a lot. Who wouldn't?" The old floral ads on the UFAS walls were so impressive, I knew the booth would take Best in Show. I wanted to enter it in some other design competition, though. It would do Hart's ego some good. "Tina's been unhappy with my approach to public relations."

He grinned. "Good riddance to them then. We don't want them anymore."

I loved this new side of Hart. Not just the sale itself, but his newfound confidence as well. His shoulders were straighter. He even seemed taller.

"You can say that again," I said, thinking how much I detested doing Tina's work. "You going home now?"

He said he was, then preoccupied himself with tightening the caps on his markers and wrapping his oil-laden brushes in tin foil. When he was satisfied that his stage was clean, he reached for his brown Berber V-neck and threw it over the shoulder of his plaid cotton shirt.

"Better put that on and be prepared to run to your car. The temperature's continued to drop outside." For all I knew, it could have started to snow by now.

"We're going backwards, aren't we?" he said. "I thought spring was here to stay."

"Me too," I said. "I guess it's what we get for thinking."

He was walking toward the Stonewall doors when I thought to ask him if he'd seen Ollie Smith.

"I don't know Ollie Smith," he yelled back. "Should I?"

No reason he should have.

"You coming?" he yelled again.

I gave him a halfhearted wave of my hand, then pointed up at the dark, reflective glass high on the wall. "Naw. You go celebrate your sale. I've got to check in with UFAS before I go."

By the time I was on the elevator going up to Tina's control room, I'd decided that Ollie Smith was a liar. What did I expect? Any man capable of calling a serve out when it's squarely center to the service box is capable of lying on the job as well. Tom had said as much when we'd discussed Ollie in the past. I'd completely dismissed him as I approached the UFAS door.

There was nothing I could promise Tina. Well, only that Joel Fineman would be in the *Observer*, although not as the stand-alone piece I was sure she expected. Merilee would mention FloraGlobal, though. When she says she'll do something, I can count on it. I had tried to get a tape from Tina. I could tell her that. I had that effort in my defense since I had called her, after all. Not answering the phone was her fault. She'd probably say I should have walked back up here. If she said that, I planned to stand stone-faced and say nothing. She'd deserve whatever the television station chose to do with my release. They'd probably show homophobes picketing the Center, so, in fairness, I needed to warn her about that. But I wouldn't tell her what I really hoped and that was, of course, no tape, no UFAS, and no mention at all of Joel Fineman's death.

I knocked while simultaneously opening the door. Almost immediately three uniformed officers converged on me from the front and both sides. A dozen or more similarly dressed policemen and women were rubber-gloved and conducting what I'd grown to recognize as crime scene analyses. I saw Tom standing next to where Tina was sitting. With him were two younger officers I'd often seen down at the station. Directly behind Tina was Jeep Ford, the department's security specialist, whom I'd seen earlier, charming the homophobes and deflecting the bugs.

"Hold up, guys," I heard Tom say. "She's here for a reason. Let's hear why."

I'm rarely at a loss for words since I use them to make my living. When Tom Thurgood and Jeep Ford turned to face me, however, what I saw by their sides left me mute. Tina Mauldin's white tunic shirt was a deep crimson. Every solitary bit of it was crimson—even the sleeves. She was spread facedown on her control board, arms extended there too. The glasses she wore on the top of her head lay beside her right hand. They were broken at the nose and hooked on a control switch. Her thin, black curly hair exposed the white of her scalp at the crown. The same deep crimson had filled in closer to her neck, though, giving her hair at that point a purple cast.

"Sydney?" Tom's voice seemed to have grown louder. "Why'd you come up here now?"

"I came to report," I was able to say. "I've been working for Tina."

He nodded. "When's the last time you saw her?"

"Around three," I said more clearly.

"Up here? Did you see her up here or somewhere else?"

"Here," I said. "She was fine," I added, then felt stupid for having said it.

"Anybody with her at the time?"

My mind was flooded with the image of her here. I couldn't think. I closed my eyes and tried to picture the room as it had been two hours earlier. Gradually, I could see the UFAS execs eating sandwiches behind Tina and me. I told Tom about them and how it looked like they'd been grabbing a quick bite

"They probably left right after I did," I said. "Oh, a technician was working on some wiring and one of the mascots was on his way in as I was leaving."

"A mascot?"

"Two people dressed up like bugs are working the show," I said, knowing how stupid it must have sounded to these people. "Tina hired them so they reported to her just as I did."

Tom nodded and waited silently.

"A short, stout man dressed like an orange ladybug was here."

Tom took a deep breath, letting it out slowly through his nose. He didn't say anything for a minute. He didn't look at me either. The people who were examining the carpet and furniture continued to poke and prod, occasionally lifting a hair or crumb with a small pair of tweezers. The officers beside me shifted uncomfortably, waiting for Tom's direction.

Finally, Tom raised his eyes to mine. The green always prominent in them had turned so dark that his eyes appeared black. I tried, but I couldn't read them.

He nodded to the men beside me. "Let her leave now. We know who she is."

To me he said more softly, almost a whisper really: "I'll talk to you later."

I mouthed "Tonight?"

"Yes," he said, but so quietly that I heard only the hiss at the end.

9

Ollie was inside the front lobby talking to a young information officer I'd seen at times with Tom. I walked right past them, and neither saw me. At least, they didn't acknowledge me.

I was surprised to see that no snow had fallen, so certain I'd been that it was beginning. Charlotte's rush hour traffic had begun, though, and was at its most aggressive as I attempted to reach the parking lot on the other side of Stonewall. Even when I had a red light, the right-on-red crew closed my small window of opportunity. Four light cycles came and went before I lucked into a napping banker and sprinted across to where I'd left the Trooper after lunch.

Before getting in the car, I paid the attendant and asked for a receipt. He was a redhead through and through, the kind whose freckles have merged and whose eye whites are pink. I noticed his gait was slow and he held his arm against his body. As he handed me my receipt, I looked into his eyes and saw dullness there. Something cold and wet fell on the back of my neck, making me shiver. If this was a snowflake, it was solitary because no others showed in the lights that had just come on at the corner of the lot.

"Just rain," the redhead said when he saw me wipe my neck and look to the sky.

"Feels like snow," I said, and pulled the skimpy collar of my wool blazer up under my hair.

"A piece of rain," he said. "You got yourself a big old piece of rain, is all." He grinned then, sharing with me not only his optimism but also the dark gap where his right front incisor once had been. But his grin was genuine, and, to me at that moment, it was the most comforting smile I'd ever seen.

In the twenty minutes it took me to drive the six blocks home, the pieces of rain had turned to small globs of slush, like ice cubes just starting to form. The roads weren't slick yet. Temperatures had dropped so rapidly during the day that the asphalt still held the warmth of yesterday. I knew, though, that once darkness fell, the roads would ice over for sure.

Tom and I had planned our last practice for tonight. Not against another doubles team, thank goodness. Just against each other with my children, George junior and Joanie, stepping in every once in a while. Surely Tom wouldn't make it tonight, not in time to play tennis anyway.

By the time Tom did arrive, the kids and I had built a fire in the living room fireplace. I'm a single parent with a sixteen-year-old daughter named Joan and a twelve-year-old son, George junior, named after his clandestine father. I say clandestine because George senior keeps himself at a distance from his kids' lives even though he lives in the same town we do, plays tennis at the same tennis club, and even shows up sometimes at the neighborhood grocery store the same time we're there. But he doesn't show up where his kids live very often and makes no attempt to do or say what most people would consider basic fatherly things.

So I play that role as well. George senior left us when George junior had just turned two. One night, during those first horrible months, I was watching a news magazine television show, and it ran a report on a study of infant recognition of male and female voices and the importance of hearing both to the infant's development. Even though George junior was beginning to toddle, I didn't want to take any chances. I'd go into his room at night when I was sure he was fast asleep, and I'd lower my voice as low as I could make it go, and I'd talk to him. One way or another, I've been doing that ever since. There's not much I'm sure of in life, but there's one thing I know: I would do anything, become anyone, to give my kids their best chance at life.

All three of us had on our flannel pajamas and bathrobes, and I'd decided to fry bacon and eggs for sandwiches. I hadn't told them about my day. I rarely do. Usually because it'd bore them. A day like this day, however, would do the opposite.

I was flipping my own eggs in my grandmother's big black iron skillet when Tom came in the kitchen door. In spite of the roaring fire in the living room, both kids had taken their sandwiches downstairs to the family room and the television.

He laughed when he saw me. "You'll be hard-pressed to hit an overhead in that heavy bathrobe," he said.

"You're kidding, Tom. You don't really expect to practice tonight, do you?" I slid the spatula under the egg, then slipped it onto the toast on my plate. "Want a sandwich?"

He nodded.

"Bacon's draining on the paper towels," I added as I broke another egg into the hot pan for myself.

Tom spread some mayonnaise on his top piece of toast, shook so much pepper on his egg that I sneezed five feet away, then laid three pieces of bacon atop it and took his plate to the kitchen table. Before sitting to eat, he removed his topcoat and hung it up in the hall closet.

"How did you know to wear that tonight?" I asked. "The morning started out like spring."

"The forecast said it was coming, Sydney. It was on the news this morning. Coming up out of Atlanta."

"What exactly is 'it'?"

"Ice turning to snow. Two or three inches accumulation. Nothing much."

"Enough to stop us in our tracks," I said as I brought my sandwich to the table and sat down with him to eat.

"Charlotte is a bunch of sissies," he said as if he didn't live here. "A dusting closes the place down."

"It'll be the headlines," I added. "City Braces for Snow!"

His hesitation broke our lighthearted rhythm. "I doubt that," he said, and, of course, he meant that Tina Mauldin's murder would replace it.

It amazes me, how we're able to compartmentalize the events of our lives. How we can jump so easily from one experience to another, with no seeming residue of the first seeping into the makeup of the second. I've heard of high-powered officials moving from heated office sex to cabinet meetings on the other side of their office doors and of mothers insisting that their children brush their teeth just after some godawful tornadic disaster has ripped through their homes. I'm not sure I understand the politicians' ability to segregate, but I do understand the mothers'. There is great comfort in routine. Once I'd reached my home and my children this night, I'd been able to lock away the sight of Tina Mauldin's body. I truly had not thought about it after I saw my children's faces at my kitchen door.

Tom's simple "I doubt that" had removed whatever roadblock I'd set up inside my head. As I pushed a piece of crust across some pooled yolk on the side of my plate, I saw her body again. I resisted the image, but it pushed its way into my head in spite of my best efforts to stop it.

"Sorry you had to see that," Tom said, as if he'd been inside my head. His hand had come to rest on mine.

I put my fork down, took my napkin from my lap, and put it on the table. I couldn't eat any more of the sandwich.

Only then did I look up at Tom. He has more empathy in his eyes than most people have in their hearts. The green is deep and liquid, like a mountain pond on the edge of a forest. I know I can go there to rest, to renew. Sometimes I want to just stare at his eyes, to be with them the way I'd be beside that pond they so resemble.

"What happened to her?" I asked, and broke the spell I'd miraculously cloaked myself in since seeing the body of Tina Mauldin some two hours earlier.

"Somebody hated her enough to stab her five times in the neck and shoulders." He breathed deeply, then let it out slowly.

I felt warm all of a sudden, felt my face flush, then subside. I hadn't liked Tina myself. His words had made me aware of that. An irritating guilt came with it.

"What was it? A knife?" My voice sounded too high to me.

"A short one," he said. "But long enough to sever her spinal cord."

I grimaced. "One of those UFAS executives?"

He shook his head. "I doubt it. I can't imagine it was over a business dispute. Far too much passion for that."

I rubbed a callus on his thumb, not looking into his eyes. "How did you get away?" I asked.

"I had plans," he said, and swung his right hand across his lap in a backhand motion.

I sat back and laughed. "What plans? Not our tennis practice?" I picked up both our plates, took them to the sink, and ran water over them to keep the yolk from sticking too badly.

He nodded, not seeming able to understand the humor I saw. He clasped his hands together on the table. "They know I'm scheduled off for a long weekend. I've got two backups and asked for Jeep's help too since he's involved already. Right now they're getting in touch with all the people from that company who're here for this show."

"FloraGlobal," I said as I watched the sink fill with suds.

"FloraGlobal?" he repeated. "How do you know those people?"

"The people are UFAS," I said. "Stands for United Floral Associates Symposium. The show they're putting on is called FloraGlobal. They hired us to help put this show on," I said.

"They a Charlotte company?" he asked.

"Richmond," I said. "They needed lots of help pulling this floral symposium off."

"Symposium?"

I chuckled. "Sounds nice, doesn't it? Really, it's just an upgrade on trade shows. It's supposed to imply there'd be an exchange of new ideas." I finished drying the last of the plates and put them in the cabinet by the sink.

"Why didn't you put them in the dishwasher?" I could hear more interest in this question than in the one he'd asked about floral symposia.

"The yolk. If I didn't get it now, it would have left a film."

"Even after the dishwasher?"

I nodded and smiled. "That's been my experience. Even after the dishwasher."

Tom returned to his seat at the kitchen table. "Is there?" he said, once settled.

He'd lost me now.

"Is there an exchange of ideas at the show? Is that what people are doing? Exchanging ideas?"

I wiped my hands on the lapels of my flannel robe and returned to the table. "I don't know. Not really. The floral industry's a great big international dogfight. There are two or three groups vying to control the whole thing. UFAS is the newest player in that fight and probably has the best shot at control."

Tom tapped his fingers on the table and nodded his head to whatever tune was playing in his head, although I didn't recognize its rhythm. When he had finished with his music, he pushed his chair back, spread his long legs apart, and put his hands in his pants pockets. "Naw," he said with mock seriousness, and grinned. "Don't tell me Mom and Pop aren't growing those long-stemmed beauties I buy at their shop."

"Who'd you buy long-stemmed roses for?" I asked.

He laughed. "Hypothetical, Sydney. Just hypothetical. Seriously, though, who grows all those flowers?"

"Mostly South Americans, from what I can see. Brazil, Argentina. Used to be us, but the whole floral market's shifted down there in the last couple of years. The countries closest to the equator have the best growing conditions so they can produce the healthiest flowers, the best color."

He looked down at the back of his own hand, then up at me again. "So," he said, "if I were to send you

All-American roses, the likelihood is they'd be from South America rather than North. Is that right?"

"There is greater likelihood of them being from South America than of you actually sending them to me." Tom Thurgood had never sent me flowers, and the chances that he ever would were scarcer than seeing a star on a night like tonight.

He tapped his hand again on the table, then put it back in his pocket. "I didn't think that sort of thing meant anything to you, Sydney. Seems sort of old-fashioned for you."

"I love flowers," I said. "Why's that old-fashioned?"

Silence sat between us on my kitchen table. I thought how nice an arrangement of flowers might look sitting there instead.

"Somebody has sent me some," I said, and smiled, remembering my conversation with Sally. "Sally told me an arrangement had been sent to the office this morning. Don't know if they are roses, but it certainly means somebody appreciates me." I looked at him carefully and wondered for a tiny second if it had been Tom who'd sent those flowers and if all this befuddlement about flowers was to surprise me.

Tom cocked his head, didn't look at me. He didn't ask me who I thought the sender might have been either. I dismissed the wishful thoughts in my head. He wasn't even curious. I sometimes think he's not capable of jealousy. Maybe that's good. Maybe it's not.

He stood up slowly and put his hands in the small of his back and began to stretch. Uh-oh, here it comes, I thought. And I was right. His arms began to flail in what would have looked to the uninitiated like random motions. But the sweeping, full-arm movements had a purpose. He was warming up for tennis. I really couldn't believe it.

He was flexing his shoulder and back muscles with arm extended above his head and bent at the elbow, while he leaned over and peeked through the pulled curtain on the top half of my kitchen door. "It won't give us any trouble until after midnight," he said as he looked out.

"You're not still thinking of playing tonight, are you?" I said but knew by now that he was.

The kids and I put on warm-up suits while Tom doused my wonderful fire.

The three of us waited in the kitchen while Tom retrieved his tennis clothes from the trunk of his car and changed in my bedroom. Joan looked at me and said, "This is stupid to be going out tonight"

"I agree," I said.

"Tom's crazy, Mom," my astute daughter added as we continued to wait.

"No, he's not," George junior said defensively. "He wants them to win, that's all. They have to practice."

Joan merely shook her head.

"Any athlete knows that," George junior said, knowing perfectly well that those were fighting words to his sister. I braced myself for the usual sibling bickering.

Surprisingly, she didn't take the bait. Normally, if George junior says anything loaded with implications like that, Joan fights back, at least has to say that she's more of an athlete than he'll ever be. But tonight she didn't. I decided she was either too tired or was actually growing up. I thought about it some more as I sat there yawning. Eventually I came to the conclusion that perhaps the two are synonymous, exhaustion and maturity. If they are, I told myself, I was very, very mature.

Getting to the Charlotte Indoor Courts was a lot easier than getting back from them two hours later. Even though the drive is a mostly straight shot down South Boulevard, black ice had formed by ten when we left to come home. The kids and I took it upon ourselves to act as helmsmen, harbingers of approaching danger. "Watch out," I'd say. "A big one on your left in twenty yards. Stay to the center." George junior hung over Tom's shoulder the whole time and so startled him with one loud warning that he almost lost control of his Honda.

"You'd better stay here tonight," I said to him when we were safely back in my kitchen. Tom Thurgood lives twenty miles from me on Lake Wylie, a large bulge in the Catawba River, straddling the line between North and South Carolina. His only domestic responsibilities are two golden retrievers, who, frankly, mean as much to him in his own way as George junior and Joan mean to me.

When he just looked at me, I added, "Won't Rosie and Red be okay one night?"

"They can make it just fine," he said. "I wasn't planning on going home tonight. I need to go back to the Law Enforcement Center and get this case headed in the right direction."

"What can you possibly accomplish this time of night?"

"Lots."

"Like what?"

"Like assessing its solvability, for one thing. I don't really have a handle on it yet."

We'd been standing in the kitchen while we talked. Now Tom headed up the steps to where the third-floor bedrooms are in my tall, skinny house. The kids had already gone up to get ready for bed. I put some water on for hot chocolate, found a bag of miniature marshmallows in the pantry, and was stirring the steaming drink when he returned.

"Will any of your team still be down there this time of night?" Tom usually worked alone. Not having full control would be hard for him. If I'd had any doubt about the importance of tennis in Tom's life, sharing this case confirmed it.

"Jeep said he'd wait for me and fill me in."

I looked at him. "Jeep will understand that tennis took priority over Tina's death?" The second I said it I wished I could take it back. The comment was meant to make him feel guilty. "I'm sorry," I added. "That wasn't called for."

Tom stood at the door, his arms loaded down with the heavy jersey of his warm-ups and his size thirteen tennis shoes. "Sydney, if I didn't look on what I do as a job and not some mission, I would have burned out by now. It was one of the first things I learned when I joined the force. And Jeep helped me learn it."

"How'd he do that?" I reached into the bag of miniature marshmallows for the first time. They'd all hardened, felt like a bag of decorative garden pebbles. I pitched them into the trash can under the sink.

He stood there, no hint on his face that what I'd said offended him. "Jeep's sister killed herself." He said it softly.

I was shocked by a statement so unexpected. "God, Tom. I asked you how Jeep helped you see the force as a job."

He held his hand up, then nodded his head. "It *is* what I'm telling you. I'm getting to it." He shifted again. "When my wife, Carol, died, Jeep told me about his sister and how the experience would have destroyed him if he hadn't had his garden. Jeep loves his garden. He told me early on, 'Find something you love and be adamant about your right to do it. Otherwise, this stuff will eat you alive.'" His eyes were moist. So were mine.

"So I found tennis," he added, and smiled again.

"You surely did, Tom Thurgood," I said, and smiled at his grinning face. "If you ever need anyone to testify to that love, just have them call me."

We both laughed. He reached over and rubbed my shoulder, almost dropping his shoes.

"Why's Jeep been working the show?" I asked. "I've seen him with those bugs and I saw him with the protestors too."

"Ah, the bugs."

"Did you find the ladybug?"

"As we speak, a search is being conducted for the insect." He laughed and shook his head. "How can you take this kind of work seriously?"

I sipped the hot chocolate. It had grown lukewarm. "My work's just as serious as yours. The bugs are peripheral." I swallowed another small sip and smiled at Tom. "Now they're your peripherals. Just be grateful the ladybug walked into that room and not the bumblebee."

Poor Tom looked tired and confused.

"What about Jeep? Why is he at the show?"

Tom shifted the clothes and shoes he was carrying and put one hand on the doorknob. "The city's been nervous about those protestors. Don't want them getting out of hand."

"But they're just bigots, Tom," I said, and realized how crude I must have sounded. "I mean Jeep's always dealt with the really big events, hasn't he, like when the President comes to town?"

He nodded. "Well, we're city employees and the city is nervous. About its number one asset: its image. Besides, if Jeep's security unit only worked when someone like a president—any president—was in town, he and his guys would be out of work most of the time." He turned the knob and pulled, letting a sharp, wet draft inside the house. "And the UFAS show is the biggest event in town right now," he added as he started to go. "We'll need his unit on a case like Mauldin too."

I kissed him quickly and looked into his eyes. "Flora-Global," I said. "The show is FloraGlobal, remember? The organizers are UFAS."

He repeated the names to himself again. When he saw me shiver, he pushed the door against its jamb, but without letting it catch. "I like to see the chief keep Jeep busy. He's been down about his health and the retirement . . ."

"Is he being forced to retire?" I asked.

Tom's features dropped. "No, actually it's Jeep himself. He knows he can't go on. Some days he can't even walk."

"He looked like he was hurting this morning. The limp was pretty bad."

"One quick question, Sydney," he said just as I was turning to leave the kitchen. "Right off the bat, can you think of anyone who didn't like this Tina Mauldin?"

"Right off the bat, Tom, I can't imagine why anyone would."

"Would kill her?"

I shook my head. "Would like her." I was shocked at myself for saying it out loud.

He looked surprised too. "She was your client."

I stirred my chocolate with my index finger, then held the finger between my lips for a second. "Doesn't mean I had to like her. You don't like the mayor. You told me so yourself."

He left without saying anything more. I held back the curtain at the kitchen door and watched him slip once while walking to his old gray Honda. Then I turned the outside lights off, locked the door, and went downstairs to watch the eleven o'clock news.

Tina would have given the newscast a mixed review. In spite of the work she had directed me to do, Joel Fineman's death wasn't mentioned. As the self-appointed guardian of Joel's dignity, I was grateful for that. However, the FloraGlobal Show was part of the lead segment. Just what Tina would have hoped for. The anchor even called it by name. But I don't know how Tina Mauldin would have felt about herself. The anchor didn't mention her by name. She didn't even call her an executive, as she probably would have if Tina had been a man. Worst of all, her beloved UFAS didn't get a plug. The female anchor's lead-in was simply "Woman Murdered at FloraGlobal Show."

10

I've had my old black Trooper since 1988, the first year Isuzu gave the engine six cylinders instead of four. In those early years I got a kick out of picking up my employees on snow days when most of Charlotte stayed home. They would always grumble when I'd arrive cheerfully at their front doors.

This attitude was particularly true of the salesman, whoever he or she happened to be at the moment. Inevitably, that person would say, "I can't call on anybody today. I don't have a car."

Those words were my cue to smile and say, "I'll take you. Don't worry."

"Nobody will be there for me to call on. Why did you insist I come in with you?"

To which I'd answer, "Make some phone calls."

"They won't be in to take phone calls," he or she would say adamantly.

And, finally, I'd say, "So what? Just think how impressed they'll be tomorrow when they come to work and hear your message. 'That guy's impressive,' they'll say. 'Next time we have some advertising, let's call Allen Teague!' "

I'd lost several of these salespeople along the way. In fact, eventually I've lost every salesman Allen Teague has ever had. What can I say? They're only on commission. Not true employees, so they won't take direction. We just keep getting new ones. One of these days I'm going to figure out what I'm doing wrong.

Two things were different today from those early snow days. Well, maybe three because the kids would come to work with me when they were younger and school would be closed. I'd left them at home this morning. The most important change over those early years was that everybody was driving four-by-fours now. So the roads no longer belonged to me. That, in itself, took much of the fun out of picking up Sally and Hart. And, secondly, Allen Teague didn't have a salesman right now. We were in between, and that was usually fine with me—except I missed the teasing on a day like today.

I was glad it had snowed three inches on top of the ice. If it hadn't, eight-wheel-drive wouldn't have been enough to keep us from sliding. At the end of work today, though, we all knew it would be bad. The snow would either melt onto or pack down upon the ice during the day, probably a combination of the two. A bit before five, the sun would turn its rays to a slant and the melting snow would freeze upon the already frozen. If I didn't get away from work early, I'd end up playing bumper cars with everybody else. And I've discovered if you pick up your employees for work, you must take them home too.

I thought about today and what I had to do. First, go to the office to catch up on a few things. Then over to the Convention Center with Hart so he could go back to performing for all those female florists who seemed to be taken with him. If the day went as I hoped it would, leaving early would be a cinch. Nobody would be judging how I looked today so I'd worn jeans, an oversized chenille sweater, mid-calf boots, and my heavy parka.

I felt a sharp pang of guilt when I realized I was grateful I wouldn't be under Tina Mauldin's thumb.

Sally, Hart, and I sat inside the Trooper in Allen Teague's parking lot off East Boulevard for at least thirty minutes while I fielded questions about Tina Mauldin's death.

"I swear I don't know anything," I said three or four times as they kept probing.

"What about Tom?" Sally said. "What does he think?"

"Last night he knew less than I did, although I'm sure that's changed by now."

Hart said, "You wouldn't expect a woman like her to die like that, would you?" He looked to me for confirmation. "She seemed awfully cold to me. Like she wouldn't know anyone well enough."

I agreed. "I think it's odd too. Hard to believe she could arouse that much passion in anyone." As we sat, the window steamed up. The temperature outside was a mere twenty-seven, but the sun's strong rays pressed against the condensation, causing the delicate film to sweat in places and disappear.

"She was passionate about computers and things like that," Sally said. "Maybe she was killed by someone else who was passionate about the same things."

Hart nodded at Sally. "That makes good sense."

"Yes, it does," I said, "except for the mess. Y'all didn't see it, but whoever killed her ruined her control board."

"How so?" they said together.

"Blood. It seeped down into everything. I'm sure all those keys are ruined."

"I spilled Coke on my keyboard last fall. Remember, Sydney?" She turned to Hart, who looked to be having as hard a time as I was listening to Sally compare her Coke spill with the bleed out of someone's body. "Nobody could fix it," she said to him. "We had to order another one." She turned back to me. "But the new keyboard wasn't expensive, was it?"

"Not much," I said, and opened the Trooper door. "Tina's keyboard is built-in, though. And I don't think it's a Packard Bell."

Walking to Allen Teague's back door, the three of us slipped in unison since we were holding on to each other for balance. Sally continued to chatter to Hart. I decided she had missed us this week.

At the back door, Sally said to me, "Oh, Sydney, you haven't seen your flowers."

I fiddled with the key, which has always been difficult to get just right in the door. "You told me about the arrangement, though. You even read me the card."

"But you don't know about the second one. It came just before you called for those press releases yesterday, and I simply forgot to tell you." She turned to Hart and winked. "Sydney's not telling us something, Hart." She turned back to me. "Come on, Sydney, who is it? Something's going on that you're not telling us."

"There has to be some mistake," I said. I finally heard the magic click of the key catching its groove and pushed the door open. "That's the only explanation I have. Somebody somewhere is sitting there without her flowers 'cause they were delivered here by mistake."

"Wow! Some mistake," Hart said as we entered my office and gazed down at the two exquisite arrangements.

My conference table seats eight. It was taken over by the two arrangements. Hart immediately reached out to one particular flower, carefully lifting it by its exotic petals.

"What do you call this one?" he asked me.

I was distracted and didn't answer right away.

"Do you know, Sydney?"

"It has a funny name, but I can't remember," Sally answered when I didn't.

"Bird-of-paradise," I said evenly.

"This one's so exotic it grosses me out," Sally said as she touched the phallic form of a bright red anthurium.

The two of them removed their heavy coats and gloves and Hart his scarf. Sally put her coat in the closet, then went into our small utility room to make the morning coffee. Hart draped his apparel over one of the chairs beside the conference table.

"We're not going to be here long, are we?" he said, his hand still on his scarf.

I didn't answer. I couldn't.

He looked up at me then. "Sydney?"

I was staring at the two arrangements.

"Sydney, you okay?"

I wasn't but didn't know how to tell him.

"Why haven't you taken your coat off?"

I slowly began to unbutton my coat. Breathe deeply, I told myself. Think, Sydney. Who did this? Why?

Hart had come to my side, had touched my elbow. I felt his gaze on my face, but it was his physical touch that jolted me partway out of my shock.

Sally had returned to the room and was saying something about some magazine insertion orders that were due to go out.

"Something's wrong with Sydney," Hart said to her as he continued to hover.

Now the two of them stood with me, one on each side,

working together to remove my coat without much cooperation from me.

"What is it, Sydney?" Sally said. "You seemed fine just a minute ago."

"The flowers," I said.

My knees truly wobbled as I approached the two arrangements. They couldn't have been more different: one exotic, the other as traditional as the centerpiece at a southern wedding. I had seen them both before, of course. The exotic one was so large that it reached almost to the edges of the three-foot-wide table. Its clone had been the same width. The zebra grass and lily turf gave it a wistful and natural nest, almost the way you'd expect to come upon it on a South Sea island. The birds-of-paradise, anthuriums, and Peruvian daffodils rose out of it gracefully. The more sedate arrangement was all white and mounded toward the center in traditional British style. White irises, white freesias, and white campanula were intermingled with fanciful daisies and pert white dianthus. My instincts had been right: Joel hadn't designed this one. The tall, clear plastic cardholders that rose out of both arrangements looked to me like devils' forks.

I turned to Sally. She was still standing with Hart beside the chair where my coat lay discarded. "Which one arrived first?" I asked her.

Her clear blue eyes held mine as she joined me at the table. She could tell by looking at me that something was terribly wrong. Her normally upbeat expression was now tinged with worry, reflecting my own state of anxiety. She reached for the card on the white arrangement and handed it to me.

"This one," she said. "It's the one I read to you over the phone."

I hesitated before I took it. I wasn't so much afraid of

this one as I was of the other one, though. After all, I knew what this one said.

"What does it say?" Hart asked as he joined us at the conference table.

I removed the card and read it out loud.

" 'When words are not enough'?" Hart repeated and cocked his head, first in my direction and then toward Sally.

"The same as Joel Fineman's card," I said. "He had it with him when he died." I held the card in one hand and its small envelope in the other. I turned the envelope over in my hand. My name was written in blue ballpoint ink across it. The name of the shop was printed in the upper left-hand corner above the printing of a solitary red rose.

"Do either of you know a florist by the name of Suzannah's Flowers?" I looked at Hart and at Sally, but their expressions told me they didn't.

I walked to the other side of the table where the large arrangement majestically sat. I put the first card back in its envelope and laid it on the table under the arching zebra grass of this display. I took a deep breath.

"I'll find that florist in the phone book," I heard Hart say. "What was it again?"

Out of the corner of my eye I saw him leaning over my desk, fumbling with the phone book. Hart looked nervous.

"Suzannah's Flowers," I said. I peered at the envelope of the second arrangement before touching it. "This one says Suzannah's too."

"I've got it right here," Hart said. "Suzannah's Flowers, Central Avenue." He looked up at me. "It's pretty far out Central. Who do you know way out there?"

"Nobody I can think of." I watched Hart writing the address and phone number on the top leaf of a pink sticky pad, then tearing it off and folding the sheet over its glued portion. He gripped the tiny piece of paper in his right hand as if someone might try to steal it.

Sally had been looking from the exotic arrangement to me and back again. "Are you going to look at that one?" she asked with a tone in her voice I recognized as fear.

I nodded, dug my upper teeth into my lower lip, and reached for the second card. I felt like a player of Russian roulette. My name was written across the envelope with the same blue pen as the first. I opened it, swallowed hard, and read it:

Fresh Cut Just for You

I mumbled the phrase to myself a couple of times, completely forgetting the two other people who were waiting almost as anxiously as I had been.

Sally took the card from me and read it out loud for Hart to hear.

"I don't understand," I said, my voice shaking. "What does this mean? Who would do this?"

"Do what?" Sally asked. "Who would do what?"

I looked at Hart, who had closed the phone book and was walking over to me. His eyes shared the same innocent confusion Sally's voice had held.

"Help me get these off the table," I said to Hart, as I picked up the white arrangement and moved it to the floor in the farthest corner of my office.

While Hart moved the larger one to the same distant floor space, Sally and I poured ourselves coffee and a cup for Hart as well. We all three returned to the conference table, where we pulled out our chairs and sat. Neither of them said a word. They were waiting for me to explain.

So, as best I could, I did explain. But I could explain only what I myself understood, and that was very limited. I told them first about the card in Joel's casket spray and how I hadn't recognized it as a gift card. How I later came across an arrangement in his show booth, and it was just like this white one.

"And the card had been removed from the card holder so that explains the source of the note I found yesterday right after he died. That note said . . . it said the exact same thing this one says."

" 'When words are not enough'?" Sally was staring at the white arrangement.

I nodded even though she wasn't looking at me.

Hart said, "Could Joel have arranged his own? That's what he did for a living . . ."

"No," I answered. "That would be too much of a coincidence . . . particularly in view of the other one." I looked at them both lying in the corner of the room. Having them removed like that had cleared my head considerably.

"What's so strange about the other card?" Hart asked, and looked from me to the large exotic arrangement in the corner.

"Yes, I think it's much prettier than the white one. You know it costs more." Sally was sipping her coffee, not really catching what I was trying to tell them.

I nodded in the direction of the second arrangement. "That is the exact same arrangement I saw in Tina Mauldin's control room yesterday. I looked at it only briefly, but who could forget an arrangement that unusual?"

"Good Lord," Sally said, and sipped from her suddenly rattling cup.

Hart whistled softly. "The cards. Were they the same too? Did hers say 'fresh cut just for you'?" He winced even as he said it.

I shook my head. "I don't know." I shuddered. What a terribly sick joke it would be if these same words had been on her card as well. Was whoever killed her playing some kind of macabre game with all of us? Had other people received these duplicate cards and arrangements or only me? And if only me, why?

"Does this mean Joel Fineman was murdered too?" Hart asked.

I shrugged, then stared into his concerned eyes. "Probably. But how will we ever know?"

He nodded, a pained expression on his face.

"This person is downright evil," Sally said in typical understatement.

"I'm going to find out who sent you these." Hart stood and returned to my desk, where he opened his hand and dropped the sticky note onto the desktop. He spread it with his two forefingers, squinted at his own writing on a crimped paper, mouthed the number to himself, then picked up the phone and dialed.

"Are you calling that Suzannah's place?" Sally asked.

Hart put his finger to his lips, then abruptly began to talk into the phone's mouthpiece. "Yes, my name's Sydney Teague," he began, much to both Sally's and my surprise. "Someone has sent me two beautiful arrangements from your shop, but the person's name wasn't put on the cards. Can you please check your records and tell me who sent them." He was silent for a few seconds while Suzannah or her representative said something. "Yesterday," Hart said. "They were both delivered yesterday . . . Yes, that would be the seventeenth . . ."

Sally was chewing her knuckle. She was also staring at Hart. He turned his back to us while he waited for the answer to his question.

"Yesterday was St. Patrick's Day," I whispered to Sally. "I hadn't realized it had come and gone, had you?"

Sally shook her head slowly. Her knuckle remained in her mouth. She looked more worried than she had last time I'd looked into her eyes.

I touched her hand. "Sally," I whispered more loudly,

"there's nothing we can do about any of this. We need to breathe deeply and relax, okay?"

She smiled tentatively.

"That's better," I said. "Now tell me. Did you wear green yesterday?" Why I went on like this with her at that moment I'll never understand. When I look back on it, though, I think maybe this small talk was my rendition of the mother with her home blown away who insists that her children brush their teeth. I was absolutely determined to chitchat with Sally.

"You forget? Well, you're not alone. I forgot, too, even though Tom and I are playing in this St. Patrick's Day Tournament."

Hart's voice had been soft and polite in the background. Now it rose considerably and came between the illusion of normalcy I'd so carefully created. Sally and I were forced to listen to him argue. "No," he said with clear indignation, "I don't understand why you can't tell me. . . . No, it makes no sense to me. I received them. It seems to me I have a right to know who's sending me flowers. . . . Anonymous affection? No such thing. Try anonymous harassment!"

But he wasn't getting anywhere. It was pretty obvious from where we sat that Hart wasn't going to prevail.

I mouthed "Forget it" to him, but he kept on anyway. He raised his voice an octave each time he made the same request with different words until finally slamming the receiver down in disgust and defeat.

"I'm sorry," he said. "They wouldn't tell me. Store policy."

I smiled. "I never would have known."

First Sally then Hart laughed with me. Not hearty laughs, but laughs nonetheless. By that time, we all needed it.

"Now let me make a call," I said, and exchanged places with Hart at my desk. "I'm going to find Tom Thurgood. He'll get to the bottom of this."

They both nodded.

First I called his direct number at the Law Enforcement Center. His machine was on and I got his standard message: away from his desk, leave a number or call the switchboard if this is an emergency. I decided it was, even though "emergency" may have been a bit too strong a word.

I called the switchboard and identified myself. I am on Tom's "list." Each officer, at least in homicide, gives a short list of people to the switchboard, with whom switchboard is told it's okay to share that officer's whereabouts. I'm on Tom's list with his mother and his veterinarian, so the glamour of this list grows thin very quickly. Half the time Tom fails to tell switchboard where he can be reached. She knew today, though, so I thanked her and hung up.

I looked at Hart. "Anything you need to do here before we go to the Convention Center?"

"Odds and ends, but nothing big. Nothing that can't wait until the show ends tomorrow."

"Good. That's where Tom is. I should have known."

Hart went upstairs to call a printer or two to set a quote in motion for a client. He also needed to pick up more white markers from his art room. He'd been through three already, he said, and might need as many as three more to finish the faux blueprint in the Garrett booth.

While I waited for Hart, I called my children. I needed to hear their voices. My heart pounded as the phone rang ten times before Joan answered. I'd obviously waked her.

"Mom," she whined. "You said we could sleep late. It's only nine o'clock."

"I know, I know. I'm sorry, honey. You can go back to

sleep after you check the doors. I'm not sure I locked them. Go check for me while I wait."

"You always lock the doors, Mom."

"Just check," I said anxiously. "I'd feel better if you would."

She sighed as she lay the receiver sloppily on what must have been my bedside table. I heard it clunk its way over uneven stacks of paperback books before clanging onto the floor.

"All locked," she said breathlessly on her return. "Can I go back to bed now?"

"Of course, honey. I'll call again at lunchtime. You and George junior might want to get the puzzles out of the hall closet."

"Good-bye, Mom," she said impatiently. "Have a good day. I love you." Except for the "I love you" on the end, Joan sounded like me getting rid of a salesman.

I poured myself a half-cup of coffee and thought about having a cigarette for the first time in a month. Quitting had been harder in some ways than quitting Scotch. My mind had cleared when I quit drinking; it had become muddled after quitting the cigarettes. I kept waiting for my concentration to come back. So far, it hadn't. I was grateful I hadn't hidden an emergency pack because, at that moment, I would have smoked one without even knowing it.

I sipped the hot coffee and tried to focus on what I'd seen in Tina's control room the night before. The shock of seeing her had been so great that I found it hard to remember anything but the purple hue at her neck. I closed my eyes; I even pressed my hands to each side of my head, hoping to reactivate whatever connection my nicotine-deprived brain had lost. I could then see the cops milling around in the room, their magnifying glasses and tweezers in rubber-gloved hands. I also saw a man crouched in the corner, hunched over an entanglement of cables. Then I realized I'd seen him there earlier in the day, not that night. And the ladybug. He'd gone into the room just as I left. The technician had been there then too. So had the UFAS executives. I couldn't separate all these people from the room as I'd seen it the night before. I couldn't remember seeing the flowers that night at all.

12

Where had Tina's flowers gone? I worried about them the entire time I was driving to the Convention Center. Anyone carrying an arrangement that large and unusual was bound to have been noticed.

"Don't you think someone would have noticed?" I asked Hart for reassurance.

We were sitting at the intersection of East and South Boulevards, waiting for two wrecker crews to remove a Nissan Pathfinder and a Ford Explorer, both of whose macho approaches to snow driving had rendered two crunched front grills.

"Under normal circumstances, of course, someone would have," he said. "But at the FloraGlobal Show?" He laughed and looked over at me. "Where we're going I bet I've seen fifty arrangements even larger than that one."

Dammit. I hadn't thought about that. A person carrying flowers was the most common sight at Flora-Global. "Why would her killer take them away? If he went to the trouble to have the flowers sent, why take them away?"

"Maybe he's afraid they'll end up as evidence against him. And, of course, he doesn't want to get caught." Hart shifted himself around on the seat until he was able to lift the tail on his navy all-weather coat. He pulled out a handkerchief and began wiping the accumulated condensation from the windshield.

The last of the two wreckers headed down South Boulevard, its patient suspended at a forty-five-degree angle from the icy road. I slowly crossed the intersection toward South Tryon Street. "He may not want to be caught," I said, "but he's trying to send some kind of message."

"To whom?" Hart's thin eyebrows had pulled together.

I turned right on South Tryon Street and got in line behind a city slag truck. It looked and moved like a World War II tank.

"To me, for one. Why else would I be receiving these arrangements too?" For a brief moment, I was afraid of my own question. What if I were being warned of my impending demise just like Joel and Tina? I think Hart was thinking the same thing because the silence between us for two whole blocks was uneasy.

"Just thank God he's only copying his messages to you. The people who've received the originals haven't fared so well." Hart didn't look at me when he said it.

"But why am I even being copied? What does he want me to do with it?"

Hart didn't have any ideas either. Why had I been chosen by this killer? These arrangements amounted to notices of his crimes. By now I was convinced that Joel had been murdered as well.

"We don't even know it's a man," Hart said. Then he

pushed my heat-control lever to the defrost position. "No wonder it keeps fogging up. You had it on heat." He said it like no normal person would have chosen heat at a temperature under thirty degrees.

The Charlotte Observer was on our left as we stopped at the light before turning right onto Stonewall. I wondered briefly if Merilee had made it to work in this mess. As soon as I turned, I wished I'd stayed home. The Convention Center was two blocks down, but the traffic was backed up in all directions. I could see the sign carriers from here. There were more of them than yesterday, maybe seventy-five as opposed to yesterday's fifty. They looked like they'd gone to Kinko's and had their signs done professionally. No more handmade posters. And they were singing loudly. "Onward! Christian Soldiers," I think it was. Maybe the singing helped keep them warm, but I bet it had more to do with the TV satellite vans that were parked curbside.

I looked at the watch on Hart's wrist. The show would open at ten and it was now nine forty-five. The congestion at the Stonewall Street entrance was ridiculous. Besides the satellite vans and the protesters, a steady stream of slowly moving cars formed three or four lanes of traffic instead of two. A crime lab van was wedged between two satellite vans. Show participants had already arrived and taken most of the spaces near the Center. Someone had plowed the lot where I'd been parking, leaving at least a fourth of it nothing but a mound of ice and snow. The "full" light flashed at me as I approached it. The red-headed attendant stood in front of the Trooper with both hands raised for me to stop. I backed out but not before noticing that Tom and his peers had taken the prime spots.

I circled the huge block surrounding the building two times looking for space in a parking lot but came up empty each time. At least part of this jam was perpetrated by Charlotte's finest, taking the finest spaces from the rest of us.

Hart was as frustrated as I was. "What about underneath the building?" he said.

"That's for show setup. We don't have cargo." I was seriously thinking about going home and dragging out the jigsaw puzzles.

Hart held his three white markers in his left hand. He pushed them in front of my face. "Yes, we do," he said. "I'm building a booth and have the materials here in your Trooper."

The Convention Center is flanked by Brevard Street on the east, Stonewall on the south, College on the east and Second Street on the north. A narrow, dark serpentine roadway runs under the Center from an entry ramp at the intersection of Brevard and Stonewall to its exit ramp onto Brevard at the other end of the block. The Trooper was spinning its slush-laden tires in yet another full lot across Brevard Street when Hart came up with his brilliant idea.

"There's no place to park under there," I said.

"Are you sure of that?" Hart said.

"I thought all they had down there were those high loading docks for big trucks."

Even as I expressed my doubt, I drove the Trooper out of the lot, pulled up to the light at the corner, and slipped down into the wet concrete hole where we had no business going. Once committed, there was no turning back. It's a good thing the tunnel was one-way because the curve of the wall, together with the width—or lack of it—of the road, never allowed me to see more than ten or fifteen feet ahead. I felt like a pinball that someone else had set in motion.

I'd been right about the docks: twenty-two of them plus five or six wide ramps, leading to either storage or show entrance. About half of the docks were occupied by eighteen-wheelers or fewer, although nothing so pedestrian as a four-wheeler like my Trooper. I didn't know if trucks were scheduled to pull into the empty docks at any minute or not. Nor did I know if there was even a way to know. I knew it wasn't posted publicly.

"Which slot, Captain?" I said to Hart, since he'd shown so much confidence in everything else recently.

"Why don't you pull into the last one down there on the end," he said, while pointing toward the farthest dock. "If the truckers aren't preassigned slots, don't you think they'd back into the first empty space?"

"Hart, you're making eminently good sense." I did as he said and, once backed in, found myself eye-level with the loading dock. Rather than walk out into the path of some larger pinball coming around the tunnel's bend, we did what all sophisticated advertising executives would do under similar circumstances. We climbed onto the hood of the Trooper, then up onto its tallest part above its seats, and jumped onto the cement landing above. I was glad I'd decided to wear pants.

I didn't expect to see anyone in the loading area now that the show had started for the day and, fortunately, I didn't. Five or six small forklifts sat idle. I told myself that if Hart and I could get away by four-thirty, no one would be the wiser for our minor rules infraction.

"What's Rhyne Garrett going to say if we leave early?" Hart said, sounding more like his old cautious self.

"He doesn't own you."

"He thinks he does. He says he could put a child through a year of college for what he's paying you for my services here."

I stopped and thought about that. "Maybe in-state university tuition, but not any of the private ones. Besides, what you've done for his name recognition will end up putting all three of his kids through someplace like Duke." I looked at him. "Won't you be finished sometime today?"

"He wants me to draw it out until the show closes at noon tomorrow. I told him it'd be hard, but I thought I could do that."

"So he'll disassemble the whole thing the minute it's complete," I said sarcastically.

"The nature of performance art," he said with a matter-of-fact tone.

We walked through a maze of partially assembled metal booth skeletons, rolled carpet, and innumerable boxes, mostly empty. Some of the boxes were actually crates that had probably housed the large walk-in coolers some people were selling and other people were using at the show. A good many of the boxes looked like coffins; at least, they were the right size to be coffins. South American long-stemmed flowers are shipped in these eight-foot-long boxes. I noticed that most of them had been knifed two or three times on top. I'd heard how Miami customs inspectors would walk the docks down there randomly slashing these things in their daily search for illegal drug shipments. Sometimes some delicate-stemmed flower would be ruined by this process, reduced to six-inch stems or less. Trade show veterans affectionately called this whole area we walked, between docks and booths, the "boneyard."

The moment we pushed open the heavy metal doors into the exhibit hall, I heard my name over the PA system. "Sydney Teague, please come to the UFAS show booth," it said.

I took a deep breath and steeled myself for what I knew would be a difficult day. Before we went in opposite directions, I told Hart I'd come by the Garrett booth for him at four.

"Good luck on getting him to let me leave."

"I'll think of something. We'll need to pick up Sally too. The roads will be slick by then and the traffic will have started." I paused for a couple of seconds and thought about the situation while I held onto his bulky navy sleeve. "On second thought, make it three forty-five."

He shook his head as he walked away from me.

The UFAS people were in a panic. Tom and his team had taken over their control room upstairs. A man who had been Tina's assistant had taken over the public relations function. I say "man" advisedly because, even though he told me he was a Virginia Commonwealth University graduate, he was pushing twenty at most. Knowing, as I did, Tina's fondness for control, I would have bet his decision-making experience on the job amounted to no more than what he would wear to work every morning.

His name was Jerry, although I couldn't remember his last. He was a compact five seven with curly, almost kinky, brown hair, a big dimple in his left cheek only; and he was fitted with the same horn-rimmed black glasses that Tina had sported. He'd worn a bold red tie with his conservative gray suit, a nice mixed message for a day like today.

"What am I supposed to do?" he asked. His voice was higher than I'd remembered it, the only other time I'd met him. "Those cops are up there acting like gods. My executives are wrecks. They're calling us one by one to answer their questions. And, to make matters worse, the Hornets' mascot is coming here after lunch."

"Why does that make it worse?"

"What do I do with him?"

"You don't have to do anything. Let him entertain the crowd. I'm sure that's why the city has asked him to come. They're not too happy about what's happened here either, you know." I unbuttoned my heavy parka and wondered for a second where I'd hang it.

"The mayor's office didn't really give me a choice about it. The woman said we needed a quality insect from what she'd heard. I have to agree with her there."

"I think she's right," I said, hoping Jerry would do well in his new role. "Hugo will fit right in with the mascots you're auditioning. Let the city help you ease whatever tensions people have over what happened."

Jerry's shoulders drooped, making him closer to five six. "You think so? You really think that'll help?"

I nodded. "Where are your bumblebee and the ladybug?"

He stood tiptoe and looked over the people milling around the front of the booth. He shook his head. "According to the schedule we set up, the ladybug is supposed to be here now. I guess he's late. Then that damn bee comes at eleven."

I smiled at Jerry. "Had a run-in with the bee?"

"I stay out of her way," he said. "That woman is dangerous."

I wish I'd stayed out of her way, I thought. "Which one of you hired those two?" I asked.

"Ms. Mauldin found them somewhere. I assumed she knew what she was doing. She always did know what she was doing." He paused but not out of sadness. I think his nerves were getting to him. "Both of those bugs give me the creeps, though."

"I think it's safe to say that Tina's forte was wiring, not

performance," I said, hoping he wouldn't think me disloyal for saying it. "Don't worry. The show's been great. A big hit. The crowd's having a wonderful time. I bet half of them don't even know what happened to Tina."

"I find that hard to believe," he said, while adjusting his glasses. His voice grew deeper as we talked, back to the timbre I'd remembered.

"You have these people captive. They're here all day. They go back to the hotel and flop from exhaustion. Then they get up and spend the rest of the evening in a restaurant. Most of them aren't watching television or reading newspapers."

"I hope you're right. We don't want the show spoiled for anyone." His seesaw voice had gone up an octave.

I patted him on the shoulder before I turned and walked away. "Jerry, I like your tie," I said.

The police had one of their own outside the elevator. The other two entrances to the control room were a set of stairs around the corner and a long, narrow hallway on the upper level, which effectively separated this room from the Center's registration and restaurant level. They probably had officers at those entrances too.

She recognized me but I didn't her, although I tried not to let on. I asked her if Tom was in the control room. I needed to talk with him, I told her.

She nodded. "They're questioning one of the Flora-Global people." She looked at her watch. "He's been up there twenty minutes and that's how long the other one was there. He'll probably be down in a minute."

"UFAS," I said.

"Beg your pardon," she said.

"The people. They're employees of UFAS. They put

on the FloraGlobal Show." Why was I hell bent on cor-
recting everybody on this technicality? For some reason it
seemed important to me.

She gazed pleasantly at me.

"Never mind," I said. "It's not important." And it wasn't.
Not to her anyway. It was clear to me, though, that I still
thought of myself as the agent of UFAS. I felt as responsible for the success of the show as Tina had, and now that
she was gone, even more so.

"Get over it," I mumbled to myself.

"Huh?"

I shook my head apologetically.

The radio hooked to her waist cracked static as the elevator door slid sideways and the pale UFAS exec stepped
out. He could have landed a part as a zombie on one of
those wonderful movies of my youth. He walked right
past us, without so much as a nod.

"You can go up now," she said to me as she put the radio back onto her belt.

I made a point of looking first at the table where the flowers
had been. It hadn't been my imagination. They were gone.
And I was sure they'd been gone the night before too.

"You look like you've seen a ghost," Tom said. "What's
going on?" He was sitting in Tina's chair and looked out
of place there. Two other plainclothes types were wiping
off the table where the flowers had been.

"There was a gigantic arrangement of flowers on that
table yesterday," I said, pointing. "Did you see it?"

All three of them nodded. Tom said yes. "It's over at
the Law Enforcement Center. In the evidence room." He
swiveled toward me as Tina had done yesterday. "Why?"

"Was there a card?"

He raised his eyebrows. The two other officers looked

at him. "Why, Sydney? What do you know about that card?"

"Then there was one," I said and walked closer to Tom.

He offered me the same chair I'd declined to sit in yesterday. I sat and stared at Tom. He was waiting for me to say more.

"I received the same flowers," I said. "I'm positive our cards said the same thing. 'Fresh Cut Just for You.' "

Now Tom looked as if he'd seen a ghost. His easygoing confidence disappeared. The two other officers came over and stood beside him so they could stare at me too. They all nodded, first at me and then at each other.

I told them about finding the flowers in my office this morning and about seeing them yesterday up here just before Tina died. When I said I was positive Joel Fineman had been murdered too, Tom leaned forward so far I thought he would lose his chair. I started with finding the card in Joel's casket spray at the design competition but not even realizing it was a gift card; told them about Sally telling me I had flowers with the same phrase written on it and how that had just confused me at the time. I told them how I'd seen an all-white display in Joel's booth yesterday, a display missing its gift card.

"When I walked into my office this morning, Tina's display wasn't the only one on my conference table. A white one just like Joel's was there too. Its card said the same thing Joel's card had said: 'When Words Are Not Enough.' "

All three of them were perfectly still when I finished. Even Tom. One of the officers whistled softly.

"I know the name of the florist," I said. "I thought we should go there and talk to her."

Tom's first word through all my telling was the following: "We?"

I nodded.

Tom continued to stare at me but leaned back in the direction of one of the officers and asked him if anyone had been assigned to the florist on Tina's card yet. That officer walked to a credenza and flipped through a clipboard. He called out a name I wasn't familiar with. "According to the schedule, he's supposed to check it out this afternoon."

"Stop him," Tom said, still looking at me. "I'll check it out myself." Then he finally spoke to me. "What's the purpose of you going along?"

"What do you know about flowers?" I asked him. "Last night you said they were superficial. Isn't that the word you used?" The two officers stared at Tom just as I was doing.

"I don't need to know anything about flowers," he said defensively. "Why would I need that?"

"Whoever's doing this is somehow connected to this show. It's a floral trade show. Floral," I repeated for emphasis. "Nothing else makes any sense, Tom. I can help you ask the right questions. You don't have anybody who can do that for you."

I watched him think. He was trying to figure out how to talk flowers without me. His green eyes had grown darker as we sat there, and his normally casual manner was long gone. The two other officers watched him too.

"Let's go then," he finally said to me.

13

Tom called the medical examiner's office from the car to get an autopsy started on Joel, an autopsy with a detailed toxicology component. He spoke with the ME himself, who asked Tom to hold while he located Joel's body.

While we waited, Tom squeezed my hand. "The perp's not after you, Sydney. He would have tried something by now."

I was silent. I wasn't absolutely sure about that. Something in Tom's voice didn't sound so sure either. It occurred to me that he was letting me ride with him to Suzannah's more to protect me than to use my knowledge of the floral world. I was on the verge of asking him that when the ME came back on the line.

"Joel Fineman's on the way to Atlanta as we speak," the ME said. "We tried to stop it, but the plane took off at ten-twelve."

I looked at my watch. It was ten thirty-six.

"Get him back up here, will you?" Tom said.

"Doing one better," the ME said. "We'll reroute the

body to Chapel Hill and let the state throw the works at him. Our toxicology panel's limited. Theirs isn't. Anything in particular they should be looking for?"

Tom looked at me. I shook my head and shrugged.

Tom said, "Anything connected to the floral trade. People who deal with flowers and florists themselves. The kind of chemicals they might use. That's probably the place to start."

"Any witnesses to his death?" The ME's voice was starting to crackle as we moved through heavy traffic at the intersection of Central and Eastway.

"I was there," I said to Tom, who looked startled.

"Just a sec," he said into the receiver, then waited for me to give him some particulars.

"He was flushed and sweating. He might have been dizzy and short of breath. It was hard to tell. I was in the audience. He was on a stage."

He gave that information to the medical examiner while I watched a wreck occur inside a strip shopping center's parking lot. It wasn't even ice-related, unless the silver-haired driver who backed her Suburban into the brand-new Volkswagen Bug was distracted by the thought of maneuvering the road. Whatever the reason, the poor VW owner must have been inside one of the shops. The Suburban's driver didn't even get out of her car to survey the extent of the damage she'd done. She knew it was more than a dent, though. I could tell by her furtive glances around the lot. Of course, she didn't notice Tom and me in the bland navy Toyota fifteen yards away.

We sat at a light the entire time this drama unfolded. Tom was still talking to the ME, although the content of his conversation had bypassed me once I began to watch the woman in the Suburban. Our light turned green just as the Suburban pulled away from its victim and headed toward the exit lane onto the large thoroughfare and ultimate freedom. I pulled the idea pad I keep for client brainstorms out of my pocketbook and wrote down her tag number. I pulled my seat belt off so I could twist around enough to get the VW's license too.

Tom had finished talking to the ME by the time I finished writing. I ripped the piece of paper from its wire binding and stuffed it into the pocket of Tom's camel-colored sport jacket.

"I'll be damned if that bitch will get away with that," I said, almost to myself.

He patted his pocket as he continued to steer with his left hand. "What's this?" he said without removing the paper.

"The tag number of a woman in a Suburban who thinks she's gotten away with destroying a poor Volkswagen. I watched the whole damn thing just now." I was so angry that my trembling hands were having a difficult go at rebuckling my seat belt.

Tom pulled the sheet out, looked at it briefly, and put it down on the seat. "You can come down to the station and give a witness statement, if you want."

"Why can't I just give it to you?"

"Not my job, Sydney." He continued to drive. A minute or so later he said, "If I had time, but I really don't."

"I hate that," I said. "I really, really hate to hear that from you. Wrong is wrong, Tom. You know it. You have the power to stop that woman right now if you want to. But, oh no, you play the protocol game and pawn it off on some poor traffic cop." I picked up the sheet of notebook paper and returned it to my pocketbook.

He pulled into Suzannah's Flowers, a one-and-a-half-story red-brick building that looked as if it had once been someone's home. He put the Toyota in park and turned to face me.

"You're nervous and scared, and I understand that. You'll be okay." He unhooked his seat belt and added, "And so will the owner of the Volkswagen."

"It would take you thirty minutes at most to track her down and cite her, dammit . . ."

He grabbed my gesturing hands. "The reason I won't go find the woman in the Suburban is because someone else can do a better job of it. I'm not going to step into someone else's territory any more than I'd want someone stepping into mine. The reason we are sitting in this parking space right now is because someone is sending floral announcements of murders." He paused until I looked at him. "Murder's what I do, remember?"

As I opened the car door, I was shaking. Even now, I don't think it was entirely fear. I remember feeling very cold, but, as Tom would remind me, fear feels cold. But so does twenty-six degrees and dropping, with wind that pushes inside your clothes and stays there to chill your shoulders and run the course of your spine down to your heels.

Tom came around to my side of the car and pulled me close to him. Although he was wearing only that wool sport jacket and I the heavy parka, his warmth was truly radiant. His heat followed the same path the chill had taken on my body. By the time he released me, I felt ashamed of my reaction, both emotionally and physically.

Almost as if he knew, he said, "I might really need your help in there. I want you to jump in if you think of something to ask."

I managed to smile. My gratitude was deeper, though.

This location on Central was a mixed bag of gas stations, Vietnamese grocery stores and restaurants, secondhand shops that had once been homes, like Suzannah's, and cheap shopping strips filled with marginal retail businesses. A large, homemade COME IN sign hung from a nail on a thick wooden door that was painted white. The paint on the door was cracking, I noticed, as was the white trim edging the fifties' casement windows.

Bells hung from the inside of the door and tinkled softly as we entered. What once had been a living room and a dining room alcove were filled with knickknacks of the decorator's trade: small porcelain figurines, brass and copper spittoons and fireplace tools, embroidered pillows mostly with garden themes, and vases of every description. Stashed here and there in baskets and vases were bunches of silk hydrangea and eucalyptus branches. The air was almost stifling in its combination of scents. Potpourri, both loose in bowls and filling small pillows, was thrown into the mix as well. If the space hadn't been so small, it wouldn't have overwhelmed the senses so, but I watched Tom rubbing his nose as we made our way through the decorative maze in search of Suzannah.

We found the woman behind a large laminated kitchen counter where she had set up an assembly line of carnations and floral tape. Little boutonnieres lay by her elbow. She looked about my age, maybe older. The tips of her brown hair were gray. Her glasses were halfway down the bridge of her nose in lieu of the bifocals she probably needed.

"I hope you don't mind if I work while we talk," she said. "A wedding tonight. We need to deliver before the roads ice over again."

Tom and I nodded. Then Tom removed his identification and extended his long arm over the counter with it in the palm of his hand so she could see it clearly. He said, "Detective Thurgood, Charlotte–Mecklenburg police." I wondered why he hadn't said "homicide." Was that information something he regularly held back in situations like this?

"Oh my," the woman said, dropping the fistful of carnations she'd been preparing to wrap. "What's the problem, Officer?"

"No problem" was Tom's immediate reply, and he smiled at her.

I watched her shoulders drop as she relaxed.

Tom glanced at me, then back at her. "This is Ms. Teague. We just want to ask you about some flowers someone ordered from you."

She nodded at me briefly, then looked up into Tom's face. "Okay, Officer." She pushed the carnations and tape to the side, then wiped her hands on the black apron she wore.

"Are you Suzannah?" Tom asked her.

She shook her head. "My mother. She's gone now, but I saw no reason to change the name. I'm Jenny." She extended her hand to Tom but not to me.

Tom pulled a piece of paper from inside his coat lapel and glanced at it briefly. "Do you remember an order sent to a Joel Fineman and another one to a Tina Mauldin? Both were sent yesterday to the UFAS show at the Convention Center."

"The FloraGlobal Show," I interjected. He'd said for me to jump right in.

Tom nodded as he continued to look at Jenny.

"Oh yes." She smiled broadly, then quickly stopped, a jumble of confused expressions fighting for dominance on her face. "A florist doesn't forget orders like those easily," she continued. "Probably the biggest single direct order we've ever had here."

"The same person placed them both?" Tom's question was close to a statement.

"And a whole lot more," she said, almost defensively. She was probably afraid Tom had the power to take her money away.

"The name Sydney Teague," Tom said. "Do you remember several orders sent to her?"

I tried swallowing but couldn't quite do it.

"Him," she said. "I've talked with Sydney Teague, and he was a man."

I interrupted. "I'm Sydney Teague. A man, a friend of mine, called you for me this morning. He was trying to find out who's sending me these flowers."

She looked even more confused for an instant. The room was silent. I couldn't see Tom's face for his reaction.

"It was Hart, Tom," I said.

He didn't acknowledge my comment. Instead, he continued waiting for Jenny to answer him. So far, I hadn't contributed much to this interview. The silence seemed awkward to me now.

"Yes," Jenny finally said, "Sydney Teague is to receive an arrangement every time one of these other people does."

Her use of the present tense scared the hell out of me. It meant there were more arrangements to come.

Tom seemed suddenly more intense. His words became fast and clipped. "How many total arrangements were in this order? One order? It was one order, wasn't it?"

She nodded quickly, aware of the change in him.

"So one order spread over several days?"

Nodding again, she said, "Placed Monday morning. He wanted them to start going out on Tuesday, but I couldn't get some of the flowers he specified that quickly."

"Total number of arrangements?" Tom asked again, but quietly this time.

Only then did she push her glasses back up her nose. She wiped her hands again on her apron and walked to a desk in a corner of the room where she pushed back a tab on a metal vertical-flip file. She pulled out two flimsy sheets of white paper about half the size of a standard piece of copy paper. The papers were attached to each other with an oversized paper clip. She brought them back to the counter.

"Let's see here," she said, letting her glasses slide back down her nose as she studied the papers before her. "The man's name was Lewis. He called the order in Monday morning. I took the order myself."

"First name?" Tom said.

She looked back at the paper. "Doesn't say. Unless he's a house account, he probably paid with a credit card." She walked back to the flip file and removed a piece of paper lying in front of the rest. She used her index finger to scroll down a list of twenty or so names. "Here it is," she said. "He used a Visa. I can get his first name off that receipt." She walked back to the desk, pulled open a drawer and lifted what looked like a check box from inside. Then she shuffled through the receipts in there until finding the one she wanted and bringing it to the counter. She turned it around for Tom to see.

I leaned toward the counter so I could see too. The name Jenny had written on the Visa slip said C. R. Lewis with a Selwyn Avenue apartment address. I knew a lot of people who lived on Selwyn, but I couldn't place anyone with the last name of Lewis.

Tom looked to me for an acknowledgment or some kind of indication that I knew the name.

I shook my head. "No," I said.

While Tom and I still stared at the Visa slip, Jenny pulled the larger sheets back in front of herself. "He called in early on Monday morning. Sydney Teague was to get four arrangements, three of them delivered immediately after arrangements were sent to three other people. The fourth one she gets alone. So that's seven deliveries altogether." She picked up a pencil and made four checks on the paper. Then she looked up at Tom. "We've delivered over half already," she said. "After the two on the truck are delivered, we just have the one left. Do you want me to cancel it?"

I expected Tom to say yes. He's a cautious man who doesn't put anyone at risk unnecessarily. His delay, therefore, threw me. His eventual answer threw me even more.

"I don't think so," he said. "When does the next one go out?"

"It's on the truck now," she said, then looked at me. "Well, they both are. One for you and one for Barry Firth of the Grocers' Floral Alliance. All of these have been delivered down at the big FloraGlobal show at the Convention Center." She opened her hand in my direction. "Yours are going to you at an East Boulevard address except for the last one." She checked the paper again. "Yes, here it is. Your last one comes to you at the Convention Center too. In care of Garrett Floral Supply."

"What does the one on the truck look like?" I asked.

"It's another big one: three-dozen yellow glads with galax fill. Quite dramatic." She smiled the smile of all professionals who love their work. "Looks like rays of sun all shooting skyward."

I was smiling with her, forgetting for an instant that she was describing a murder announcement.

Tom wasn't though. "Write the Visa cardholder's name and address down for me," he said abruptly. "Also today's recipient and his organization."

"I know Barry Firth, Tom," I said.

He didn't hear me. He acted, in fact, as if I wasn't there.

Jenny bit her upper lip, pushed her glasses up with her forefinger, took one of her business cards and wrote Firth's name and the Grocers' Floral Alliance on it with her pencil. She pulled another card out of her apron pocket and was beginning to write Lewis's Visa information when Tom stopped her.

"The last one," he said urgently. "When does the last one go out?"

She looked down at the paper again. She was beginning to show signs of Tom's urgency. She dropped her pencil on the floor, bent to pick it up, and her glasses slid off her nose entirely. She caught them in her hand with the pencil. "Tomorrow morning. His instructions were 'just before noon.' " Then she picked up the Visa slip, extended it some distance from her eyes, and held it firmly. Tom's nerves, and probably my own as well, had rattled her beyond acceptance. Jenny was determined to get her composure back.

"The show closes at noon," I said to Tom, although I was watching Jenny write numbers on her business card. I looked up at him then and saw that he was staring at me. I couldn't tell if he was worried or not. His eyes were so intense that they made him seem angry at me.

"Is this Barry Firth at the show today?" Tom asked me.

I nodded. "I think so. The grocers have one of the bigger booths, a real presence there. Besides, they've spent the week working a deal with the South American growers. Barry's been critical to that."

"What kind of deal?" Tom asked. A hint of command had crept into his tone.

"Bulk buying. Negotiating on behalf of the country's grocery chains. Half of them anyway."

Jenny gasped. "Bulk from the South Americans?" Her brow knit itself together. She put the Visa slip back in its box and handed Tom the business card. "Damn them." she said, then seemed shocked at her own words. "Sorry," she added. "But they'll all see the death of us yet. Florists don't stand a chance anymore."

Tom let the comment slide by him, but I didn't. She sounded just like Peg to me.

Tom and I spoke at the same time, he asking to use Jenny's phone and I asking what my solo arrangement looked like.

In keeping with some kind of tradition we'd established, she heard Tom but not me. She directed him around the counter to a phone on her desk. He dialed what I assumed to be the UFAS control room because he asked to speak with Jeep. While he was talking, Jenny stood staring at me with profound confusion in her eyes. I understood exactly how she felt.

She said to me, almost in a whisper, "I know something awful must be going on, but this was the biggest single order we've ever had—not counting weddings."

"You've already filled six of the seven," I said. "You won't lose that no matter what the police decide to do about tomorrow's order." I then repeated my earlier question, the one drowned out by Tom. "Tell me about the arrangement for me, the one that's to go out tomorrow. Have you completed it?"

"Heavens no. It'll take me and my daughter all night. We can't even deliver the wedding I'm working on because of it. My husband will have to do it and he hates delivering weddings." Her eyes regained the concentration they'd momentarily lost, devoid of the anxiety she'd shown over potential lost business and crimes untold. "It's quite an unusual arrangement, to say the least. It calls for a series of wire forms over Oasis foam in the shape of hearts. Three-dimensional hearts at that." Her hands began to move along the proposed imaginary lines of the arrangement—mounding, swooping—showing how smaller hearts would grow off a large, center one. "Short-stemmed red carnations are to make up the heart bases."

"Put in with picks?" I wanted her to know I understood her business.

She nodded and smiled. "We'll need hundreds of carnations." She paused and gazed into my eyes. "This man thinks an awful lot of you. The labor alone will cost more than today's glads in its entirety. And let me tell you about the really special touch he asked for. Centered on each of the smaller hearts, he wants geometrics fashioned out of white carnations. You know, a triangle on one, a circle and then a square on the two others. I can probably balance only three smaller hearts. He said that would be okay."

"You talked in this much detail with the man who placed the order?"

"Oh yes," Jenny said. "He was very, very particular. He knew exactly what he wanted for all four designs."

"Isn't that unusual, particularly for a man?"

"Maybe, but not that unusual. Men know more than they used to. And . . ." She hesitated, seeming to size me up for receiving her next words. "And, gay men send lots of flowers to their friends these days. They are probably our biggest customers. They always know what they want."

"Weren't half of these recipients women?"

"Oh, you can't judge the order that way. Gays simply

like flowers. Gay men send as many arrangements to women as they do to men." She smiled brightly. "I find they usually like women a great deal and use flowers to communicate that. Whoever this is thinks highly of everyone, especially you, to spend the money he did." She whispered, "Over five hundred dollars for the lot."

"Wouldn't you say he knows floral design well?"

"I guess so," she said. "Sort of old-fashioned, though. Lord, I haven't seen a big splashy heart theme like he wants since Elvis died, maybe even before."

Tom had finished his call while she was talking and came back to where I was standing on the customer side of the counter. He quickly thanked the woman named Jenny, whose last name I never learned. He put his hand in the small of my back to direct me toward the door.

"Just a minute," I said, and looked at Tom. "What about the message on the final two?"

We both turned to Jenny, who looked down at her order sheet again. "Yes, here they are. For Firth, it's 'Flowers Are the Food of Life' and yours today says that too. Your special one tomorrow, Ms. Teague, says 'Broken Hearts Don't Heal.'" She looked embarrassed. "Uh-oh, whose heart did you break? Some guys never forget, you know."

"Do you think it means that?" I asked.

Her expression was knowing. Then she nodded. "Seems a shame to take away your surprise on getting these, you know. It's half of the pleasure of receiving flowers, don't you think?"

Not this time, I thought to myself, but nodded to her. I repeated the two phrases out loud.

Jenny nodded.

"Could you write those down too?" Tom said, still with his hand on my back.

She started to reach inside her pockets for a business

card again, when I stopped her. "Wait a minute. That's too much for the back of a business card." I pulled my idea pad out of my pocketbook, ripped out the first empty sheet, which was the one after the Suburban's license tag, and handed it to her.

When she was finished, she started to hand the paper to Tom, but I intercepted it. "Thank you, Jenny," I said, and smiled.

She looked at Tom for some sign that she'd broken the law. He gave her one of his abbreviated waves instead and a mumbled thank you as well.

We were at her front door when she called out, "So, it's really okay if I go ahead and make up the big display for tomorrow?"

Tom nodded. "Unless we call you."

She was shaking her head. "When would you let me know?"

Tom shrugged, as if creating a three-dimensional foam heart display was an everyday chore. He had no idea about these things. "Tom . . ." I began, only to be drowned out by Jenny.

"No way. If you call me tomorrow and call it off, I'm out two people working all night and over fifty dollars in carnations. And that's wholesale."

Tom looked down at me for leadership on this issue. I frowned appropriately, making it clear I was on Jenny's side on this.

"Has it already gone through on the credit card?" he asked her.

She nodded, much less afraid of Tom now that he was about to leave her shop.

"Okay, then," Tom said matter-of-factly. "You'll be paid." He pulled a business card out of his pocket and held it up. "You've given us what we need to solve this thing. We really appreciate your cooperation."

"You haven't even told me what Mr. Lewis did wrong. If that's his credit card number you have there, what could be illegal about sending these flowers?" She looked hopefully at Tom, then to me said, "You'll agree with me, I know. About the nicest gestures I've seen in a long time." She stared at Tom again.

He merely smiled at her, as if she'd just thanked him for something. I recognized the expression on his face. I'd seen it myself from time to time. I knew how confusing it could be and how frustrating to the person asking him the question. And now that I knew it was purposeful on his part, I wanted to scream whenever he did it. I felt sorry for Jenny. She deserved some kind of answer.

"Sorry," I said. "Can't talk about a case in progress." Tom nudged me out the door.

Out on the stoop, he laughed. "What TV show did you get that line from, Sydney? 'Case in progress,' " he repeated, a mocking tone in his voice.

His attitude made me mad. "It's what you always say to me," I said seriously, and walked ahead of him to the car.

14

On the ride back, we didn't talk much. Tom said the situation looked under control to him. He'd dispatched two homicide detectives and four backup patrol cars to track down the man named C. R. Lewis.

"Should have him in custody even before we get back," Tom said. "The only thing I'm worried about is Firth. If we can find him before Lewis, then this whole thing will be behind us."

"Is it really that simple, Tom? Why would this Lewis man want to kill these three people?" I didn't count myself on the list, although I'm not sure why. There was no reason not to and every reason I should. Denial is a powerful tool in the hands of the experienced.

Tom's willingness to explore the possibility of my being in danger was even more remote than my own. He really seemed to believe this strange case was all but wrapped up. In retrospect I think it was wishful thinking on his part. Savannah was looming, after all.

"Sydney," he began in a polite but definite lecture

tone, "I used to think there had to be a reason people murder. Maybe at one time there was. Back when our caves and our women were sacrosanct. Back when our territories were more defined, and people made sense like animals make sense. Murder's different today. I guess people still think they have reasons, but you ought to hear some of them. 'He looked at me funny.' 'She whispered behind my back.' 'She knew not to talk to me like that.' And my favorite one of all: 'I was in a bad mood.' " He looked over at me and squeezed my hand in his. "Murder's a stress reaction today. I've even heard of stress as a defense."

I let go of his hand and unzipped my heavy parka. It seemed terribly hot in the Toyota. "But those are the random acts," I said. "This is anything but random."

"No, it's not random, but once he's arrested, I'd guarantee you his reasoning won't make any sense. And he's probably being arrested as we speak."

"What about Barry Firth?" I asked. "Are your people looking for him right now?"

"Yeah." Tom looked at his watch. It was the only time during the drive that he looked at all worried.

"Why do you think he's sending me one by myself tomorrow? I'm not sure I want an answer to that, though." And the strange fact was, I really didn't.

The car slowed, then came to a stop at the light at Eastway. Tom didn't say anything until the light turned green and we were moving again. I got the feeling he didn't want to look at me.

Finally he spoke at least. "I'll ask Lewis, how's that?" He laughed, but the sound was too short, too dry—not really a laugh at all.

A long strand of golden retriever hair extended from Tom's jacket sleeve. I picked it off and held it up.

Tom looked at it, then back at the road. "Rosie's hair," he said.

"How do you know it doesn't belong to Red?" I asked.

"Too light," he said. "Red's hairs are red."

"Makes sense," I said. "I wish everything else did."

Tom didn't say anything. Neither of us did the rest of the ride.

It was eleven-thirty by the time we returned to the Convention Center. The sun that had been bright earlier was dull by then. The fresh blue of the sky had been so promising. Now it resembled the low gray luster of a cheap aluminum pot.

The redhead let Tom park behind his own car in the lot across from the Center. Although grateful we didn't have to walk far in the slosh, the taxpayer in me took note of the favoritism.

"I think it's going to snow again," I said to Tom as we crossed Stonewall. The air seemed wetter to me than it had earlier.

"No way," he said without looking at me.

"Pollyanna," I said without looking at him either.

The snow removal trucks had gone for the time being, but the TV satellite vans were still straddling the curb in front of the Center. Homophobes were continuing to mill around with their Kinko's signs. They were fewer than earlier as well as less organized and less adamant. No cameras were rolling at present, that fact probably explaining the decreased animation among the group.

Because of their good behavior I expected to see Jeep Ford among them, working his calming magic. I mentioned to Tom how good he'd been out here yesterday, how he'd charmed those lizards like a snake.

"The force is going to miss the hell out of Jeep," Tom

said. "His retirement's June first." Then he reminded me he'd pulled Jeep to work on the mess happening inside.

My sometimes AA buddy Curtis was there, though. He even spoke to me this time. Tom stopped with me.

"Haven't seen you around much, Curtis," I said in AA code. "We've all missed you." These simple words were code for "we all know you're out drinking, so you'd better get your act together and get back with the program."

"I was over at Christ Church last night," he said. His eyes were no longer red, and his face was clean-shaven. Curtis was sober for the moment, and I was glad to see it.

I introduced him to Tom.

"I didn't get your last name," Tom said.

"We don't have last names," I said quickly, and winked at Curtis.

Tom knew by now that the lack of a last name meant AA affiliation. He used to act awkward—shuffling or gazing at the ground—when I introduced him to another alcoholic. Now he just smiles and shakes hands as he was doing with Curtis.

The pleasantries were short-lived, however. With absolutely no warning whatsoever, two patrol cars and a navy Toyota like Tom's pulled onto the wide sidewalk no more than ten feet from where we stood talking. Two more patrol cars stopped in the street, their lights flashing but sirens silent. Curtis and I turned in their direction as a half-dozen cops poured out of their cars into the group of protestors. I glanced briefly at Tom. Even he looked confused.

One of the cops yelled, "There he is," and ran in our direction.

He grabbed Curtis so violently that Curtis's sign fell out of his hands. The rest of the policemen, including at least one plainclothes detective, converged on him. In no more than ten seconds Curtis had been handcuffed behind his back and read his Miranda rights. I was overwhelmed by the sheer speed of it all.

If it hadn't been for the reading of his Miranda, neither Tom nor I would have understood the reason for this onslaught of law enforcement. But the detective said, "Curtis Roger Lewis, you have the right to remain silent . . ."

"Oh my God," I said. "C. R. Lewis. Curtis is C. R. Lewis."

"What did I do?" Curtis whined. He was looking at me when he asked, as if I'd been the one to set him up.

I looked into his panicked eyes and saw not only confusion but fear there as well. The fear I saw wasn't of the police only. He was a man afraid of himself. I'd seen that expression in drunks' eyes before when memory fails them but experience says something bad has surely happened. How much booze did it take to forget deeds as gruesome as these murders?

"Call my wife, Sydney," Curtis begged.

"I didn't know you had a wife," I said, feeling confused and stupid.

"Hattie. You know her. Call Hattie."

"Hattie's your wife?" I said in disbelief. Hattie's one of the stalwarts of my regular Saturday night AA group. She's been going to the same group I have for almost as long as I have—over ten years. She's spiritual, open-minded, and wise. I'd never seen her speak to Curtis during his sporadic visits to our group. I couldn't believe she was married to him.

"Close you mouth, Sydney," Tom said when they had taken Curtis away. "Is it that much of a shock? The guy obviously hates gays."

I was hardly listening to Tom. I still couldn't believe the wonderful woman I knew as Hattie L. was married to this man. And what did he mean by "the guy hates gays"? Tina wasn't gay that I knew of and I certainly wasn't.

"The guy's an active drunk, Tom. He couldn't have done this."

"He didn't seem drunk to me."

"Maybe not today," I said, "but drunk's his normal state."

The camera crews, who'd all been inside looking for action, came rushing through the glass doors just as the patrol car carrying Curtis pulled away. Tom and I watched as, one by one, they jumped into their vans, like a posse jumping on their steeds, and followed a bewildered and shackled Curtis to the Law Enforcement Center.

"I need to call his wife," I said.

Tom said he was going to see if his men had found Barry Firth. "I feel certain we caught this in time," he said, making Curtis sound like a progressive disease.

"Will you let me know?" I asked with no confidence in Tom's certainty.

"About Firth?"

I nodded. "The rest of it too. When you figure the whole thing out."

"You know I will. Where will you be?"

"Garrett Floral Supply, if the owner will let me use his phone." I sighed heavily. I must have looked confused by the turn of events.

"Sydney, you don't have to be alcohol-free to plan and execute murders. In fact, a hefty percentage of murders involve alcohol. It fuels the hatred."

"Sounds like the random ones," I said.

He shook his head. "No. Not always. They plan while they're sober and get drunk to execute the plan."

"My memory of the process is different," I said. "When I was drinking, I must have planned the deaths of a hundred people all told. When I'd sober up, I was afraid to get out of bed."

I stared into his confident eyes and tried to share what he was feeling. I couldn't. "It doesn't make sense," I said.

"I told you it wouldn't make sense. It never does."

"Sydney Allen, tell me about this murder you have over there. Ollie Smith is running around the newsroom like it's Christmas morning." It was Merilee Gillespie on the phone. She'd called my office so much this morning, she said, that Sally finally gave her the number to Rhyne Garrett's booth.

I sat in one of Rhyne's director's chairs with Rhyne glaring at me as if my sitting down had halted the flow of his business. I hunched over and looked at my feet rather than his angry eyes.

"Tom says it's over," I said to her. "I'm not sure I agree, but he's the cop, not me. They arrested a picketing homophobe, a guy who's been hanging around all week."

"Wouldn't you just know it, hon? There's been steady violence from that corner, but you don't read much about it. I almost hate to say it, but something like this will at least bring that violence to light."

Even looking at the floor, I could feel the intensity of Rhyne's eyes on the top of my head. I told Merilee I'd have to hang up.

"I want you to see the story on Joel Fineman and the others," she said quickly. "That's really why I tracked you down."

"When's it going to run?"

"Sunday. A big splash. I'm real proud of it. How about lunch tomorrow so I can share it with you?"

"Can't do it. The show's closing at noon tomorrow," I said as I looked up and smiled at Rhyne. "As soon as I can get free after that, Tom and I are going to grab my kids and head to Savannah for the weekend."

Rhyne mouthed for me to get off. I mouthed back that I was.

"Shoot." Merilee sounded really disappointed.

"Breakfast. Let's do breakfast," I said. "IHOP on South Boulevard at eight. How's that?"

It was fine with her and a good thing too because if I had not hung up then, I believe I would have lost Rhyne Garrett as a client. And since Hart was so proud of having snared us his new silk line yesterday, I would have alienated Hart as well.

"That is a business line." He glared at me.

"Sorry," I said. "It was a business call."

"Not my business. You need to get a cellular phone like everybody else." As he reprimanded me, he stood with his hands folded behind his back. He looked like a proper English butler announcing the rules of the house.

Today Hart had suspended a straw wreath, wrapped in decorative ribbon, from the metal poles. His audience had swelled to a small throng. I smiled and nodded in the direction of Hart's audience. "Your idea worked," I said. "His admirers have grown daily."

Rhyne didn't return my smile. Instead he said, "When's it going to rub off on business?"

I stood up. "I don't know when, but I guarantee that it will." I tried smiling at him again and pointed down at his phone. "May I make two more short phone calls?"

"No, you may not."

Hart smiled at me pleasantly as I gathered my large pocketbook to leave. "Come back later," he said over his shoulder. His voice was bolder and fuller than I'd ever heard it. Was he catching a cold or a new level of confidence?

His audience parted for me, even stared at me in awe. The way Leonardo DiCaprio's mother must get stares when she's with her famous son.

Peg was alone in his small, exquisite booth. Although Allen Teague was his agency, he'd outfitted the space himself. It was one time I didn't argue the superiority of our skills. In fact, if Peg had possessed Hart's graphic knowledge, he could have probably designed his own ads and brochures as well.

His backdrop was mostly white with gold and silver stenciled accents. The few arrangements he'd chosen to display were green, although in many shades of green, except for gilded curly willow interspersed throughout. All the other florists, both retail and wholesale, who had booths at the show had gone overboard with color. Instinctively, Peg knew they would and had chosen his elegant but understated theme accordingly.

"The prick," Peg said. "That stuffy, anal prick. Of course you may use my phone. Talk as long as you want. Brevity is the soul of the devil in these matters."

"I do plan to be brief," I said. "Don't make me into the devil, Peg."

"Then I didn't mean it, dear. Whatever you do is always divine."

He was reclining in the corner on a gold damask chaise, a piece with the look of old money. Except for the simple gold-rubbed straight-back I pulled from the other corner, it was the only seat in his booth. Peg wasn't looking for customers here. He was making a statement to the industry. He didn't need them.

The phone sat on a small but ornate Italian table of various inlaid woods and paint patterns. Even the phone looked antique. It was white with gold trim and a rotary dial face. As I awkwardly dialed my children, I tried to remember the last time I'd used a phone like this.

Joan told me she was reading, but I could hear the television in the background.

"Who's watching television, then?"

"Your son," she said with the dry but droll tone of an old-fashioned schoolmarm.

I had to chuckle. "Put him on, please."

"Don't you have anything better to do than watch television?" I asked when he picked up.

"Like what, Mom?" He really sounded perplexed.

"Like reading, for one thing."

He was silent.

"Or the puzzles. Did you get out the puzzles?"

"I've done them all," he said with a definite childish whine.

"I like to do them every winter," I said. "Doing them once doesn't make them any easier the second time around."

"Huh? If you can't get any better, Mom, why do them at all?" His voice was starting to get that early adolescent edge to it.

I watched Peg sip what was probably tea from a beautiful porcelain cup. I sighed out loud, then spoke into the receiver: "Read a book, George junior, or do your homework, if you're desperate. But turn off that damn television. I'm going to get a lock on it if you don't stop watching so much."

After we'd hung up, I sat there wondering if he ever paid any attention to me.

"Kid problems?" Peg asked casually.

"Not really. Not any more than usual." A white porcelain bowl of off-white buttermints sat on the Italian table. I took one and laid it between my lips.

"I don't know how you do it, Sydney. Running Allen Teague, raising those two kids alone. You amaze everyone who knows you, do you know that?"

It was highly unusual for Peg to turn sincere on me like this. I wasn't sure how to handle the compliment.

"Open up," I said, and pointed to his mouth. When he did, I lobbed a buttermint into it perfectly. "You embarrass me, Peg. Anybody'd do the same. We live the lives we're given."

"Some of us choose," he said abruptly. "Some of us orchestrate our lives down to its most minute detail." He lifted another buttermint, studied it for a second, then put it in his mouth. "Like cream-colored mints against white porcelain."

"May I use the phone one more time?" I asked, as directly and simply as I could.

"Be my guest," he said while still sucking on the buttermint.

"Do you mind if I call information?" I held the old-fashioned receiver in my hand.

"Only way to get a number in this booth. I didn't bring a phone book."

"C. R. Lewis on Selwyn Avenue," I said to the automated voice. I don't know why, but I watched Peg for recognition when I said the name. His expression didn't change. In fact, he looked bored.

I'd never done this before, told a woman that her husband had just been arrested for murder. I felt that little wire in my chest, the one that dangles there trying to prepare you for the unexpected. I wondered what the protocol on my delivery was. Should I announce it like a death? More like a wreck? Or matter-of-factly, as if Curtis was down at the grocery store and therefore would be late coming home?

I opted for death. I mean, how much worse could a phone call get? As I listened to the ringing, I leaned toward Peg. "I hate having to make this call," I said. I showed him the perspiration on my hand.

Just as I said that, Hattie L. came on the line. I recognized her voice from hundreds of hours of AA meetings. She was shocked that I'd be calling her, she said outright. Not as shocked as you're about to be, I thought.

She asked my last name again, then how I'd figured out what hers was.

I swallowed hard. Hold it, Sydney. Back up. You can't say you heard her name during the reading of her husband's Miranda rights. Get Hattie back to the beginning. There was nowhere we could go with this conversation.

I took a deep breath. "Hattie, Curtis has been arrested for murder."

I held that breath for a full minute. Hattie took almost as long to speak as I did to start breathing again. When she did, though, her tone was matter-of-fact. She didn't even ask who was dead. Her questions were simple and direct: When did the arrest happen and where was he now? Her response had been a grocery store response, after all. We talked for a few minutes more, she the calm one and I offering nothing in return. Some people do serenity better than others. Some of us have to re-create it every day of our lives.

"I'm afraid I've perspired on your phone's receiver," I said to Peg when I'd hung up.

He stood and reached for a handkerchief on top of a stack under his counter. "I told you I keep these things handy. Can't have enough handkerchiefs." He wiped the residue of my nerves from the receiver and put it back in its U-shaped cradle.

"I feel as if I'm dumping all over you, but I have one

more favor. May I leave this heavy coat here? Rhyne Garrett's not loving me today. I'm not welcome in his booth, so I'm sure my coat isn't either. I'm beginning to feel like a polar bear in Georgia." I dabbed at the perspiration trapped under my chenille sweater.

He helped me off with the parka without saying a word. Then he hung it on an appropriately antique hall tree. He didn't ask me any questions about my call to Curtis's wife. Not even who Curtis was. But even more odd was his lack of curiosity about whom he was accused of killing.

I decided to leave it alone. I had too much on my mind already.

15

I had that antsy feeling I get when something needs to be done but I don't know what it is. It's like a call to action, complete with internal horns and sirens going off in my head. Almost any action on my part will quell these feelings. So I decided to walk the Convention Center floor. And, if Tom hadn't done so already, to find Barry Firth in the process.

Peg's booth was toward the front of the exhibit hall, across from FloraGlobal. Grocers' Floral Alliance was in a corner toward the back. Although my boots and jeans were out of place amid the upscale dress of most of these florists, walking the length of two football fields, or what seemed like it, was easier because of it.

The Center appeared as crowded today as it had been yesterday. Automatically I thought how pleased Tina Mauldin would have been. Here she had ice and snow over the city and a full house in spite of it. No matter what I thought of her personally, I had to give her credit for knowing her business.

Thinking of Tina led me to thinking of Tom up there in the control room. For the first time since her murder I wondered about her control board, her "electronic toy" so marred by her blood. Was it still working? I looked above me to that black window and wondered if the police were taping everything as Tina had done. Had Tom's crew been able to salvage what she'd taped already? And, if they had, was there at least some evidence of Joel's murder? Only then did I realize Tom hadn't shared any information with me today. Surely he'd have gathered some evidence by now.

I kept walking, passing every level of sale in the floral trade: from off-brand foam and pick manufacturers, through wholesale distributors of casket saddles and plastic bouquet holders, all the way up to the big stuff like walk-in coolers and personal greenhouses. I realized for the first time that even though I'd helped plan this show, I'd never really experienced it the way I was doing now. I watched two men in a ribbon-manufacturing booth crinkling bows with a proprietary, awkward-looking small machine they were trying to sell to retailers. Two booths down, a woman was demonstrating the process of gilding flowers. She was wearing a wet suit, the kind you go scuba diving in. Only hers was metallic gold. As I passed, she dipped fresh roses into a bowl. I didn't see the roses reemerge, but I heard the small group assembled all say "ahhhh."

A Wisconsin-based cheese company offering mixed gift baskets of flowers and food had a booth set up to look like the set of *The Sound of Music*. Garlands of spruce and edelweiss were roped around the booth's perimeter. Cardboard-backed faux walls were plastered with Austrian mountain scenes even though they were just a tad under five feet tall. Not a good visual considering the

Center's wall height restrictions. A Christmas incense mix filled the air, but March was too soon after to turn me on. I know a young man who specializes in aural marketing. I'd try to remember to tell him my reaction to this particular ploy.

An older man and woman were in the booth, he in lederhosen and she in an ornately embroidered red apron with an equally ornate white blouse. They were offering all who passed by them their new product. I had to admit it looked delicious: ripe olive and walnut Brie torts. They were decorated with a confetti garnish of edible leaves and flower petals and cut into bite-size pieces. Just as everyone else who had gathered around was doing, I reached to pick one up from the woman's tray. Once I had the delicacy in my hand, however, I couldn't bring myself to eat it. Saliva caught in my throat. I choked.

"Is something wrong?" the woman asked.

"No. I'm fine . . . I'm fine. Something just caught in my throat. These look delicious." But my body felt something before my mind could give it a name. All of a sudden, I was afraid.

She smiled. "They are, dear. They're from Wisconsin."

I backed away, then walked to the middle of the hall where the crowd would shield me from her view. I reached into my pocketbook, pulled out an old wadded-up piece of tissue and wrapped the Brie in it. It had hit me just like that: What if this tiny bit of cheese, or something like it, had killed Joel? What if a tiny drop of some godforbidden lethal poison had been folded into this Brie?

I headed for the closest ladies' room and waited my turn for a cubicle. Once inside, I flushed the cheese down the toilet. Then I washed my hands for five whole minutes with steaming hot water. It had hit me the way grief does— unexpected and always from the blind side. Someone had made a list of people and was methodically killing them one by one. Until Curtis Lewis confessed to these crimes, everything and everybody I saw became suspect. I had to look out for myself. I didn't intend to be this killer's last victim.

So, putting myself on automatic pilot with the grocers' booth programmed in as my destination, I renewed my walk through the hall. I walked dead center, not wanting to come too close to anything floral or anyone florist. Not three minutes into my flight path, I saw Barry Firth's shocking white head of hair moving toward me. He appeared to be alone. Why hadn't Tom assigned a bodyguard by now?

I'd known Barry for twenty years, since he was a cub reporter for *The Charlotte Observer*. In those days I was a free-lance copywriter. Occasionally I'd write a feature for the paper too. I'd met Barry on a visit to the *Observer* for one of those feature assignments. Eight or ten years ago he'd ventured out into public relations work, and by then I'd started Allen Teague. Once or twice over the years we'd even shared clients—those rare ones in Charlotte who can afford both advertising and public relations. He'd been head of PR for the Grocers' Floral Alliance for about three years.

I wouldn't really have called Barry a friend, though; nor would he have considered me his. We were more like directional features for each other. You know. The big oak on the corner that's always been there. When you see it, you know to take a left. When I would see Barry handling PR, I knew the company was a solid one. His particular skill was bringing folks together in the art of the deal.

He saw me and waved as he approached. I pretended I hadn't seen him. I don't know why.

"How could you miss this head of hair?" His laugh was

self-deprecating, and his hair was indeed memorable: pure white, thick, and brushed back off his forehead. Barry was about five ten at the scalp; with his hair, a true six-footer. His hair had been starting to turn even back in his newspaper days when he was in his late thirties. It had turned completely white at about the time he went out on his own. I liked to tease him that his hair was his only drawing card and that my little firm had to produce in order to be recognized. He'd always respond by telling me to dye my hair purple. See if that'll pull in the clients, he'd say.

"I see your hair's still unimaginative, Sydney," he said, and grinned. "So you're still having to do good work to get noticed, eh? You can chalk this show up as one of your better projects. Rumor has it you and your art director are responsible for much of the success of FloraGlobal."

"That's unusual," I said, trying not to show the uneasiness I was feeling.

"What's unusual?"

"To be the subject of a positive rumor. Unfortunately, rumors are usually false and this one's no exception. Many, many people put the work in on FloraGlobal."

"You're modest, Sydney," he said.

"No, I'm not. You know me better than that. I'll take it if I deserve it. This time I don't. My art director does, though."

A woman carrying a large plastic FloraGlobal shopping bag bumped into my shoulder then tripped on Barry's foot. We were standing smack in the middle of the show's equivalent of Times Square and got whatever we deserved in angry stares and smashed toes. Barry touched my elbow and directed me into the closest booth.

"So what are you doing out here on the floor, Sydney? This is the first time I've seen you here. I figured you'd taken your money and run."

"I wish I had," I said, and forgot to laugh.

He stopped smiling himself when he saw I'd taken his words seriously. "You mean what happened to the UFAS PR woman?" The window was at least a hundred yards from us, but he looked in that direction anyway.

"Tina Mauldin. Yeah, that'll ruin a show," I said, and regretted my sarcasm immediately. "And, before her, Joel Fineman."

"Poor Joel. He was one of the great ones, wasn't he?"

I nodded. "I was there when he died."

"How's Peg Corbeil taking it?"

I wondered exactly what he meant. "Okay, I guess. He was with me."

"No show of guilt?"

I shook my head. "Why should he?"

"The scene Tuesday." He said it like I should have already known what he was talking about.

"What scene, Barry?"

"You didn't hear about it? I thought everybody heard it directly or heard about it. He broke it off with Joel and Joel didn't take it so well." He was surveying the vast room while he talked.

"What?"

He returned his gaze to me and smiled nervously. "We were all here setting up. The two of them were in the middle of the aisle calling each other every name in the book. It was obvious what it was about."

"I didn't think Peg and Joel had been lovers for a while now."

"Well, you thought wrong, Sydney. They've been off and on as long as I've known them. Peg has obviously found someone new." He licked his lower lip. "Joel was none too pleased about it."

I didn't know what to think. In fact, I felt sort of numb.

"Sydney," he said, suddenly animated, "I think I just helped close the biggest deal of my life. Have you heard what we've been working on?"

"I've heard something. A bulk deal, right?" I was grateful to throw the focus back on him.

He crossed fingers on both hands and looked toward the high ceilings. "Please, please, God, let it be done. All that's left are signatures, and, with any luck, we'll have those tonight over dinner. I've been down at First Union all morning with our lawyers and the ones the South Americans hired."

"No hitches?"

"None that any of us could see. Their lawyers just needed to take the numbers back to them for approval; then it's a done deal."

"A price break for the grocery stores?"

"Is it ever!" He could barely contain himself.

"How good? Don't withhold from me, Barry," I teased. I knew he'd tell me no matter what I said.

"Let's put it this way. Six months from now a bunch of fresh flowers will cost no more than a bunch of spring onions."

"Damn. Some bulk deal. No one will have an excuse not to bring flowers home, will they?"

He folded his hands behind his back and rocked a bit, a broad catlike smile on his face. "That's the plan, Sydney. That's the plan."

I watched the passersby, a good majority of them working florists, and knew how devastating this deal would be for them. I thought of the florist named Jenny I'd met this morning and how prophetic her words had been. They'd all be paying more for flowers wholesale than those of us at the grocery stores would be paying retail. This was a no-win deal for them.

"Say good-bye to FloraGlobal then," I said, feeling the bitterness all these florists would feel. "No reason to ever have this thing again."

Barry laughed, then slowly saw that I was serious. "Don't pull that crap on me, Sydney. I'm sick of the whiners. I'm surprised to find you among them."

"I'm not whining," I said. "I'm stating a fact. This industry won't exist after your perfect deal goes through. No one will be able to compete. No one." I stared at him, totally prepared to strike down any mumbo jumbo he was planning to send my way.

"Come on, Sydney Teague," he said, now as angry as I was. "What happened to progress? I've never known you to be a reactionary. Change isn't good or bad, dammit. It just is. Your comments sound like the damned threats I've been getting."

Those words stopped me cold. My anger completely disappeared. "What threats, Barry?" I heard my own voice wobble.

"Aw, nothing." The exuberance was completely gone now. His shoulders had drooped. "I've been getting notes from some kook."

"Do you mean here at the show? Or before now? What do you mean?" The words rushed out of me.

"For about a year," he said, but looked more frustrated than worried.

"Who? What kind of notes?"

"If I knew who was sending them, I would have had the jerk arrested by now. I've gotten four of these things over the past year. The notes are generic hate, with a pretty pitiful attempt at poetry." He stopped and stared at me. "The world's full of crazies, Sydney. We've always known that, you and me. It's just different when they zero in on you."

It was clear to me that no one had told Barry about the list of floral deliveries, and as much as I didn't want to be the one to break it to him, I knew I had to. "Barry, it's probably the same guy. He was just arrested a few minutes ago outside. A guy sending flowers with threats."

"What are you talking about?" Confusion replaced his anger. "What guy? What flowers?" He rested on the heels of his shoes, not about to go anywhere until I made myself clear.

"Someone's been sending flowers to people here at the show," I said carefully. "Earlier today I saw a list of who was to get these flowers, and your name was on it." I took a deep breath. "The notes aren't threatening, but the sender isn't kidding. He killed Joel Fineman and Tina Mauldin. The police arrested one of the picketers outside the show."

His eyes, which had been so intensely focused on me, shifted to the ground, but not before I noticed his jaw clench.

"Traced the credit card right to him," I said.

He raised his head again and nodded while peering deeply into my eyes. If I were forced to give his demeanor a name, I'd have to call it resignation.

"What? Sydney? What are you trying to tell me? Someone's trying to kill me?" He leaned toward me. A piece of his thick white hair fell onto his forehead.

"Have you received any flowers in the last hour or so?" I sounded to myself like airport personnel inquiring about luggage possession.

"The gladiola?"

I nodded. "Yes, they're glads, yellow glads."

His bold white eyebrows knit themselves together. "I saw them when I got back from the bank. They were for me?"

I nodded again and watched him closely.

"How long ago was that?"

He thought for a second, then shifted his stance. "No more than ten minutes. My staff didn't know the man who delivered them."

I shook my head. "He's not the one. He's just the florist. Or the husband of the florist." I steeled myself and added, "Those gladiola are this guy's calling card. He's letting you know he's ready to strike." I felt a chill when I said those words. Quickly I added, "But he's been arrested now. Soon we can relax."

He was shaking his head. "How does this creep sign his notes? Does he say, 'You kill the flowers and I'll kill you'?" His laugh was very ragged. He saw the shock on my face and suddenly stopped. "That's what he said all four times. Silly, but I've always thought he was completing 'Roses are red. Violets are blue.' " He nodded and raised his eyebrows, waiting for me to confirm.

"No," I said. "Your glads say 'Flowers Are the Food of Life.' "

He seemed to relax. "How stupid," he said. "That's no threat."

"Yes, it is," I said. "He's done it twice that we know of—with notes almost as inane."

"Well, then it's pretty obvious why the police want to see me," he said. "They're waiting in the UFAS control room." He automatically looked up there.

"I know," I said. "I knew they were looking for you. Thank God they called for you."

"My staff said an officer came to the booth. Told them to send me when I got back."

I studied his face for some clear sign that the seriousness of all this had sunk in. For a moment, I thought it had. Slowly the bafflement I'd seen evolved to something I couldn't easily label. He clenched his jaw again. "Dammit!" he said all of a sudden. "I'm not going to be scared off."

His anger was the last thing I expected. Fear, yes. But not this resurgent anger.

"Nobody's going to stop this deal, Sydney. It's the best damn deal I've ever been a part of." His jaw was fully set now, not just momentarily posed. Barry had become as territorial as a male lion with a dwindling food supply.

I thought I saw something else, though. I recognized the urgent anxiety in his eyes, the unwillingness to look clearly at something so unpleasant. In it, I saw myself.

I think, in the long run, Barry Firth and I were a lot alike.

16

I followed Barry to his meeting with Tom. I made no attempt to keep up with him. I couldn't have even if I'd wanted to.

He was demanding an explanation from Tom and Jeep by the time I entered the control room. Tom was doing most of the explaining while Jeep stared through the window at the crowds.

"We can't be certain, of course," Tom said, "but we have plenty of reasons to believe he's the perpetrator of these crimes."

"When will you be certain?" Barry demanded.

Tom hesitated long enough to get Jeep's attention. The two stared at each other for a moment—as long as it took to share a short, sarcastic laugh. "One hundred percent certain?" Tom said as if from an old, familiar script.

Barry nodded, his jaw still locking on solid resolve.

"When he confesses or when he's convicted. Either one's good enough for me." Tom's eyes were level with Barry's as he said it. Jeep looked at me instead of Barry, and nodded. I wanted to tell him I hadn't asked the question. He didn't need to explain anything to me. I looked away with Jeep still staring at me.

"Look," Tom said, his tone now empathetic, "I know how you're feeling." He walked over to the round table and pulled out a chair. "Why don't you sit down here a minute and we'll talk about it." He pulled another chair out and motioned for me to sit down too.

I sat immediately, but Barry hesitated. I watched his face during his brief internal struggle. When he finally did sit in the chair across from me, he appeared to have lost some battle. The resolve that had wound him so tightly let go like a yarn ball tossed to a litter of kittens.

Tom took the third chair. "Have a sandwich with us. We've put in an order from the College Street Café. There's plenty for all of us." Without waiting for Barry's response, he said, "What can we get you to drink? We're limited to the vending machine's inventory out in the hallway. Not bad, though. Even has orange juice if you don't like the carbonated stuff."

His uncharacteristic chatter finally got Tom what he wanted: a normal response out of Barry. "Water. I'd just like some water, if you have it."

"Should be easy enough," Tom said as he leaned back and reached for an empty pitcher on the cabinet shelf behind him. He nodded in Jeep's direction. "Sergeant Ford, will you do us the honors? There's a water fountain beside the drink machine." He held the pitcher with one hand, waiting for Jeep to take it.

But Jeep hadn't heard him. His eyes seemed fixed on the floor below.

"Jeep?" Tom shouted. "Some water for Mr. Firth."

I would have jumped if Tom had yelled like that at me. Jeep slowly looked back over his shoulder, then relieved

Tom of the pitcher and left the room. I noticed that same limp as he did.

Tom smiled at Barry. "You'll have to excuse Sergeant Ford's preoccupation. He heads up our Special Security unit and twenty of his folk are down on the floor along with twenty of mine, looking out for the two of you." He chuckled, more to himself than in sharing. "Think old Jeep ought to tell them all to go to lunch now while we've got both of you up here?"

Despite Tom's feigned affability, I resented how he was communicating our predicament. He made it sound like we'd done something ourselves to bring it on.

Barry looked at me with the first honest worry I'd seen on his face. "What do you mean by 'both of you'? How's Sydney involved in this?"

Tom let Barry figure it out on his own during the silence that followed. Barry continued to stare at me. Finally he said, "Are you on this list too? The list you say you've seen?"

I nodded slowly, still feeling the intensity of his stare.

"Goddamn," Barry said slowly. He sounded disgusted.

A thin, young and very black girl entered the room without knocking. She carried a large round tray with a round platter taking up most of its surface. At least twenty halves of club sandwiches formed a wheel circling the platter. A cup of upright triangular-fold napkins served as its hub.

"Clubs," she said without looking at any of us. She put the platter in the middle of the table, retrieved the check from a pocket at the hip of her starched blue uniform, slapped it down on the table, and recited "forty-eight twenty-six, gratuity not included."

Tom stood up, fumbled in his wallet, counted out two twenties, mumbled something to himself, then looked over toward Jeep, now back at the window. "Got a ten?"

Jeep shook his head.

The girl tapped her foot.

"I've got it," Barry said, pulling his wallet from his pants pocket. He added a ten to the two twenties Tom had already put on the table.

The girl crossed her arms and shifted her weight to the left hip and leg, like someone settling in for a long wait. "Gratuity not included," she repeated.

"Keep the change," Tom said, pulled out his chair again, and sat.

"Humph," she delivered. The girl grunted like a pro.

I stared at Tom, who didn't seem to realize his "tip" represented a mere three percent of the price of the sandwiches. I dug into my pocketbook for another ten, which she accepted without so much as a smile before disappearing down the hallway.

Something was definitely wrong with Tom. I'd grown to think of everything he said and everything he did as being very deliberate. It wasn't like him to not tip appropriately; it wasn't like him to crack the remark about dismissing officers either. Especially to laugh about it when he did. And his incessant chatter. The chatter made no sense at all. I'd known him to talk this much only when the subject was tennis or, on rare occasions, when he was extremely nervous about something. But that was usually again about tennis. Never had I seen him go on the way he was talking today.

If I had bothered to think about Tom's behavior in any more depth than I was doing, I might have figured things out before I did. If I had followed my own reasoning as far as it could take me, at least one life might not have been lost. Maybe even two.

Barry didn't give Tom much room to talk while we ate our sandwiches. He asked question after question of both

Tom and me. What was this all about, to which neither of us dared hazard a guess. Tom restrained himself enough to let me tell Barry of my own experiences: Joel's death, the crumpled gift card, flowers delivered to my office almost simultaneously, the same message. While I was telling him about Tina's flowers and the cruel, ironic message, he flinched—almost as if someone had thrown a punch at his face and barely missed.

"You received the same note?" His voice was deep, but hollow.

"The same flowers too. I found them there this morning along with the flowers like Joel's."

Gradually, as I talked and he asked questions, a kind of kinship formed between Barry and me. We became like two prison camp inhabitants, both having fought in the same war, both trying to survive whatever fate we shared now.

Tom watched us. Jeep had yet to join us at the table. He seemed to be looking for something down on the floor. Tom would occasionally look in his direction. Slowly I became convinced that the two of them knew something they weren't telling either Barry or me.

Barry swallowed hard. "This list with our names on it. Tina's name was on it? And Joel Fineman's?"

"They were the first two," I said slowly, confirming what I'd told him before.

He asked where I'd seen this list and that's when Tom took over the conversation again. While he was telling Barry about our visit with Jenny at Suzannah's Flowers, I picked up half a club and walked the few steps to where Jeep still stood at Tina's control panel and window.

"Here, Jeep," I whispered. "I hope you're not letting us—Barry and me—keep you from eating."

Jeep seemed almost embarrassed by that little bit of attention. He shook his head, raised a hand up, then let it drop. I found his mannerisms endearing. I'd understood from first meeting him why Tom liked Jeep so much. Not one drop of ego in the man's soul.

"I'll wait," he said, then pulled at his belt. "Trying to cut back too."

"You have to eat something." I held out the sandwich again. "And a club's not much."

"Eat it, Jeep," Tom said. I was surprised he'd heard our whispers in the midst of his conversation with Barry.

To oblige both Tom and me, Jeep did take the sandwich. After one bite, though, he held the rest of it in his right hand until Barry Firth left the room.

I returned to the table to hear Barry ask Tom which one of us was number three on the list.

"You're three and Sydney's four," Tom said evenly.

Barry looked up at me. "Those glads?"

I nodded.

"What flowers are you being sent?"

Leave it to the industry spokesperson in Barry to ask that question. I don't think anyone else would have under the same circumstances. I told him about the odd foam-based three-dimensional hearts I was slated to receive. I even described the triangle, square, and circle that were to sit in white relief against the red carnations that would make up the hearts.

He didn't react to the archaic design, even though I'd emphasized it so as not to stress its purpose. He listened intently, then turned toward Tom and took a deep breath. As he did, Tom bit into his sandwich.

Barry blurted out his history of receiving other, more threatening notes this year. How he'd ultimately dismissed them as competition toying with him or even someone in his own grocers' organization, someone jealous of this deal he was about to close.

"Sounds like somebody's been trying to tell you something for a long time." It was Jeep. The intrusion surprised me since he hadn't been involved in the conversation at all.

All three of us at the table turned toward him.

"What do I know though?" His half-smile was sheepish. He shrugged and turned back toward the window, the sandwich still in his hand.

Barry turned back to Tom. "Do you think those notes and these are connected?"

"We'll check it out," Tom said without commitment.

Barry stared at Tom a full minute. I thought, at the time, he was deciding, as I had, that more was known than was being said, and that both Tom and Jeep seemed to be playing a game with us similar to good cop/bad cop. Only this one was dumb cop/dumber cop.

Finally, Barry put the palms of his hands on the table-top and eased himself up slowly. As he did, he said to Tom, "Where's this Lewis character? Anybody trying to get him to come clean about all this?"

Tom began to nod and continued to do so—only more slowly—while he answered him. The two best interrogators he had were with Curtis at that moment, he said. They'd either get it out of him quickly or warm him up enough for Tom to take over this afternoon.

"If he's our man, we'll break him, Barry." Tom stopped to look at his watch, then back at Barry. "I don't think you have anything to worry about."

Barry pushed himself away from the table entirely. "Why do you say that?"

Tom glanced at me, but he made no eye contact. His

focus returned to Barry, and he said, "According to our man's schedule, you should have been dead before now."

The last thing Barry Firth said to any of us before leaving was a very sarcastic "some consolation." The poor guy's jaw was quivering in spite of his mocking tone.

As he closed the door, Jeep pulled the radio from his belt and began telling one of his men that Barry was on his way. "Pull Smith over and the two of you stick to him like glue. Don't let him out of your sight. Better yet, just introduce yourselves and tell him to pretend he's the President for the afternoon and you're the Secret Service." He stopped to chuckle at himself before continuing. "If he balks at that, then drop back again. Got all that?" Jeep held that club sandwich the entire time.

"Will you finally join us?" I said to him when he'd finished talking.

He assessed the sandwich in his hand as if it had sprouted there and not been delivered by me some ten minutes earlier. He bit into it as he limped to the table. I pushed one of the napkins in front of him as he sat, just in time to catch a nasty-looking yellow thing, which, on closer inspection, I deemed to be a slice of winter tomato.

"You okay, Jeep?" Tom said to him. "Leg bothering you?"

"My knee today." Jeep ran his hand down his left thigh, then straightened back in his chair and ate his sandwich. As he leaned over the napkin, I saw an odd lump on the outer rim of his ear. It was larger than the various barnacles and skin anomalies aging people invariably get. In fact, it was large enough to call a cyst but looked too much like bone itself or cartilage to be one.

"What you looking at, Sydney?" Jeep said when he saw me staring at it.

Embarrassed by my own rudeness, I looked down into my lap and pulled either a strand of pink chenille or a hair from one of Tom's dogs off my denim thigh.

"I've been wanting to ask you something, Tom," I said. I sought his eyes so I wouldn't have to look into Jeep's.

Tom mumbled a mouthful of encouragement.

Jeep seemed to have tuned us out again.

"The two people I saw in here yesterday besides the UFAS execs. The guy in the corner there," I said, pointing to where some cables lay coiled and unattached to anything that I could see. "He was fooling around with those cables. Could the UFAS people describe him?"

Tom showed mild interest, which was stronger than he'd been showing. "Did you get a good look at him?"

"No. He never stood up."

"Too bad. The FloraGlobal guys never took a look at him either."

I bit my tongue. Really bit it. Damn Tom. Why couldn't he keep the company straight from the show they were putting on? I stared at him a second or two while I thought about whether or not to correct him again. Oh hell. They were, after all, my clients.

"UFAS guys, Tom. The execs in the room worked for UFAS. When you talk about your car, your Camry, you call it a Camry, don't you? You don't confuse the Camry with the company that builds the Camry, Toyota, do you? You don't ever call the Toyota Corporation the Camry Corporation? Camry's the brand name and Toyota's the company that builds that brand. So, you don't call the people who work for UFAS FloraGlobal execs; you call them UFAS execs."

Tom stared at me as if I were a book whose pages he didn't want to read.

So what? The world's not interested in brand nomenclature, but I thought Tom would at least fake an interest. I conjured up the sweetest smile in my repertoire.

"Yeah, but sometimes I call my Camry a Toyota because it is." Tom glanced at Jeep. "What about your Blazer, Jeep? Ever call it a Chevy?"

Jeep grinned. "Cut it out, Thurgood. Sydney's just perching on her nest. She's the mother hen to all these floral companies. Their empires might fall if we get their names mixed up."

"Why is my work such a joke to you two? Neither one of you knows anything about companies or image or advertising or sales." I was building to a point I wasn't clear on myself so I was glad when Tom interrupted me.

"Jeep knows," he said. "He's from a retail family. You pegged me right though. I'm just a farm boy." He laughed. I couldn't believe how much he seemed to be enjoying himself.

"Farm boy or retail boy, it doesn't really matter. I think you're acting strange about this case. Two people are dead. I'm on the same list they were on." I leaned forward, not more than a foot from Tom's face. "Tom, what's going on here?"

Tom's eyes met mine for five seconds before he dropped them abruptly. I waited in silence for him to say something.

Jeep waited too, both of us staring at Tom.

Finally, Jeep said, "Tom wants to close the show, shut the whole place down. It's a good idea, but the chief won't let him."

Tom continued staring at the tabletop.

"Is what Jeep's saying true, Tom? When we were at the florist's shop this morning, you said you weren't going to shut the show down. What happened to change your mind?"

"It's just too dangerous," Tom said and only then

looked at me. "There are too many people out there. Protection's close to impossible."

"What about Curtis Lewis? You seemed so convinced he'd done all this."

"He might have. I hope so," he added. "But if he didn't . . ." Tom seemed almost sick with anxiety and worry. It was such an abrupt change. Frankly, I preferred him this way right now.

"If he didn't," I said, "then the only way to catch the person responsible is just to play it on out. Isn't that right?" I glanced from Tom to Jeep and back to Tom. Neither one of their expressions told me anything. "Except for maybe Joel's autopsy," I added, but didn't know if that was true or not.

"Parts of that will take weeks," Jeep interjected. "The most important parts anyway—the poisons."

"Why's that? Why does that take so long?"

Jeep answered me again. "If he ingested something that killed him, it'll take weeks to break down in his tissue. Some stuff won't, but a lot of stuff will."

"Then it'll be too late," Tom said in a monotone voice, as if reciting something he'd been saying to himself for an hour.

"What about fingerprints? Have you tried matching Curtis's to anything in here?"

Tom took a deep breath. "We haven't found any fingerprints that don't belong. We haven't even found the weapon that did this." He glanced toward Tina's empty seat when he said that.

"A knife? I thought you said it was a short knife."

He raised an eyebrow. "Merely supposition at this point. We need time, and we don't have it."

I turned back toward the control board. "What about the tapes. Is her setup still working?"

Tom shook his head. "Ruined."

"So, you've got two murders that you have no real evidence for?"

Tom's answer was indirect. "If you think about it, Sydney, we have no real evidence that Fineman was even murdered. You're making an assumption based on its linkage to this one."

"And you're not?" I glared at Tom, then turned to Jeep. "What do you think? Do you think the show should be closed?"

"What do you think, Sydney?" he said, more serious than I'd seen him. "You understand these people. What do these messages mean? If anyone can figure them out, it's you." He saw my frustration and added, "Something needs to happen, doesn't it? Or we're going to have some real problems."

I looked back to Tom. "I'd say my kids will have some real problems." I know I probably sounded either flip or sarcastic, but I meant it as a cry for help.

Tom sat up from the slouch he'd been in. He reached for my hand. "That's why you're not coming here tomorrow if Lewis hasn't confessed."

Maybe Tom had a plan after all. I trusted this man. He wasn't going to let anything happen to me if he could help it. I didn't expect Curtis Lewis to confess, but the possibility allowed me to function for now. I squeezed Tom's hand in gratitude.

Jeep was staring at our hands. He looked sad. I let go then. I didn't want to make him uncomfortable.

"What about the ladybug?" I looked at Tom first and then Jeep.

"What about him?" Tom answered.

"Find him?"

They both shook their heads.

"Did anybody tell you about him? Did the UFAS execs

tell you what he did after he entered this room? I know the execs were still here when I left."

Tom shook his head again. "That's when they left." He had picked up a pencil. Now he put it down on the table.

"All of them?" I asked. "In unison?"

Tom nodded.

"Don't you think that's odd?" I asked, and looked at Jeep and then at Tom.

They both nodded that they thought it was odd.

"Why in unison?" I asked Tom.

"I was hoping you might know why he was here."

"How could I know anything? I just passed him as I was leaving. Those execs know, though. Did you ask them why they all left?"

"Yes, I asked them." He squinted as if he was getting a headache. "They all told me the same thing: because Tina Mauldin asked them to."

17

I left the control room feeling more vulnerable than I had in my whole life. No matter what Tom said about shielding me, how could he really? How could he stop a person he knew nothing about? And even if I stayed home tomorrow, didn't come here at all, I'd be afraid the person would come looking for me. That would put the kids in jeopardy along with me. I couldn't stand to do that, not under any circumstances. What choices did I have? If staying away from the Center was no safer than being here, then I had to help myself.

The elevator opened to a wild scene. Hugo had arrived. Since his visit had been promoted, kids were everywhere. Little kids, maybe four or five on average, scampered about the convention floor like puppies in pursuit of butterflies. They jumped and fell; they ran and fell; they got up and fell again, breaking into spasms of giggles and sheer pleasure at being in the presence of "Charlotte's bug." Hugo, with his electric teal uniform and bulbous white trademarked hands, was the only constant on

Charlotte's pro basketball team. Until recently, he'd even merited a portrait covering the entire south side of the First Union building. I wondered who he was.

I didn't wonder enough to spend any time in the middle of this mayhem, though. I noticed the big female bumblebee standing off to the side of the crowd. If I had to guess her mood, I'd say she looked jealous. God help Hugo if she got near him with her heels. The ladybug wasn't anywhere near here that I could see. I hoped he'd show up soon. If I could find him or if Tom's men could find him, maybe he could tell us something to put a stop to it all.

The only time I'd been to Joel's booth had been late yesterday with Peg. Then, I'd had no notion of what had actually started with Joel's death. We'd rushed through the place so quickly, I could recall it only vaguely. I wanted to go back there.

By the time I reached the booth, the Center seemed unusually empty. I assumed everyone had gone to the front to see Hugo. The monitor where Peg and I had seen Joel's brave new Web company was black. Someone had turned it off, but that didn't surprise me. The Convention Center had its own security and maintenance people, as did the UFAS people. Any one of them could have turned off the monitor once they heard Joel had died. But what about his employees? Why hadn't any of them been here since Joel died? Peg implied Joel's help was low-level; maybe they hadn't come with him from Atlanta for the show.

Maintenance people hadn't been inside the booth, though. If they had, surely they would have watered Joel's displays. All of them were wilted beyond revival. You can let them go just so far.

When I saw the trash can, still full of calla stems, I knew for sure no cleanup crew had been here. I picked up the trash can and looked out into the wide center walkway. When I didn't see anybody, I turned the trash can upside down and emptied the callas onto Joel's floor in hopes of finding a magic clue. Some of the stems had begun to ooze, as decomposing vegetation does, but nothing else was in there.

I had my heart set on finding the stack of papers I'd seen in the booth yesterday, but they were nowhere to be found. Damn. Why hadn't I taken the tiny bit of time needed to look the papers over? Again, I thought of Peg. He knew Joel. Hell, he knew Joel much better than he'd been willing to let on, if what Barry had told me was true. Surely he could help me answer these questions. The papers probably had something to do with the new Web business. Maybe they were contracts Joel had in hopes of signing up all these florists while he was working the show. I would have brought contracts if I'd been in his situation.

I sighed as I looked around the small space. I suddenly realized I *was* in his situation now, only I knew what was about to befall me and Joel hadn't even been warned. Or had he? If Barry had gotten threats for a solid year, and if this was the same person sending notes now, it stood to reason that Joel had received those earlier threats too. Except the reasoning stopped there. I was on the list, too, and I certainly hadn't been receiving notes for a year. My temple began to ache.

As I tapped my fingers on the back of the chair where Joel had obviously trimmed his callas, I looked to the table before me. There sat the two coffee cups. The one closest to me must have been Joel's. The angle of the handle was such that a right hand extended from my same angle would have put it down just as it was now. It had been drained to a gummy base of nondairy creamer and a minuscule amount of undrunk coffee. The other was completely full, its dark brown liquid coated in filmy residue. Obviously, Joel hadn't been alone yesterday morning. While he cut his stems and inserted his picks and shaped his design for competition, someone had sat with him.

Except the visitor hadn't touched his coffee. The cups were from somebody's personal giveaway collection. They were mugs really, the kind I get when I register for a conference or enter a tennis tournament. The kind I order for clients every day of the week. Joel's mug was a cheap white ceramic with a red inscription. It said *NC Arboretum*. The visitor's mug looked older and more substantial. I pulled a tissue out of my pocketbook and covered the handle before lifting it. This mug was definitely heavier than Joel's. The color looked to have been baked into the clay in some kind of glaze-firing process. I knew nobody did that anymore with the giveaways. It cost too much. So, I knew it was an older mug. The color pattern dated it too: powder blues and pinks mixed in random swirls, a fifties look. The color had faded a lot in places and the poorly differentiated light blue words were mostly impossible to read. It advertised a florist, and it didn't take any brains on my part to figure that out since the only word I could decipher was "Florists."

I could read the tag line, too, or enough of the letters to fill in the ones missing. The tag said *Say it with Flowers!* There was too much missing from the florist's name, though. All that remained was part of a capital "W" and a lower case "i" after that. Since the swirling pattern was intact where the missing letters had been, I decided the words had been painted on rather than stenciled during the firing process. For a costly 1950s mug, this thing sure was tacky. But, of course, I reminded myself, fifties svelte was always tacky.

I knew I had a clue here, maybe even two. But I didn't know what to do with these mugs. I looked around for a coffee source. The Center sold coffee toward the front of the show, up near the FloraGlobal booth. The visitor's mug was so full, nobody could have walked that distance and not spilled some of it. If Joel brought coffee to the show yesterday, surely there'd be a thermos in the booth and there wasn't. I was left with only one explanation: The visitor had brought the coffee as well as the creamer for both Joel and himself.

The tissue I'd been holding in my hand was torn and wet. I'd perspired all over it. I wiped my palms with what was left and threw it in the trash can.

By now I'd become convinced this coffee had killed Joel. Something else was mingled with his nondairy creamer and coffee, something strong enough to stop Joel's heart in a matter of hours.

I couldn't figure out how to get these mugs to Tom, though. Not without spilling the old, cold coffee left in the visitor's mug. I sat there and thought about what to do. I could hear a familiar Charlotte Hornets' cheer in the distance but not a lot else. None of the booths down on this end had phones so I couldn't call Tom.

Finally I decided to pour part of the visitor's coffee into Joel's trash can so it wouldn't slosh all over me while I carried it. Whatever would be found in eight ounces would surely be found in four ounces. I pulled my sweater sleeves down over my hands, used them as mittens, and handled the mugs that way.

The closer I got to the front of the hall, the less I could think. The noise grew and so did the numbers of people. I was bumped by a man in a hurry, knocking as much as a teaspoon of the coffee onto my sweatered fingers. Every show goer in the place seemed to have converged here. A wall of people stood ahead of me, all talking loudly and all with their backs to me.

An odd version of "Tiptoe Through the Tulips" blasted over the loudspeakers. Rather than the light, melodic tones I'd always associated with the song, this one was bump and grind. I hoped new boy Jerry hadn't made this decision. Music like this would showcase the wrong talents of the bumblebee. Who knows what she'd do with this rhythm? So far, the children were laughing at her.

I couldn't work my way past the people. I couldn't see over them either. The audience was five or six bodies deep all the way around to booths on either side. I determined I could barely slip into a booth at the back of the crowd, but I wouldn't be able to go farther. Not with the mugs in my hands. I hooked a short utility ladder with my boot and dragged it to the back of the crowd. It was just the lift I needed to see why the crowd had gathered.

I couldn't believe the scene. My disbelief wasn't at the bee. I expected something bawdy from her, bawdy putting it mildly. She was strutting the floor like a turkey in heat. Her long, powerful legs were stepping high from the knee, her butt so tight it seemed to curve upward, her neck almost double-jointed as it bobbed forward then backward like a light bulb whose socket is broken. At every refrain, she'd stop to shake those wings of hers at the shoulder blades. What shook instead was her chest, no matter how far back she threw those shoulders.

The surprise was on the other end of the open hallway. The ladybug I'd seen yesterday was gone, truly gone. In his place was a petite girl no older than my sixteen-year-old daughter, Joan. She wore gray tights, ballet shoes, and a dark blue tutu. Along the outsides of her arms she wore lifelike feathers in black and gray and, on her head, a feathered cap culminating in a pointed rubber beak. She was dancing with Hugo in a traditional, although fast-paced, two-step.

Where was my ladybug? Even in a crowd as big as this one was, orange is an easy color to spot. There wasn't any orange anywhere. I kept looking, though, because I couldn't believe he'd disappear.

A man's booming voice streamed over the top of the music. It was a circus voice, pregnant with itself: "Which will it be, ladies and gentlemen? The powerful and regal queen bee or the dainty, sweet hummingbird? The choice is yours. Boys and girls, you can vote too."

I heard a little boy scream: "A hummingbird's not an insect, you dummy!"

I chuckled; certain others had heard him too.

The crowd began to disperse, with only a few entering the show booth to vote. I noticed Jerry greeting those who did. Good for him. Tina would never have stooped so low.

I decided to survey the exhibit hall one last time. Then I'd return these six inches given me by the little ladder. That's when I saw him. He wasn't wearing orange; in fact, he had on a tweed sport jacket and dark brown pants. His pale yellow turtleneck bunched at his neck, though, and his brown limp hair was a day dirtier. The ladybug saw me just after I saw him.

He was looking for someone himself, if I could tell anything from his eyes. They were darting back and forth, his squat little head moving frantically. He was pushing himself up on his toes, straining to see as many of the people gathered as he could.

Suddenly, all his movement stopped. His eyes came to rest on me. Like someone hailing a cab, he lifted his arm in my direction, pointing his finger at me as he did.

Although afraid, I was still drawn to him. He, more than anyone else, had some of the answers I needed.

The spread between us was about fifty feet. Twenty or thirty people still milled around in that space, although most of the children were gone. I stepped down from the ladder as quickly as I could without spilling. Although I could no longer see him, I knew exactly where he was. I walked in that direction, all the while assuming he was walking toward me too.

When I'd seen him, he'd been standing by a steel girder. It was one of scores of girders supporting the room's thirty-foot height. It took me no more than two minutes, three at most, to reach that girder, but he was gone. I shifted the two mugs to the same hand, hooking my fingers through their handles, then I touched the steel pole, held on to it, and peered to its other side. He wasn't in any of the directions I looked. The man had just vanished.

I did see two cops, though, one in uniform and one attempting undercover. The undercover was a woman. The brown wool suit, complete with sterling dogwood pin on her lapel, was to blend her in with the florists, I supposed, but it wasn't enough for me. Her black shoulder bag was one I'd seen before, so it must have been a police issue. The radio she was talking into couldn't pass for a cell phone either. I watched her eyes as she talked. I followed them to the doors that led to the underground road and loading docks.

As much as I wanted to talk to him, I wasn't going into that place alone. If the police were to catch him, and they certainly were better equipped to do it than I, then he could tell Tom what I hoped he would have told me.

18

I entered the control room without knocking, assuming Tom and Jeep would still be there. They weren't. Instead, I found four homicide detectives playing what looked like hearts at the table and a female officer, the one who'd held me at the elevator this morning, standing watch at the window. All five of them stopped and stared at me.

"One of those for me?" cracked a detective whose head was both bald and wrinkled. He glanced at the three other men and laughed.

"It's evidence," I said, but the men at the table showed no interest.

The woman officer told me that Tom had been called downtown and that Jeep was on the floor.

I looked at my watch. It was after two already. I wondered if Barry had left the building. If I'd been he, I know I would have.

I felt like a cancer victim with a lowball chance of a cure. Time was paramount if I was to survive. Time and luck and the skill of the pros who were helping me. My time was running out. Less than twenty-four hours, the way I saw it. Luck had never been my long suit either; in fact, I'd learned never to count on any. I would have expected better from Tom and his men, though. He'd seemed distracted and scattered during lunch, and his homicide crew would rather tell bad jokes and play cards. Who was off the mark here? Was I imagining the danger I was in?

"May I give you something for Tom Thurgood?" I chose to ask the woman because, frankly, I couldn't speak to those men in a civil tone.

She nodded. The detectives returned to their game.

I joined her at the control panel and set the two mugs down where Tina used to prop her elbows.

She retrieved thick plastic bags from a box on the floor just to the other side of the card-playing detectives. One of them glanced over at me, then stared at the woman as she put the cups in separate evidence bags and the brown liquid in another. Afterward, he scratched his head. He must have been the dummy.

"What are these?" She'd sealed the bags and was poised to write on one with a black marker.

"I know. I'll bet they're coffee cups." It was the same flip detective. He laughed at himself, but no one joined him.

"They were in Joel Fineman's booth," I said. "Detective Thurgood will know what to test them for."

When she'd finished writing, she put both plastic bags in a larger padded black bag that looked to me like a child's knapsack.

"Will you take it now?" I asked.

"I have the floor until Sergeant Ford gets back." The two of us turned and together looked through the glass. I'm sure she was looking for Jeep. I don't know why I turned that way too. What I saw was Hugo. He'd just returned from a triumphant tour of the exhibit hall. Like the

Pied Piper, he commanded an entourage of children as well as quite a few adults. He held up one of those Mickey Mouse–size hands and waved at someone standing just under our window. I leaned into the glass and peered straight below us to where he was waving. All I could see was the top of someone's silver hair.

"Call Thurgood about it," one of the card players said to her. "If he wants, one of us can take it down."

While the female officer got Tom on the phone, I followed the movement of the woman with the silver hair. She waved back at Hugo, then walked toward him. I could see her more clearly once she'd moved away from the wall beneath us. By the time she reached him, I knew who she was. She didn't even have to turn around for me to know. Just a bit of the profile gave her away. I'd seen that side of her this morning. I couldn't believe it. Here was my hit-and-run that Thurgood wouldn't arrest.

"I'll be damned," I said to no one.

I turned around just as the female officer was breaking up the card game. Tom had told her to send the evidence bags downtown, she was telling them, and one of the cardsharps would have to do the honors.

"Which one of you is going?" I asked.

The one who'd been dummy was pushing his chair back. "I'll go," he said flatly.

"Can you wait just a sec? I'm going to bring you one more thing to take downtown."

I left the room to make my first ever citizen's arrest. While I waited the few seconds for the elevator, I pulled my notepad out of my pocketbook and ripped off the page with the tag numbers on it. I could feel the adrenaline soar inside me. Maybe my luck was changing. At least I'd get closure on something today.

She was standing next to Hugo when I reached her.

The two were posing for a photographer, who acted miffed as I entered his viewfinder.

"Who the hell do you think you are?" the photographer screamed.

Hugo grabbed my waist with one of his large white hands, pulled me close to him, kept smiling for the photographer and said to me, "Smile, doll. Look good for the camera."

On Hugo's other side was the silver-haired woman. She was smiling for the camera, a toothy, lipstick-encased smile, a smile speaking more of her self-importance than her natural warmth. Who was she? Was I supposed to know her? And Hugo, that cute, mute mascot of the Charlotte Hornets. I was beginning to care less who he really was as he dug those fingers into my side.

"Thank you, people," the photographer said. "I need your name," he said to me.

"You're under arrest," I said to the silver-haired woman before she could walk away.

She tried to anyway, so I grabbed her angora sweater at the elbow. It stretched two feet before she thought better of leaving. "I'm serious," I said. "We saw you hit that VW in the parking lot at Central and Eastway."

"What?" she said, acting genuinely surprised. "Don't you know who I am?"

Whoever she was, it wasn't enough for Hugo. He'd slinked off to join a group of departing parents and their children. I figured out why when the camera started flashing again.

"Come with me," I said to her. "If you don't, there'll be pictures in the paper neither one of us wants."

She obliged. The two of us walked briskly to the elevator leading to the control room. As we waited for the elevator she said, "Officer, please understand. The ice was everywhere. I couldn't help hitting that car."

I decided not to correct her assumption about me. It was that assumption, after all, that was making my mission so easy. So I played the part, although in retrospect I hope subconsciously. "No excuse for hit-and-run" was one of my lines. The worst, however, was "You know better than that, ma'am." Grade B seventies film dialogue all the way to the control room. Fact is I had no idea how to conduct a citizen's arrest. I was calling on the only language I knew.

The cop, whose name, I discovered, was Charlie, took her off my hands. The poor guy looked traumatized when he did, though. I gave him the sheet from my idea pad, the sheet with the tag numbers on it.

Hopefully the silver-haired woman had insurance to cover what she'd done to the Volkswagen. It was really all that I cared about here. Charlie said he'd take her over to the Law Enforcement Center, where he promised to deliver her to Tom along with the evidence bags.

She'd begun to snicker at me toward the end. "I'll have your job," she said a couple of times, still thinking me an officer of the law. When the cop named Charlie piped, "This wasn't my idea," I began to suspect she wielded some kind of power.

The three of us left the control room together, they heading toward the lot at Stonewall and I back into the mayhem of the show. I won't say I felt good about what I had done, but I did feel I'd done what was called for. In fact, I felt if I hadn't done it, no one would have.

I could see Peg's booth clearly from where I stood. Not only was he there, but he appeared to be working. It occurred to me then that in the five years I'd known him and as strong as his reputation for design was, I'd never seen him actually do the work. I headed in that direction, although I knew even then that I needed more from him than design tips.

"How can I create beauty at a circus like this?" he asked, his exasperation showing in the bead of sweat on his forehead.

"But you have, Peg," I said. "Look at it. Stand back over here where I am. It's a gorgeous arrangement."

It truly was. He'd filled an oblong vase, about three feet long and a foot wide, with fifty or more of the most exquisite lilies I'd ever seen. Either daylilies or Asiatics, I couldn't tell which since he'd removed their leaves. They were packed so tightly as to form a continuous sheet of lemon yellow except for a wave of aubergine lilies arching at an angle through the center. The effect was unique—typical of Peg Corbeil. Quite sophisticated too. I told him so.

"So it'll do for a grown-up's birthday party?" He stood beside me admiring his own work.

"A birthday party?" I laughed. "I guess so. A very uptown birthday party."

"You don't see it then?"

"See what?" I asked.

"It's a banana split, Sydney. Don't you see it?"

When he said it, I did see it all of a sudden. The "chocolate syrup" even "dribbled" artistically down one side.

I held his upper arm with one hand and patted his back with the other. "You're brilliant, Peg. Absolutely brilliant. Nobody's close to your level of genius."

He folded his right hand over mine on his arm. "I hope not, Syd. If they were, I'd have to do them in."

His remark, although seemingly meaningless, hit me as if it had been physical. I shuddered.

"You cold?"

I shook my head and rubbed my arms with my hands. "I'm sorry. Forgive me, Peg. I know you didn't mean anything by what you just said. But, honestly, I'm beginning to suspect everyone."

"Suspect everyone of what?" he asked, genuine bafflement coming through in his voice. "You mean Joel? Did the police decide it was murder?"

I had to really think about that to answer him. "No," I said, and was a bit confused by the truth of that simple word. "I guess they really haven't yet." I realized I hadn't told Peg anything about what was actually going on here. He hadn't seemed curious either. After hearing what Barry had to say about Peg and Joel, I wasn't sure I trusted Peg with my thoughts.

"And that Mauldin woman was no competition for anyone. Not as a designer anyway." He walked back to his lily display and straightened the aubergine that dribbled.

"I thought that dribble was on purpose."

He jabbed it in just a little. "It is," he said. "Just not so much so."

I thought I knew Peg well. Until today I would have bet he didn't mean those words about Tina as callously as they sounded. I would have said he was simply sorting events to see if they affected him in any way. I would have said he was practical, not selfish.

I came out of my reverie to see Peg staring at me.

"It bothered you, didn't it? What I said about the Mauldin woman?"

"It's okay. Really, it's okay." I sighed. "Actually, I want to ask you a question or two about Joel." I joined him at his "banana split."

"Shoot," he said, removing a lily that displeased him.

"Remember that small stack of papers in his booth yesterday? It was on the table."

"I think so." He wasn't looking at me.

"It's gone," I said. "Could his employees have taken it?"

He shook his head gently, the lily stem horizontally perched in his mouth while he rearranged its neighbors. When he was satisfied, he stuck the lily back down into the display and stood back. He cocked his head and smiled his elfish grin, pleased with his effort.

"Why do you say no?"

He didn't answer right away. I held my breath, hoping the truth would roll out of him.

He finally looked at me. "Why do you care? Those papers have nothing to do with you."

"You took those papers, Peg. Why?"

He pushed up on the arrangement with the palm of his hand. The gesture reminded me of what women do to their new perms. "How can you ask that, Syd? His plans were despicable." He stood back, studying his art from a distance. He cocked his head. "I thought you and I agreed on that."

"I don't remember how I felt about it."

He reached down into the bucket at his side and pulled out a deep red lily. It may have been the most vibrant red I'd ever seen in a lily. He held it above his display, made a clicking noise in his mouth and said, "Too big. I'll need a diploid here."

"Is that for the cherry?" I asked, fascinated by his process.

He nodded.

"The color's right, Peg."

"Yeah. The tetraploids have the best color. No doubt about it. But the damn tetraploid flower is too big." He turned to me and grinned. "Too big to be a cherry anyway."

"What's the difference?" I chuckled at his artistic dilemma. "I mean between the tetraploid and the other one?" I'd forgotten the name.

"Diploid," he said. "Chromosomes. Tetraploids have double that of diploids. Makes them bigger, showier, and they have the rich colors. All these are tetraploids. All with forty-four chromosomes, courtesy of colchicine. The diploids are God's doings. I wish he'd made me a bright red."

"Colchicine? I thought that was a medicine."

"It is. I think it's used for gout. We use it to breed these big babies, though." He fondled one of the aubergine, chocolate-looking flowers as if it were a lover.

I blurted out, "Why did you lie to me about Joel?"

He straightened and pulled his chin into his neck in exaggerated offense. "I make it a point not to lie. I'm surprised you think I would."

"Dammit, Peg. Barry Firth told me you and Joel just ended a long relationship. Barry said you broke it off Tuesday."

"Did I ever tell you Joel and I had never been lovers?"

"Not in so many words, no, but you didn't volunteer the truth of it either."

He shook his head, turned his back to me. "Barry's got a big mouth. He ought to go back in his closet."

"What?"

He ignored my question. He knew that what he'd said about Barry startled me. I think he got a kick out of jolting me like that. "Too bad we can't isolate what the colchicine does," he said. "I mean give us size without color change or the color in a nice small flower. I've tried to manipulate the properties myself, and I couldn't do it."

I was impressed against my will. "Your talents never cease to amaze me, Peg. So you're a scientist too." Until now I'd never known him to touch flowers, much less genetically alter them.

"I'd rather buy the perfect flower than make one, darling Syd." He began to walk toward his chaise. "Believe me, I don't like working with colchicine. The stuff is deadly." He threw his right hip and leg onto the chaise, then eased the rest of himself down and sighed. "Sometimes, though, you have to take matters into your own hands." He looked up at me then. "Know what I mean?"

After I left Peg, I used one of the pay phones outside the bathrooms to call Tom. I wasn't surprised when I was told he wasn't available.

"Can you get a message to him?"

When the detective said he could, I asked him to grab a pencil and paper. "I need to spell something for you."

The detective returned with a pencil. I watched a tall man watching me while I waited. I hoped he was guarding me instead of stalking me. "Ready?" I said. "Okay. C-o-l-c-h-i-c-i-n-e. Just tell him to check for colchicine first."

19

Hart's audience had created for themselves a theater-in-the-round. They had pulled metal fold-up chairs from wherever they could find them and formed a semicircle about the front portion of Rhyne Garrett's booth. Each lady, and I noticed they all were ladies, was holding a tiny clump of sphagnum moss tied with patented Garrett crinkled ribbon. I wondered if the favors were Hart's idea or Rhyne's.

Rhyne himself was sitting on his small conference table, swinging his legs like a bored child. The only evidence of residual anger was the white of his knuckles as he dug his fingers into the undersides of the table. His face was appropriately pleasant.

"Hello, Rhyne," I said. "Some group you have this afternoon."

Rhyne raised an eyebrow. His irritation at the ever-increasing crowd had reduced to a simmering resignation. "Wish I'd thought to charge for him," he said, cocking his head toward Hart. "He's a veritable Martha Stewart."

I glanced quickly at Hart. He hadn't heard that comment, was too involved to hear anything coming from our corner of the booth.

"Yes," I agreed, "you would have done well to charge. Not as well as you'll do because you didn't charge, though. I still think it's going to pay off, Rhyne. In the long run . . ."

He listened to me this time without all the posturing he'd shown earlier. Then he crossed his arms at the elbows, breathed deeply, and sank back on the table to listen to Hart.

Hart was talking as he worked now, a dark gray marker in his hands. Sphagnum moss was the topic of the hour. He'd just finished describing the cutting of it from trees, how an industrious group down in lower Louisiana worked dawn to dusk taking it down with machetes. He was turning to the moss's artistic virtues. "Watch the delicate twine, ladies. It moves like the curly hair of Scots. It even mats like the curly hair of a Scot."

Most of my family is Scottish, and we all have straight hair. Some of us with nary a wave. I wondered if he'd made that up.

This afternoon Hart was creating the illusion of sphagnum moss by zigzagging a series of squiggle marks on all three foam core walls. Just above each of those "blueprint" illusions, he'd shot oozing pellets from a Garrett commercial glue gun, then lightly pressed the moss into it. He'd squirted enough of the hot liquid to hold a continuing run of moss. He'd also burned several more holes into the foam core. They looked like little cigarette holes. You could see them only if you were looking straight at them, though.

I looked over at Rhyne. I knew the man well, so was certain he'd never admit it; but Rhyne Garrett was just as enthralled by Hart's performance as the ladies in the gallery. Hart showed no signs of self-consciousness. Here was a new Hart entirely. His movements were as artistic as the work he'd created on the walls. He swooped, then stooped in fluid, natural movements. When he poked or prodded or picked at a clotted grouping of moss, he did so delicately—as a bird would when building her nest.

I whispered again to Rhyne: "You ought to consider preserving these walls."

I wasn't expecting what came next. A genuine sweep of satisfaction spread across his face. "Been thinking about doing just that, Sydney. Hart's work sets us off, doesn't it?"

I decided not to smile in return. If I did, Rhyne might realize I'd smiled because he had; then he might think better of it. It's a relationship thing with Rhyne, I think. He feels we consultants should never know he's pleased with us. If we suspect it, we might charge him more for our services. All of our interactions with him are colored by this fear of his.

Instead, I held up my watch arm and whispered Rhyne's name. "We need to shut his show down for the day. I've got two kids at home alone and employees I have to drive all the way to their homes."

"They're spellbound," he said without looking at me. "We can't stop it now."

"That's exactly when you want to stop it," I said. "One of the rules of performance art, Rhyne. Stop it at the height of their interest. That way, they'll come back tomorrow."

"Well, okay," he said just as his phone began to ring. He held his hand up, asking me to wait until he'd handled his call.

I shrugged. Hart was winding down anyway. He began to talk about tomorrow's finale: ribbon adornment. A few chairs started scraping the cement floor outside the carpeted area.

"It's for you," Rhyne said, and handed me the phone. I wondered briefly if it was one of the kids.

Tom's voice had regained the warmth I'd always expected until today. "Good news," he said. "Lewis confessed." He waited for me to react.

I was silent while I thought about it. A confession hadn't really occurred to me. "What exactly did he confess to?" I asked slowly.

Tom was hesitant. Had he expected I would just accept that and move on? He chuckled softly. "Killing Fineman and Mauldin. What did you expect?"

"Not murder. Harassment maybe." I'd begun to think the flowers and the murders weren't connected.

As much as I wanted him to, Tom didn't respond.

"Wishful thinking, I guess," I said into our silence.

"I think so," Tom said. "It *was* his charge card, Sydney."

"Somebody could have stolen that. Easily. Curtis is a drunk."

"His pocket knife clinched it," he said in a rush. "Tina Mauldin's blood was on it." I heard relief in his voice.

"Curtis Lewis's pocket knife?" I was really surprised and hoping I could feel as relieved as Tom sounded. "Where did you find it?"

"On him. And not even washed very well." He stopped, cupped his hand over the phone, and spoke to someone. "Sorry," he said when he came back. "A lot of people down here are relieved."

I was going to have to get used to the idea that Curtis perpetrated these crimes. "Why did he do it?"

Tom cleared his throat. "Want me to quote him?"

"Yeah, I do."

"He said he hates all florists. To quote him, 'floral fags.' His phrase, not mine."

"We already knew that, Tom," I said, and felt irritated

suddenly. "He's never killed them before. What about Tina Mauldin? What about the threats to me?"

He hesitated. "You want the guy to make sense, Sydney? I told you he wouldn't. He says you're all 'floral fags.' He calls you 'a fag lover.' " Tom sounded irritated at me for wanting to discuss it at all. I think he wanted confirmation only that the whole affair was coming to an end.

"And Tina Mauldin?"

"He said she was a lesbian. No, that wasn't his word. He called her a dyke." He breathed heavily. "There. Do his words lend any logic to it for you?" His frustration sounded close to sarcasm to me.

"Why did he all of a sudden confess?"

"The blood match came back on his knife; I told him the results and he crumbled. It was easy then. He blamed his alcoholism. Said he doesn't know what he's doing sometimes."

I breathed deeply then, let it out slowly. Hart was putting the tops back on his markers, sliding oil brushes down into a tray of turpentine. The ladies were returning the chairs to their rightful owners.

"I don't know what to think of all this," I finally said.

"Just be grateful, Sydney. I am."

"Maybe I will be when I get used to it. I feel sorry for Curtis's wife. I know her from AA. I've known her for years." I watched as Rhyne went over to Hart, shook his hand, and patted him on the back. I allowed myself a small smile.

"She's calling a lawyer right now. The wife," he added, sounding distracted.

"Curtis didn't have one during the interrogation?"

"He waived it," Tom said. "The wife claims he blacks out, that he isn't responsible for what he does then."

"You don't agree," I said.

"You know I don't. You don't either."

"I agree he probably blacks out, doesn't know what he's done half the time." He was right about the rest of it, though. I didn't agree with her assessment that he wasn't responsible if he did it. I didn't think Hattie believed it either, but what kind of defense could they pull together in face of physical evidence like the blood? Suddenly I wished it was the same time tomorrow, and Tom, the kids, and I would be halfway to Savannah.

"Sydney?"

"I'm still here. Sorry. I was thinking how grateful I'll be when we leave for Savannah."

"Me too," he said. "With the weather like it is, I've been thinking we ought to take your Trooper."

"The weather will be fine by tomorrow," I said.

He laughed. "Where've you been? We've had three more inches since noon."

I'd assumed the snow and ice were melting like they always do in Charlotte—quickly, efficiently, as if never having fallen. "Dammit, Tom. What are we going to do?"

"For starters, someone else needs to pick up your employees tomorrow. And maybe Joan and George need to come to the Center with us in the morning. That way, we can get away quickly when you decide you can leave."

"You've thought this through, haven't you?"

He mumbled something I couldn't understand.

I asked him to repeat it.

"Thought maybe I should stay at your house tonight. Coming in from the river might be impossible in the morning."

Rhyne was busy with a new customer, one of the ladies in Hart's audience. He'd removed an order pad and was writing furiously as she talked. Hart was watching them, smiling to himself as he did.

"We're leaving now, Tom," I said. "I've got to take Hart home and Sally too."

"Hold it a sec, Sydney. Something's going on here." I heard him talking to people, asking them to hold on until he could get off. He returned to me and said, "What's going on with Charlie? What did you make him do, Sydney?"

Obviously, Charlie and the silver-haired woman had arrived at the station. I didn't want to get into this on the phone. I changed the subject. "God, I wish it hadn't started snowing again."

"We won't let it stop us. Not the number one seeds. Nothing can stop us." He sounded as upbeat as always whenever our tennis is mentioned.

I dug my boot heel into the edge of a dried piece of glue on Rhyne's carpet. Hart reached down and picked it up, then dropped it into the wastebasket a couple of feet behind me. I hadn't noticed him standing beside me. He had on his heavy navy coat. He'd even wrapped his scarf around his neck. I winked at him as I finished with Tom.

"I'll bring pizza or something," Tom said, "unless you have dinner planned."

"The pizza or something will be fine," I said, and laughed.

Tom said, "That's good to hear. Your laughter. I've missed it these last few days. It makes me feel good when I hear it."

My eyes stung. I felt a sudden rush of heat. I hung up, then pinched the bridge of my nose and felt a thin layer of tears at the corner of my eyes. I had no explanation for their presence.

"You're tired," Hart said.

"Not really, Hart." I pulled a tissue out of my pocketbook, closed my eyes to wring them dry, and dabbed the

corners where the wet accumulated. "A guy I know confessed to killing Joel and Tina."

Hart whistled softly. With him in his heavy quilted
jacket and double-wrapped scarf, the sound changed
meaning. "You sound like Old Man Winter, Hart. That
whistle is cold."

He smiled, although his eyes were all of it I could see.
"A good friend? The man who's confessed?"

I shook my head. "Far from it. I know him through AA
is all." I gathered my pocketbook and mouthed our exit to
Rhyne and his new customer.

We started what I'd grown to think of as a trudge, that
long walk to the front of the exhibit hall.

"Was he sending the flowers?" Hart asked.

The question was such a simple one. So much had happened since I'd driven us here this morning. I realized
Hart knew none of it. So I let the events spill out of me:
our visit to Suzannah's Flowers, the threats to Barry Firth
throughout the year, the flowers sent to him and me this
morning, and the final arrangement tomorrow. Something kept me from telling him tomorrow's was mine
alone, though.

Hart shook his head throughout it, his thin wispy eyebrows almost sinking to the sockets they framed. We
paused between the UFAS booth and Peg Corbeil's. Short
little Jerry was barking orders to a show attendant, a boy
in his early twenties. Peg's booth was empty. It didn't surprise me. He really had nothing to sell here, nothing but a
you'll-never-match-me superiority.

"Oops. My coat. I almost forgot it," I said. Hart waited
in the center of the hallway while I retrieved my parka and
put it on.

"Tina's underling has turned into a Hitler," Hart said
when I returned. "I just saw him push an attendant out of

the booth. Both hands too. The boy turned his back and the new guy shoved him so hard the boy almost fell."

I sighed. "Jerry's heady with Tina's power. Too bad. Their visions are opposite, but their methods are the same." I shook my head. "Just what the world needs. Another jerk too heavy for his rung on the corporate ladder."

"We're through working for UFAS?"

I nodded. "Never again." I looked into Hart's eyes. "Hold me to it, okay? No matter how much they offer us."

"Don't worry. Some work just isn't worth it." He turned around, facing the mayhem again. He took a step or two in that direction.

I stood flatfooted. "Where are you going, Hart?"

He stopped and turned. "Did you move your car? It's not still underground?"

I'd completely forgotten about driving underground. I threw both hands into the air and grinned at him. "God, Hart. Remind me to tack my head on better in the morning, will you?"

We walked side by side through the thinning crowd.

"I'll secure it with one of Rhyne's glue guns," he said deadpan.

"Yeah," I shot back. "Better not leave those little holes in my neck like you did on the foam core."

"Couldn't be helped," he said. "The damn thing's hot, to put it mildly."

Neither of us could remember exactly which of the doors we'd entered this morning. There were five or six double doors along a two-hundred-yard stretch. We compromised and approached one of the middle ones.

The heavy metal moaned on its hinges, then clanged shut behind us. We were in the boneyard with its boxes, crates, metal booth structures, and carpet rolls. No wonder show people called it the boneyard. These were skeletal remains of a trade show's life, necessary for transport and protection but not of value in themselves.

Lighting was sparse and high in the boneyard. The few fluorescent fixtures hit ducts and pipe suspended from the ceiling before trickling down to us. Fluorescence throws odd shadows in situations like this. Cold shadows, fuzzy ones, a greenish-gray light brushing up on cinder block walls. Above all else, it was a drab light, not much of a light at all.

It was enough light to turn the loading docks dark, though. I felt like an actor onstage, overhead lights streaming down on him. He doesn't know if the audience is empty or full. Out there it's nothing but black. The light was above us, not out there at all. The boneyard was an extension of those docks, but the dock area itself and the roadway beyond it weren't lit. I wondered if they were supposed to be lit and if someone had just forgotten.

"I think we took the wrong door," I said, and heard an echo of my words.

"How would you know?" Hart said sarcastically. "It all looks the same."

"Didn't I park as far in as I could? Didn't you tell me to take the last slot? Remember?"

We had stopped beside a roll of carpet thick enough to cover a football field. It stood waist-high.

"I remember now," Hart said. "In case more trucks were coming."

So we turned and headed across the long room, knowing that we'd come to its end eventually.

"I broke the Center's rules, you know. What if we've been towed?" I heard our footsteps in the echoes along with our voices.

Hart's chuckle sounded eerie. "I was picturing worse,"

he said. "What if the truck whose slot we took backed in today without looking? I see it in my head."

"Don't say that, Hart. You'll jinx us."

As I was saying those words a heavy shadow blocked the sickly light, and then faded quickly. For a second I thought the lights themselves had flickered. I held Hart's wrist and looked to the ceiling behind the ducts, waiting for the light source to bleep again.

Hart's eyes followed my own to the ceiling and then the walls and then to my own eyes. He frowned and held his index finger to his lips. We stood perfectly still.

"Who's there?" I said weakly, then grabbed a fistful of Hart's thick sleeve.

"It's okay, Sydney. People work in here." Hart saw the fear on my face, then seemed to be assessing it for a second or two.

"Who goes there?" he said loudly, his preference for Elizabethan theater surfacing.

We waited in the silence that followed, Hart surveying the area between us and the car and I just staring at Hart.

A man's voice cut into that space. "The Teague woman," he shouted. "I want the Teague woman alone." It was coming from behind a large furniture box in the area where we'd seen the shadow.

Hart looked into my eyes for something I'm sure wasn't there. I didn't recognize the voice. We still didn't move.

"I'm staying with her," Hart yelled back. He squeezed my hand again.

I think I breathed then for the first time. The old Hart would have said he was leaving.

The voice behind the box was silent.

"Come out if you want to talk to her." Hart's voice was

brimming with authority. I know *I* would have come out if he'd talked like that to me.

It worked on the man too. He eased sideways from behind the furniture carton until he stood parallel to it; he was almost as wide as the box.

"You're the ladybug," I said. This day had been filled with strange surprises.

"My name's Shep Scott. I'm a private detective." He offered a thin wallet to us and moved close enough for us to see his ID. The card was what he said it was: a North Carolina–issued P.I. license. I reached in front of Hart and handed the wallet back to the man.

"I worked for Tina Mauldin. Someone was sending her hate mail." He leaned sideways slightly and returned the wallet to his pocket. "I couldn't stop what happened to her, and I feel rotten about it."

Those few words explained so much. The reason Tina made the UFAS executives leave the control booth when the ladybug entered. The reason she'd abandoned all reason in the first place and cast this man as the ladybug.

"I think I can help you, though." He glanced quickly around the space as if he didn't have much time, as if he couldn't trust the silence.

"Why are you hiding back here?" I said.

He brushed his greasy hair back with his hand. "Her killer suspects I know," he said. "He was in the control room when I gave her my last report." He hung his head. "I didn't know everything then. Obviously."

"The technician in the corner with the cables?" I said. "Was he her killer?"

He nodded, his chin slicing into the rolls of his neck.

"He confessed," Hart said. "Sydney's out of danger

now." He was no longer touching me, but his presence was reassuring still.

Shep looked from Hart to me. "Is that true?"

I nodded, but my mind was racing back to the Center's steps when I'd left for the *Observer* yesterday. I couldn't remember if I'd seen Curtis outside at that time or not.

"I bet you were shocked," he said.

I was going to ask him what he meant, when a pair of doors to the exhibit hall pitched open. The clanging of the metal mixed with the strident voice of a flirting Peg and another voice I wasn't sure of. Peg and someone else were walking in our direction.

Hart and I both turned toward the sound. When we turned back around, Shep had moved away from us.

"Stop. Come back, please," I called out. "I don't know what you mean."

The fat man faded into the shadows where I hoped the Trooper was waiting. I heard a thud as he lowered himself to the road and then the scraping shuffle of his burdensome efforts to clear the building.

20

"Is that you, doll? Yoo-hoo," Peg yelled to his own echo. "Are you in here, Sydney?"

Neither Hart nor I moved. Peg's voice bothered Hart, though. I noticed him tense whenever Peg spoke. While we waited, I heard the slow drip of a leaking pipe and the distant sound of honking horns.

If it had been just me, I would have answered Peg. In spite of his eccentricities, he was my friend. I admit I might have felt otherwise had Peg picked at me as he did at Hart. Out of deference to Hart's feelings, I stood still and silent along with him.

Peg saw us anyway. The boneyard was cluttered with crates and boxes to hide behind; but it still was no more than a flat landing for the loading docks. We saw Peg clearly when he rounded a greenhouse crate. His arm was around the bumblebee's waist as the two of them walked toward us. I squeezed Hart's arm to get him to look at me, but Peg spoke before Hart turned.

"Well, look at you two," he said. "What a surprise."

"And you two," I replied. "An even bigger surprise."

"I know that girl," the bumblebee said to Peg. "She's the one messed with my wings." They continued to walk toward us. "I mean what I said, girl." She pointed, then shook her middle finger, the one Peg was missing, at me. "I need this gig. I got child support to pay."

Something was out of sync here. I couldn't picture this woman with children. "Child support? You have children?"

"Anyone can have children, Sydney," Hart said under his breath. He turned away from the two of them as if looking for something in the darkness.

"What you say there, boy? You making 'spersions toward me?" She pushed Hart on the upper arm.

Hart stumbled slightly, then turned and stood beside me. Together, we faced Peg and the creature who was obviously his friend.

I felt something odd here, though. I was thinking it through, trying to pinpoint what bothered me. Trying to understand the relationship I was seeing.

Peg spoke three little words then, and everything fell into place. Well, sort of into place. Peg said, "Stop it, Larry."

Hart and I said, "Larry?"

"What's it to ya?" Larry gave us both a haughty glare. He threw his pelvis so far to the left that he looked like he'd broken his waist. He used Peg's shoulder for a wall and anchored his right elbow there. He held his head in his hand, adjusting his wig with his fingers while settling his skull into his palm. Once situated, he hardened his eyes, contracting them from all angles until they looked compressed—like steel. He said, "Show me where a bee has to be a woman."

Peg chuckled, but otherwise stood perfectly still. In everything, Peg reveled in the value of shock.

"Of course no one said it. The ladybug wasn't a woman either," I added. I didn't care what sex or even what species Larry was at that moment. It seemed like the whole world had shifted to the left and everyone was wearing the face of the person next door.

"Good Lord," Hart whispered to me.

I looked at Peg. "We're late getting out of here. How bad is it outside?"

Peg shrugged. "Haven't been out today. Someone said it snowed some more."

"I heard that too," I said as I looked at my watch. I had to ask it, even as I tried not to: "How do you two know each other?"

Peg winked at Larry. "A bee can't stay away from honey, Syd."

"That's not really an answer, now is it?" I asked.

Neither of them responded. I sighed, wondering why I felt the need to interrogate everyone.

"Are y'all leaving too?" I asked Peg.

He hugged Larry. "We need a distraction. They count the mascot votes at five."

"We're going to walk through the snow," Larry said. "Isn't that romantic?"

"You'll freeze your stinger off out there." I smiled at him then.

"Peggy has room in his coat for me, don't you, babe?" He snuggled up against Peg's chest. Peg wrapped his wool overcoat around him.

Larry and Peg both jumped gracefully down to the roadway while Hart and I stood on the landing beside the Trooper. To my right, I could see the light of the roadway's exit. The two men started to walk in that direction.

"Oh, one more question," I said to them.

They stopped and looked up at me. "Ask away," Peg said.

"It's for Larry. How did you know about this mascot tryout? Had you worked for Tina Mauldin before?" I knew she'd installed her detective in the role. I thought perhaps she'd set up Larry for a similar reason.

"Peggy boy here told me about it. Even talked the FloraGlobal powers into letting me try out." He ran his finger down the bridge of Peg's aquiline nose, then kissed him on the lips.

"I didn't think you knew Tina, Peg."

He stood straight, his hands off Larry, staring into my eyes. "I knew her well enough to get Larry the tryout."

"But you didn't even act like you knew Larry yesterday. Remember that? Remember when we were on the way to Mangione's for lunch and—"

"That's when you fucked with my wing, when you—"

"I'm asking, Peg," I said, interrupting Larry right back. "Why didn't you acknowledge Larry?"

"I didn't want to hurt Larry's chances," Peg said with a serious undertone I'd never heard in his voice before. "The kids and all. What if they heard he was gay?"

"That doesn't sound like you, Peg." I stared as intently at him as he had at me.

"Maybe you don't know me then, Sydney." He grabbed Larry about the waist again and the two turned away from us. They walked toward the light.

The driver's side of the Trooper was too close to the wall. When I saw it, I wondered how I ever got out that morning. We stood beside the front passenger door while I reached inside my pocketbook and retrieved my keys.

"That was a surprise, wasn't it? Peg and the bumblebee." I could hear the keys clanging around in there, but so far hadn't touched them.

"You mean their being together?" He shook his head.

"Nothing Corbeil does surprises me." He propped himself against the side of the car.

"Not what I meant. Peg never let on he knew him, did he?" Just then my thumb brushed up against the key ring. I deftly hooked it and pulled it out.

"I'm just happy Peg Corbeil has an object for his affections. Maybe now he'll leave me alone."

"He never told us he knew Tina either. I wonder why."

"It's a Corbeil!" he said, mocking the ads we made for Peg.

I pulled the latch, but the car door didn't open. "I thought I locked it this morning, but obviously I didn't. Just now I locked it instead of unlocking it." I reached into my pocketbook again, muttering as I did. "Damn. It's past three-thirty, Hart, and we're still not out of here."

"I thought you'd locked it too," Hart said.

I reinserted the key. This time I heard it unlock. I pulled the latch with the big key ring still hanging from the lock.

When the door opened, the Trooper's lone overhead light came on. I stepped up onto its narrow running board and put my knee on the passenger seat. "Here, hold this," I said as I handed him my pocketbook. Hart stepped onto the running board behind me.

I didn't see it until after I'd grabbed the steering wheel. In fact, I was holding on to it, my body extended midair over the middle console, planning to ease myself down into the driver's seat, when I looked to my body's destination. I screamed.

A dozen or more xeroxed papers lay haphazardly on my seat. A liquid had spilled on the pile. It had dripped and oozed and turned splotchy in places. The light was so weak that the liquid seemed black, the papers gray. It looked as much like ink as blood. But I screamed because I knew different. I didn't even have to think. A long pair of florist shears drove through the papers and into the seat, pinning it all like a giant custom staple.

The shears were smeared with the liquid too. Even their handles were smeared. Down the shafts toward the points, the liquid was dark and uniform. It had pooled to the paper there too.

I fell backward onto Hart, both of us landing on the cold cement floor.

"Oh my God," I mumbled as the two of us struggled to stand up.

"What's in there?" Hart brushed the dirt and sawdust off his navy coat.

I could only stare at him.

He walked around me, stepped up into the Trooper, and said the same words I had uttered. Then he whistled long and low. He struggled to remove his scarf. He said he'd use it to handle the shears.

I waited outside. I felt violated. "You shouldn't pick those up, should you?" I asked.

"Why not?" He looked back at me.

I tried to shrug. "Isn't it evidence?"

"I won't mess up any fingerprints, but if I don't get them out, we don't get home."

I agreed without saying it.

"The blood's not even dry," he said.

When I heard the shears being pulled from the seat, the sound was awful. It may as well have been pulled from my body. I even felt it in my stomach.

Hart wrapped the shears in his scarf and laid them on the backseat. Then he backed out of the Trooper again and put on his gloves, shaking his head while he did. He reached back in for the papers.

He carefully placed them on the Trooper's hood. I

stood beside him and looked at the bloody pile. Although considerable blood had covered the top few pages, those underneath were unsullied.

"Look, Sydney," he said. "We know what these are."

I made an effort to focus. When I did, I saw that he was right. We knew exactly what these papers were. "The ads," I said. "All the old floral ads. These are the ones on the UFAS walls, aren't they?"

Hart riffled quickly through the stack. "Most of them," he said. "There's one or two here we didn't use." He held them all in the fist of his hand and turned to face me. "But I'll bet you I know where these came from. I had a pile of forty or fifty of these in case I needed to repair the walls during the show. Remember?"

Honestly, I couldn't.

"You must remember, Sydney. I threw these and more into a cardboard box, and we drove them here from the office." He stood on his toes and looked over the boneyard. "I'll bet that box ended up in here. It looks like everything else did that isn't being used."

I had only a vague recollection of Hart's procedure on the UFAS walls. After I'd studied and chosen the ads for the booth, the ones he glued and sepia-varnished there, I went on to other work. But these were the ads I'd found, some of them going back a hundred years. There wasn't any question about that.

"Look at this," Hart said. He held the top page in his hand. This was the page with the most blood on it, and the shears had ripped through its center. I could barely see the ad itself, but I could tell it was one of the older ones. The visual was a woodcut rather than the photography that's dominated most of this century. But I couldn't see the ad's heading.

"Not the head. Along the side," Hart said and turned

the page so the side was facing upward. He lay it back down on the hood. With thick black marker in hastily scribbled block lettering, it said DAMMIT! PAY ATTENTION.

"To what?" I asked Hart. "To the ads? To the blood? To the bodies littering this building?" Tears seeped into my eyes, then out onto my cheeks and sides of my nose. "Oh God, Hart. What's going on here? I thought it was over."

He hugged me tightly, quickly, then released me and held my shoulders at arm's length. "It is over. This is bound to have been done before."

"Before what?" I asked.

"The alcoholic. Before his arrest."

I wanted to, but I couldn't believe his theory.

"Or by some idiot playing off what's happened."

"The blood's still wet," I said, sniffing between words. "So it can't be Curtis. They took him in hours ago. How long does it take blood to dry?"

Hart shook his head. "It does take hours when it's thick like this, doesn't it?"

"It's not paint, Hart. It's blood. Think about when you cut yourself."

"Then some idiot taking advantage of the situation." Hart sounded so sure.

I couldn't find a tissue in my pocketbook. In desperation I picked up the hem of my chenille sweater and pressed the sweater against my face. I looked back up at Hart. He was looking at me for agreement. I don't think he believed what he was saying either.

"Whose blood did the idiot use, Hart?"

21

The snow fell in fat white flakes. It fell silently and steadily. No ice upstaged its beauty; no wind mussed its uniform spread. This was a classic snow, the kind dreamed of at holidays and stenciled on cards. The kind you'd want in December, not in the latter half of March.

While still on the Center's underground exit ramp, I had to put the Trooper in four-wheel drive. Chains would have probably been preferable. At least we knew we'd make it, though. All along our short route I saw those who hadn't: cars abandoned on curbs, abandoned, too, against other cars.

Hart and I didn't have much to say to each other during the drive to the office. He'd used up his hypotheses, and I'd asked the few questions I could think of. The silence between us was born of utter confusion more than anything else. Rarely have I been so bewildered by circumstances that I can't even think of good questions to ask. In fact, the biggest question of all wasn't one that begged for an answer; it was one that begged for questions. It was "What are the questions?"

Only once did Hart speak. I know he was trying to lift my spirits, but what he chose to say felt like icicles in my soul. He said, "Well, at least this will all be over tomorrow." I hadn't told him tomorrow's arrangement was coming to me only. I decided not to tell him now, either, although I don't know why. I didn't say anything at all.

At the office, Hart said he'd go inside to get Sally. The last thing I wanted was to go inside. When I thought of my own office, all I could see were those floral arrangements spread about my conference room like funeral flowers awaiting a casket. I called Tom from the car phone instead. I didn't recognize the voice at his private extension. Tom had left for the day, the man said. I remembered then. He was coming to my house.

Exiting the Allen Teague parking lot proved no easy task. I made the mistake of backing onto an area of yard as I turned the Trooper around. My back right tire spun itself a foot deep before I shifted into four low and pulled it out.

Shadows hit the road's edges as I worked my way first to Sally's apartment and then Hart's house. I stayed on the worn tracks of the cars in front of me. Those who didn't were starting to slide.

Sally told us the third arrangement had come just after lunch. "I hope you won't mind what I decided to do," she said.

I looked at her face in the rearview mirror and waited.

"I knew you weren't exactly thrilled to be getting those things. I mean the first two were on the floor so I thought it was a pretty good bet."

"Correct so far," I said.

She leaned forward in the backseat. "And you should have seen this one today. It was so bright and cheerful, and the weather was so glum and all. . . ."

"I bet they were yellow glads, weren't they?" I said sarcastically. "Not cheerful, though."

"Not to you, Sydney," she said in a wonderfully innocent tone. "But I knew they'd cheer up somebody. So I asked the florist if he'd mind taking all three of the arrangements by Carolinas Medical."

"In this weather?" Hart was beginning to sound as negative as I.

"Of course in this weather," she shot back quickly. "The man was out in it already. It's not like he was going to have to make a special trip. It was his next stop anyway." She stopped and took in a breath. "Sheesh, you two. I thought you'd be happy. I got rid of the flowers that Sydney hates so much and made at least three other people feel better while doing it. What could be better than that?"

Hart swiveled his head toward her while not moving any other part of his body. "All I said was 'In this weather.' I was making a weather statement, not a value judgment on your altruism."

"Good," she said sharply. I wasn't watching her, but I knew she was talking to me now. I felt the air shift close to my right ear and her words felt directed. "I even got us a charitable receipt."

"I'm glad you got them to someone who could appreciate them," I said, but felt disingenuous.

The three of us fell silent for the rest of our ride to her apartment out Randolph. I saw fewer and fewer cars on the road as I drove. The shadows had begun to spread menacingly onto the lanes. When I pulled up behind a city bus at the intersection at Wendover, the driver motioned me around him as the light turned. The motor was running, but the bus's back tires had slipped slightly into another lane. The bus was still packed with passengers. I was grateful we'd gotten away when we did.

"What about tomorrow?" Sally asked after I'd unintentionally parallel-parked in front of her apartment building. "Are we working?"

"I think so," I said. "The show's not over until noon. We still have to handle our booths." I caught her eyes in the mirror. "Don't assume you don't have to, Sally."

"Don't bite my head off, okay?" She was hunched forward between the Trooper's two bucket seats the way the kids sometimes sit when they're bored from a long trip. "Honestly, both of you. I've been feeling left out stuck at the office all week while you've worked the show, but if this is the mood you've been in, I can do without either one of you."

I was turning to tell her I was sorry when I saw the knuckles of her balled-up hand press down on Hart's partially folded scarf. It had been on the seat beside her throughout the ride. My mouth was still open to apologize when she reacted.

"Yuck, Hart," she said. "Good grief." She opened her hand, turned it over and quickly looked at the backs of her fingers. "You got paint all over the scissors and your good scarf too. How in the world did you do that?"

Hart and I looked at each other, but neither of us volunteered anything. I touched the lidded compartment between our two seats where I'd placed the bloodied ads.

"I just hope it's the kind that washes out," she said.

"It is," he said.

"I'll call you, Sally," I said, changing the subject. "I won't know until morning what Peg and Rhyne and the new guy at UFAS will expect of us."

She held her hand to her nose and sniffed. "Smells like it came from an old can."

I could hear her four or five layers of clothing rub against each other and the seat as she slid toward the door. "You two get some rest."

Hart finally turned his whole body around to face her. His tone was softer. "I'm not tired," he said. "The show's been a madhouse."

"I knew it was something like that 'cause this isn't like you at all." She extended her bloody knuckles between our two shoulders, then quickly pulled her hand back. "You can smell the rust in this red. You would never let me forget it if I'd brought you that paint."

I chuckled and looked at Hart. "Sally's right about that."

She chuckled, too, confident that our rotten moods and the "rusty" paint on her hand were both products of show anxiety.

Why tell her any different? Why tell anyone more than they needed to know about something that couldn't be understood anyway?

I took that same philosophy home to George junior and Joan after dropping off Hart. It was five-thirty by then, and I frankly felt lucky to have made it. Tom's car wasn't here yet. I wondered if he'd make it at all.

Charlotte has a hard time with snow in any form. Here we had a second snow on top of the first. I couldn't remember when something along this order had happened before. Probably never. I wondered seriously if our overly dramatic mayor, the mayor Tom didn't like, would beseech the governor to send us the National Guard.

One of the beauties of snow is the lid it clamps on noise, noise you never even know is present until a snow covers it. I noticed that quiet once I was away from traffic and in my own driveway.

I am always surprised by the quiet and a little in awe of the power it represents. This particular snow seemed more powerful than beautiful to me. I think fear transforms beauty anyway. When I'm afraid, everything seems menacing. Like the lack of lights inside my home. Although the sun wouldn't completely set for thirty more minutes, there wasn't really a sun in the sky at all. It was merely dark gray on its way to black. The lights inside my house should have been on. Where were my children?

I left my pocketbook on the front seat, slammed the Trooper's door, and started running toward the steps leading up to the kitchen. Almost immediately, I fell. The snow had packed itself into the semblance of a skating rink where the shadows of the house had hit all day. In the wide expanse of the turn-around drive, there was nothing I could hold on to to pull myself back up. I was so desperate to reach the children, though, that I pushed and slid myself, scraping my palms and ripping my jeans at the knee.

When I'd slid to the bottom of the brick steps that lead up a flight to the kitchen, I grabbed the wrought-iron railing. The railing felt like a life preserver to me. If it hadn't been there, I'd have slid into the garbage cans like a swimmer caught up in an outgoing current. The steps were so slick that getting up them required all the upper-body strength I'd been saving for tennis. My ascent was difficult, like a paraplegic regaining her chair after falling.

Between the exertion and the fear, the snow's quiet had disappeared. In its stead, my coursing blood and bursts of oxygen threw enough traffic inside my head to rival Charlotte's worst jam.

Once I reached the landing beside my kitchen door, I lay there trembling, trying to get enough oxygen into my lungs to stand up and face what I'd find inside. Sweat had popped out at my hairline, making me almost feel sick in the cold. It was such a clammy feeling, almost like impending death might feel.

I took in one very deep breath, let it out, turned over on my side, and placed my now bloody fingers on the door's threshold. My plan was to ease myself up to the knob itself, then go inside. With my hand holding desperately to that threshold, I dragged the rest of my body into a heap all along it, trying my best to lie where ice hadn't formed. My next step was to reach for the doorknob, which I did by inching my palm up the door's surface.

My hand was halfway up that surface when the door suddenly gave way. I tumbled into the kitchen like a Mafia hit thrown from a fast-moving car. All I saw were two feet in white athletic socks.

"Mom?" Joan sounded as if she wasn't sure.

"Thank God," I whispered. "Are you okay, honey?"

She squatted a foot from my head, sock heels together, chino knees splayed outward.

I propped myself up on my elbows, my eyes almost level with Joan's. Her smile was tentative at first, then a short burst of sound escaped her throat, followed by dancing in her eyes and finally full-scale laughter. I lagged behind her by a few seconds, but within thirty we were both laughing without control.

Between gulps for air I was able to establish that the house had lost power several hours earlier. Along with the rest of the neighborhood, I might add—not in some sinister plot to take my children's light and warmth. Joan's laughter was both longer and stronger than mine. From it and the few words she was able to muster, I learned that the blood on the palms of my hands was now on my chin from having propped myself up.

"You have a goatee!" she said as I tried wiping it off.

By the time George junior bounded up the steps from our family room, I'd managed to turn my sprawl into a cross-legged sit.

"You've got ketchup on your chin, Mom," he said without paying much attention to me. He carried two handfuls of candles and put them on the counter. "There's more where this came from. We're good for a couple of days at least."

"A couple of days?" Joan said in disbelief. "Duke Power will have everything back on in a couple of hours." She was sitting at the kitchen table now and looked down at me, a question in her eyes. "They always do, don't they, Mom?"

"They try," I said. "Help me up, Joanie. I don't want to bloody the floor pushing off."

She stood and took my two wrists, holding them firmly and letting my hands dangle uselessly.

Once vertical, I asked her to unzip my parka too and help me slip it off. I walked to the kitchen sink to wash the blood from my hands and noticed the emergency arsenal George junior had assembled on the counter: twenty to thirty candles, fifty or more partially used packets of matches, and four flashlights varying in size from one doubling as an ink pen to one of the large lantern types. He'd also found every random battery in the house and piled them into an oversized ornately swirled turquoise and brown ashtray that I'd inherited from my parents.

"Good work," I said as I blotted my palms with a paper towel. "We may need every bit of that if the snow doesn't stop soon."

"Oh, damn," Joan said, as if our fate were all but sealed.

The house was still relatively warm, but I knew the

darker it got, the quicker the temperature would drop inside as well as outside. I dispatched George junior to our woodpile so at least we'd have a fire in the living room.

Twenty minutes later I had a strong fire going with the wood that was already on the grate and a house full of mismatched but burning candles. Joan had gone upstairs to my bedroom, where our only "traditional" phone was still working. The others, because of either their cordless capacity or their attachment to the answering machine, were useless without power. As long as the telephone lines didn't go down, Joan would be fine.

I stood at a living room window watching George junior work in the last vestige of daylight. He was pushing his fifth wheelbarrow load of firewood from backyard to front porch. I noticed his shoulders, how broad they'd become. He'd be thirteen in another month, and it showed. The wheelbarrow dipped into, then out of, a hole as he pushed it. A large log toppled onto his foot. A momentary grimace covered his childlike features, turning him instantaneously into the man he'd grow to be. I watched his mouth move in a curse I'd never heard from him and hoped I never would. I didn't know George junior even knew such a word. At that moment, he saw me standing at the window, and grinned. His lips formed "sorry." He waved to me, then pretended to throw a snowball. The bashful boy returned in a rush.

I could barely see the outline of the slag truck that puled to a stop in front of the house. A dark figure opened the heavy metal door on the passenger side, dropped down the two sets of steps to the ground, then slapped the door with his hand and gave the driver a quick wave and imaginary tip of hat. The man then turned in my direction and began to walk toward the house. He was a tremendous hulk of a man, much taller than the two-year-old six-foot dogwood he passed as he walked. He wore heavy dark clothes and a dark skullcap. I panicked for George junior, who'd disappeared into the backyard just as the slag truck caught my eye. I hoped he'd come in the kitchen door from the back rather than return to the front yard and run into this monster. Just then I heard the back door open and George junior's voice calling for me.

"Quiet, honey," I whispered loudly as I continued to watch the figure in the front yard. "There's a stranger approaching the front door." I could hear George junior's footsteps coming from the kitchen.

The stranger carried a large, dark case, the kind I'd seen hit men carry in movies. Making the figure even more ominous was the machine-gun shape along the side of the case. Chains were draped over his other shoulder, or maybe it was a rope. I rushed to the front door and locked both the dead bolt and the slip-barrel locks, then turned my back to the door and pressed hard against it. My breathing was loud, but shallow. I was close to hyperventilating from the panic I felt.

22

"Let Tom in, Mom," George junior pleaded.

I still had my back glued to the door. The man had been knocking and calling out to me for five minutes. I wasn't convinced the dark figure outside was Tom Thurgood, so I wasn't about to open the door.

"Why won't you let him in?" George junior stared hard into my eyes, just as he'd been doing the entire time I'd been pressed against the door.

"I can't be positive. The voice doesn't sound like his."

"Yes, it does," George junior said, then shifted his eyes to the door's surface beside my head. He called loudly: "Say something, Tom. Mom says it's not you."

The man didn't answer. We waited a full thirty seconds. Still no answer.

"See," I said, "it's not Tom."

"Yes, it is," he said. I wondered briefly where the boy got such belligerence.

"No, it's not. Tom would have answered. This man is afraid to 'cause he knows we can tell the difference."

George junior walked hurriedly to the living room window. "It's dark now," he said. "Shine a flashlight so I can see him."

"Get away from that window this instant, George junior! Do you want to be shot?" In spite of my fear for him, I remained at the door as if my leaving would cause it to spin open immediately.

"Shot? What are you talking about? Mom, this is crazy." George junior returned to the hallway where I had remained and glared at the door again. "Tom . . . Tom . . . Say something personal to Mom." He was yelling louder than I'd ever heard him off the soccer field. "Say something she'll know only you would say."

As soon as George junior screamed those words, I heard a thud in the kitchen, then a chair scraping as if being pushed a short distance. My eyes darted toward that door. George junior turned in that direction too. The tall, awkward-looking body of Tom Thurgood appeared in the doorway.

"Well, okay," he said casually. "Why did you arrest the mayor's wife, Sydney?" He looked from me to George junior. "How's that, George? A little personal knowledge we both share."

That's when I learned relief can be as jolting to a system as fear. The blood in my head seemed to drop to my toes in record speed when I saw him. I had to hold on to the doorknob to keep from falling. I couldn't speak; in fact, could hardly breathe.

"The front door was locked," Tom said, "so I walked around to the kitchen." He looked at George junior. "Real slippery on the back stoop, George. Got a bag of salt or some sand?"

George junior had broken into a wide grin from the moment Tom appeared. He continued smiling broadly even as he shrugged, then looked at me. "Do we, Mom?"

My mouth still hadn't closed. So the silver-haired queen of the demolition derby had been the mayor's wife. Damn.

"I couldn't get us a pizza. I had to hitch a ride. No way my car was going to make it."

I shook my head and tried to regain some composure, although I couldn't take my eyes off Tom. "Just a couple containers of Morton's table salt," I said. "What were you carrying over your shoulder?"

Tom looked confused. "You mean the tire chains?"

"Oh. Tire chains. Of course."

He nodded. "We've got to get out of Charlotte tomorrow, remember?" He sounded angry. Something was off in his tone.

"How stupid of me not to think of that first." I knew I sounded sarcastic, but the part of me that might have controlled it was still shaky. "I guess that was your tennis bag you were carrying in your hand."

"I put it down in the kitchen," he said without reacting to my sarcasm.

So now I'd accounted for the "machine gun" he'd toted as well. I didn't feel as much like a fool as I probably should have.

"You didn't answer my question," he said. He hadn't moved from the kitchen doorway. He hadn't removed his cap or unbuttoned his heavy coat.

"I don't remember a question."

George junior must have sensed the tension between Tom and me. "I'll go look for salt in the basement," he said, and quickly vanished down the stairs to our first-floor family room.

"Yes, you do," Tom said. "Why did you arrest the mayor's wife?"

I turned away from him and walked into the living room. I was beginning to feel cold. I pulled a blood-red mohair throw from the back of one of my wing chairs, wrapped it around my shoulders, and sat on the sofa.

"How was I to know that's who she was?" I didn't turn toward him when I said it.

I heard Tom sigh heavily before he removed his coat and cap and laid them on the chair I'd just taken the throw from.

"Did I get you in trouble with your chief?" I kept the sarcasm out of the question, but I didn't give a damn what the answer was.

Tom sat at the opposite end of the sofa. We could have put three adults between us.

"None of us needed the distraction," he said instead of answering my question. He had turned to look at me. I felt his eyes leveled on the side of my face.

"Was she charged?"

"Yes."

I stood and reached for the black iron poker. A large oak log had slipped behind the grate. I stabbed it a couple times to spark it, then rearranged my smaller logs on top.

"Here. Let me do that." Tom was at my side. He took the heavy prongs, reached in and lifted the oak log back into the grate, then rearranged my smaller logs on top. "There," he said. "That's better."

His hand brushed my elbow. I felt a shock. Static. From where, though? The air? Or the two of us? He returned the prongs to the tool stand, then put his hand over mine with the poker to return the poker too. I let go of it. When I did, he saw my palms and asked me what had happened.

"You were right. It's slippery out back." I sat on the sofa, curled my legs up under my body.

He stood with his back to the fireplace and watched me. "Can you grip?"

I hated that this was his first question. I nodded.

"You ought to put something on them," he said. "Doesn't it hurt?"

"Stings," I said.

"Still," he said, and sat on the other end of the sofa.

"Close the show down, Tom." I set my jaw to itself and my eyes on his.

When I was a child, we had an old tomcat named Tucker. I remember one morning seeing old Tucker in a stare-off with another cat. I was going out the door to wait for the school bus. The two of them were behind the bushes beside our front door. When I returned eight hours later, they hadn't moved more than six inches in any direction. Occasional low growls came deep from within, but that was the only indication to me that what I was witnessing was not love. Tom and I were staring at each other with that same nervous intensity when both George junior and Joan entered the living room. I wonder how long the two of us would have continued in that state with neither of us speaking.

"What are we going to eat?" Joan asked me as she plopped between us.

"I found some bags of sand," George junior said as he did the same. "I think it's what the guy who made the brick patio didn't use."

"Good," Tom said, although George junior was looking at me.

"Roasted hot dogs," I said to Joan. "If we have any." I tapped her thigh. "Go look, sweetie. If we don't have any, the best I can do is peanut butter and jelly."

Tom spoke to George junior: "Put those bags just outside the basement door. I'll spread the sand before I go to bed."

Both kids jumped up as quickly as they'd sat down, George junior to the basement and Joan to the kitchen.

She yelled that she'd found a package of hot dogs and would put them on skewers.

I took up where I'd left off, rearranging myself on the sofa by pulling my knees up under my chin. I gazed into the fire.

"You have to, Tom. Shut it down." The oak log popped, giving my words exclamation.

I didn't think he'd ever answer. When he finally did, he said, "I tried. The chief wouldn't let me before Lewis confessed. For sure, he won't now. There's no reason."

"Yes, there is." I pulled the edge of the throw from my shoulders to my knees on both sides of me, creating as much of a tent for my body as I could. "Somebody's going to kill me if you don't." I turned my head toward Tom and rested my cheekbone on my knees.

Saying those words aloud brought me unexpected peace.

Tom's features grew taut, the opposite of how I now felt. His eyes fixed on me, their normal moisture dried up, their pupils vertical slits. He cradled his jaw between a thumb on one side and the rest of his hand on the other, as if, without that support, his lower face might crumble. His face showed signs of a battle within, a battle he didn't look up to waging. I was afraid he might cry.

"I want you to look in the backseat of the Trooper," I said softly. How odd that I felt a need to comfort him just then. "You'll find Hart's scarf wrapped around a pair of blood-stained scissors. There's also a pile of xeroxed ads in the compartment between the bucket seats. The same blood's on those too."

Tom was concentrating hard on what I was saying. His face seemed to regain some of its strength as a result of it.

"When Hart and I left the Center today, those ads were lying in the Tooper's front driver's seat. Blood covered them. The scissors were piercing through them into the seat."

He continued staring even as I was telling him. He nodded a couple of times as if hurrying me toward a better ending.

"The blood was wet," I said slowly. "This was four hours after Curtis was taken into custody."

He looked away from me then. I couldn't tell if he was thinking or if he was trying to avoid my eyes. I continued telling him everything anyway, including the bold hand-printed message along one of the ad's margins.

When I had finished, our eyes locked in the first honest encounter we'd shared all day. He had gotten it. Finally, he seemed to have gotten it. I was really a target.

He asked me a question I didn't expect: "Where were you parked?"

"Underneath the building." I wondered what difference that answer could make, so I asked him.

Instead of answering me, he asked another question. "Did you see any more blood?" Then another. "Was it outside the car as well?"

I shook my head. Gradually, I realized he was determining where to look for a body. The blood had to come from somewhere.

"Did you see anybody down there?"

I looked away for a second to think, then back to him. "We ran into my client, Peg Corbeil, and a guy named Larry who's posing as a woman while he's trying to land the UFAS mascot job."

I could tell I'd confused him with the stuff about Larry. His eyes narrowed. "You mean that African American woman? The bee?"

I nodded. "She's a man. We talked to Tina's private detective down there too."

Tom leaned forward.

"Did you know that the ladybug was his cover, that Tina put him in that role so he could protect her? She'd been getting threats for the past year—just like Barry."

He looked down at the sofa cushion between us. "He didn't do his job, did he?" He looked back up at me then. "He should have stayed with her."

Neither of us said anything. I watched the light from a flame dance along the side of his nose.

"Name's Scott. He told me he knew who Tina's killer was."

Tom waited.

I shook my head. "My client interrupted us. He ran away. The man's afraid, Tom."

I wanted Tom to say something then, but he didn't. Finally, I added, "I'm afraid too."

This whole time, I think I was waiting for him to tell me I would be okay, that no harm would come. I'd expected he would, that his arms would envelope me and his words would soothe me. I was waiting to hear that my fears were illogical, that danger wasn't looming after all, that I'd failed to see some critical part of the puzzle. It didn't happen.

We'd finished eating two charred and bulbous hot dogs apiece, stale potato chips, and Coke watered down by melting ice. The kids were in their dark rooms packing for Savannah, and Tom had just rekindled the fire to roaring. I was sitting on the floor close to it, my back against the front of the sofa.

"So what do you think?" is how I worded the most frightening question I'd ever asked.

"I think the chief may change his mind," Tom said carefully. "Either he lets me close the show or you stay away from the Convention Center." I'd wanted a simple answer, but I thought this was maybe too simple. "I'm going to call the chief at home," he added. He pressed his hand down on the top of my head. "Stay put." Then he picked up one of the brass candlesticks and disappeared out of my sight to use my bedroom phone.

The entire time he was gone I didn't move. His hand had put just enough pressure on my head to make me feel jammed into myself. At least, I told myself that. Maybe the feeling was psychological. All I had to do to relieve the feeling was either extend my neck an inch or two or sit up a little straighter. I did neither, instead choosing to suspend myself just as he had left me. Over ten minutes passed.

I heard his footsteps coming from the bedrooms on our third floor. When the candle flickered against the bookcases beside the sofa, I finally moved my head to look at him. Tom stood under the arch separating the living room from the hallway.

Something about his outline told me part of the tension had gone out of him. His shoulders no longer looked stiff, for one thing. An arm came up from his side in a loose, natural way. "He's agreed to close it," he said. He walked toward me. "Thank God," he said, his voice cracking.

Neither of us mentioned the Center, the threats, bloody scissors, or even flowers the rest of the evening. We packed instead and helped the children pack, encouraging both of them to bring their tennis rackets, too, in case we found an open court during waits between matches.

I wanted Tom to tell me that I'd be safe, that he'd see to it. I wanted him to say it confidently, in such a way that, no matter what my brain told me, my feelings would accept his words willingly.

What I heard instead was an hour-long string of sports chatter between him and George junior. Not tennis, but basketball and the play-offs. If I'd been a passerby and didn't know any of us, I'd have thought we were settling in for a long weekend with nothing to do, that no trip was planned, that no snow had socked us in, that nothing of any import was on any of our minds.

Again I questioned whether I'd overreacted to all that had happened. I knew I hadn't, though. I decided I needed to segregate better, to put one experience in one box and the next in another, and to choose whether or not to look at either. I wanted to be like the mother choosing dental hygiene over tornadic anxiety.

Once, while they were discussing the work ethic of the young Michael Jordan, I decided to interrupt. Tom was saying young Michael had known early rejection, when I asked, "Do we all just dismantle our booths first thing in the morning?"

All four of us were on the couch in front of the fire again. We'd taken my grandmother's old heavy quilt off my bed and had spread it over us to ward off what now was quite cool air.

"Whatever you'd do at twelve, you now do first thing. It's over. The public won't be let in tomorrow." He gave me this information matter-of-factly, as if he were customer service and I'd asked directions to the ladies' room. Immediately he turned back to George junior and attempted to resume his story.

Joan yawned. "So we help you take down walls and leave for Savannah from downtown?" She looked from me to Tom.

"I don't have to do the labor," I said. "We've hired it out."

Tom raised an eyebrow. "Why go there at all then?"

"I have to direct how it's done. The beginning of it anyway. Hart and Sally can stay with them until it's complete."

"We have to pick them up in the morning?" George junior asked me. He covered a wide yawn himself, then rubbed his eyes.

"There's no time for that," Tom said as if he'd decreed it. "Someone else will have to get them there."

His sudden directorial air angered me. "Who, Tom? Tell me who that 'someone' might be? Would it be my chauffeur? Or perhaps you're talking about my personal assistant?"

While my indignation was merely warming up, I remembered Merilee Gillespie from the *Observer*. I was supposed to meet her for breakfast. I pushed my portion of the quilt to Joan's lap and stood suddenly. "What time is it?" I demanded of no one. I leaned over the hearth and held my wrist so I could see the hands on my watch. Ten o'clock. Too late by etiquette standards, but I had a feeling this was one protocol Merilee wouldn't berate me for breaking. With my back to the fire, I said to both Tom and the kids: "You three may have to pick up Sally and Hart somehow and get to the Center without me. I'm supposed to meet someone for breakfast."

Tom was asking me whom I'd been "fool enough" to schedule a breakfast with in this kind of weather as I left the room. I decided to treat him the way I felt he'd treated me: I didn't answer him.

I really didn't expect Merilee to want to keep our date. In fact, if she hadn't canceled in weather like this, I myself normally would have. However, I knew I wasn't feeling normal. I wanted to be in a situation that would force Tom Thurgood to act. I wanted him, instead of me, to be left with a problem. I wanted to see him work hard for a solution. So when poor Merilee started to say we shouldn't meet, that she didn't think her car would make it from Queens Road to South Boulevard, I heard myself say that I'd not only pick her up for breakfast but take her back home if she wished, as well.

Before returning to the living room, I called Sally and Hart too and told them we'd need to work, after all, in the morning. Someone other than me, although I didn't know who, would be picking them up before nine. Then I told them about the decision to shut the show down immediately. Neither of them asked me why, although I'm sure Hart knew the reason as well as I. When I told Sally, she said: "Is that normal for a snow like this? How many inches do you think we have?"

23

The night was not pleasant. Neither the temperature in my bedroom nor the man at my side made for a good night's sleep. I'd given Granny's quilt, along with my only wool blanket, to Joan and George junior and bedded them down together on our air mattress in front of the fire. Once that was done, Tom and I were left with a couple of cotton blankets and a variety of throws the length of his thighbone.

The physical discomfort didn't keep us from sleep as much as the mental one. Tom put the chains he'd brought on the Trooper's tires before he even tried to sleep. While he was outside, he spread the sand George junior had found as well. He must have been out there two hours.

That whole time, I tried to sleep. I didn't come close. It wasn't the cold that prevented me so much as all the bulk from the clothing I wore. With long thermal underwear, sweatpants, a turtleneck, a sweater, and two pairs of ski socks, I couldn't move. When I tried to turn over, I pulled all the covers every time. Finally I decided I'd be better off without them and pushed them in a heap to Tom's side of the bed. When I heard him finally shut, then lock, the kitchen door downstairs, I sat up in bed.

I wanted a cigarette badly. If I could simply light one, I reasoned, I'd be satisfied. I rummaged around in the deep drawer in my bedside table, hoping to find an old pack, even though I knew none was there. I'd thrown them all out when I quit, just as I had the Scotch when I stopped drinking. That tiny, carefully cultivated AA voice inside me said, You stupid fool. Stop kidding yourself. You want to smoke, not just light up.

As Tom entered the bedroom I was lighting a cranberry-scented Christmas candle instead of a cigarette, one of those fat candles that'll burn for two weeks straight. I looked up at him.

He chuckled. "You look as if you're settling down for a long winter's nap, Sydney. Where's your kerchief?"

I didn't laugh with him. Not because what he said wasn't funny. I'm sure I did look like something out of a kid's book. I didn't laugh because of what he was holding in his hands: Hart's bulky scarf in his right and the xeroxed ads in his left. I couldn't take my eyes off them.

Tom shook his head. "Don't let this prank get to you. Whoever was trying to scare you has lost now." He nudged a couple of perfume sprays on my dressing table until he'd created enough space to lay the evidence down.

"Lost?" I thought it an odd choice of words. I thought the same thing about the word "prank."

He walked to the other side of the bed, pushed the mountain of coverings I'd created to the center between us, and sat. His back was to me. "Sure, he lost. We closed the show, didn't we?"

"Like the show was his stage? Something like that?"

Tom nodded, then reached down to remove his vinyl boots. "Closed his curtain and sent the orchestra home."

"What if that's what he wanted all along, Tom? What if shutting down this show was his goal?" I thought it was at least a possibility. How could Tom be so certain of his own interpretation when he didn't appear to know any more than I did?

He didn't answer me right away. Finally he turned toward me and said, "You'd think there'd be easier ways, wouldn't you?"

"Now look who's assigning logic. I thought you said this whole thing wouldn't make sense when it was over."

He removed his watch and put it on the night table. "I told you that because it's how it usually unfolds." He'd been unbuttoning his coat as we'd talked. He stood and removed it, tossing it across my reading chair. He returned to the bed.

"I wouldn't take any more clothes off, if I were you. It's cold." I rubbed my hands together in spite of the fact that the scratches on my palms still hurt. I swung my legs over the side and touched my feet to the floor.

Tom lay flat upon the bed. He began to place the throws on his large body. The pink cotton blanket still lay at his side. He didn't cover himself with it. Instead he kept pulling one throw after another onto his bulk.

"Where are you going?" he said.

I stood at the foot of the bed and pressed both hands into the small of my back. Tom had almost finished covering himself. He looked like a bulging patchwork quilt. I caught myself before I laughed.

"I'm going to study these ads," I said as I took them from my dressing table. "There has to be a reason why he chose them."

"Reasons don't matter as long as it's over." He pulled a stone-colored throw under his chin. The result looked like a large napkin, the kind a person might tuck inside a shirt collar to keep off the butter from a dripping lobster.

I did laugh this time. I couldn't help it.

He grinned. "Not a lot of choice here. Every little bit helps."

"You could use the cotton blanket." I nodded at it mounded on my side of the bed.

"That's for you," he said softly.

I put the ads down and leaned over the old pink blanket. I picked it up by two corners and then spread it over him.

"What about you?"

I walked around the bed to what remained of Tom in view, his head on the pillow. I bent over and kissed his lips lightly. "I know where it is if I need it," I said.

He left his lips pursed even after I'd walked toward the bedroom door. "It'll be good and warm under here when you're ready," he said. His voice had a dreamy quality that attracted me.

"Toasty," I said, knowing that a part of me was more than ready. I opened my top dresser drawer where I keep one of those clip-on book lights and a bunch of extra batteries. I grabbed the light along with two triple-As. I slid the batteries into a side pocket in my sweatpants, grabbed the ads, and turned to leave.

"Don't stay at it too long, Sydney. It's already past midnight." His voice flattened so quickly. Almost like having two men in my bed.

"I can sleep on the way to Savannah." I shifted my own voice to match his.

"You'll wake up cramped." He was thinking about tennis even if he didn't say so.

I was going to disagree but didn't see the point. We

always seemed to digress to inconsequential detail in order to avoid what mattered.

"Blow the candle out," I said as I left.

How can the very darkest of nights grow even darker?

I didn't need to see at first. My feet knew the steps from bedroom to stairs; groggy mornings had given them practice. The stairs were a different matter. I clicked on the little reading light and held it facing downward to light my way.

I laid the ads on the kitchen table, then turned off the reading light and laid it there too. I bumped into a chair someone had failed to push under the table but, other than that, felt my way safely to the hallway and the living room.

I could see the outlines of my children in front of the embers. If I stood very still and kept my head level, I could see them both breathing. I used to watch them like this when they were infants, sometimes for hours at a time. In those days, I wanted to make certain they were still breathing. This night I didn't know why I was staring at them. After a while I walked over and covered them again with Granny's quilt. The dying fire still gave off heat. I knew it wouldn't much longer, though, so I pulled back the screen, laid two new logs on the grate, and stabbed them a couple of times with the poker. One of the logs popped as it caught. Both children moved but didn't wake. I replaced the screen and tiptoed back to the kitchen even though, without shoes, I knew my steps wouldn't wake them.

I felt my way to the back door. The top half is covered with a café curtain, which I pushed to the side enough to see out. When I put my face against the glass, however, I saw nothing outside. Nothing. No tree outlines. No sky. Not even the big black Trooper against the white snow. My experience of snow is bright, almost movie-set nights. It's part of snow's magic. I couldn't remember a night as black as this, snow or no snow.

The culprit, of course, was the storm itself. In spite of having dumped a few inches on top of the ice, it wasn't through with us. I suddenly realized the moon was missing, as were the stars. "Reflection," I said softly, "there's no reflection." It was a blessedly quiet storm, though, and since I couldn't see it or hear it, I decided it had moved on. I chalked up the missing reflection to a brand-new sliver of a moon.

That same attitude has gotten many a southerner in trouble. If there's an assumption to be made, we assume on the side of what's pleasing. It's why we often see poverty as gentility, drunkenness as creativity, and insanity as eccentricity. If close friends or family talk sideways on a subject, chances are we'll say they're sensitive on it rather than dishonest about it. I like to think I'm cynical sometimes. Enough to stay in a cutthroat business and to ward off guys out for one-nighters. But, given an option even then, I'd rather not see a reality too harsh. Not if I don't have to. That goes for storms I can't see as well.

I felt the same way about Curtis Lewis, even if I wasn't sure why. Curtis had never seemed violent to me, and I thought I'd seen him at his worst. AA meetings can bring up the dregs of a person, and Curtis's history wasn't pretty. Yet even when I'd seen him with his placard and caught him in that lie about children, he seemed harmless. There are open, obnoxious drunks, the ones who fall off the wagon with a thud. Then there're the conniving ones, who plot their dismounts with Sherlockian precision and a cunning often frightening in its genius. Curtis was clearly the former.

After twelve years of watching alcoholics come and go from AA, I've decided we conduct our lives, once sober, the same way we used to plan drunks. We either are who we say or we're not. Curtis was a gay-bashing, bigoted, lazy drunk. He wouldn't deny that if you asked him. Whoever placed these ads in my car was cunning, methodical, and capable of violence. This was a person hiding behind flower arrangements, of all things.

I finally pushed the switch on the reading light and held it over the ads. The torn one was still on top, its sloppy message to "pay attention" along its side. Even under the strong halogen bulb, the pigment had evaporated from the dry blood. It looked more like mud off a pair of shoes now.

Behind me, in the corner of the kitchen, I keep cookbooks on a low bookshelf whose top doubles as a breakfast sideboard. I shone the light on the shelves and pulled out a *Southern Living Annual*. I was already tired of holding the reading light, so I opened the *Annual* to its approximate middle and clipped the light to the top of a page. Then I laid the pile of xeroxed ads down on it.

The first thing I did was count the sheets of paper. There were fifteen ads, including the almost illegible top one. As hard as I tried, I never could decipher that top one. The others were clear as could be, however. I removed the bloody ad and turned it facedown beside my lighted cookbook.

I didn't know what I was looking for, but I was convinced it was here. I was further convinced it was a message to me from the killer. The four of us targeted had little in common—personally or professionally. Tina Mauldin was a geek, an electronic PR whiz kid. I knew absolutely nothing about her personal life, though. On the other hand, I knew Joel Fineman was gay and that gay hatred was bubbling up again in Charlotte. Professionally, Joel was an aging statesman for the florist industry. He was revered by every florist I knew. Barry Firth had one thing in common with Tina, the PR, and one thing in common with Joel: He was gay. Maybe. I admit it was only a suspicion because of Peg's snide remark.

Then there was me. Although technically my job was broader than both Tina's and Barry's, I handled my fair share of public relations too. I was only peripherally involved in the floral world, though. And even if Tina was found to be gay, I wasn't.

So what was it about me that attracted this killer? What had he wanted from me each time he copied me a death notice? Was I supposed to understand before now? Is that why this message said "Dammit. Pay attention"? Because I hadn't been and I should have?

The message had to be here in these ads. Most sheets carried more than an ad, though. All were copies of magazine pages where the ads I chose had run. If the ad was full-page, nothing more appeared. If the ad was as small as a quarter-page, I'd sometimes copied articles inadvertently.

The first thing I noticed about all the ads, the bloodied one being an exception, was their vintage. These were all fifties advertising. I could tell even without looking for content.

In those years graphic designers were drawn to a loose, sparse style. The illustrations never looked finished to me. When they rendered people, they left off the feet or the hands. The eyes would be mere slits. The theory, I think, was that suggestion was more powerful than showing. Their typefaces bothered me even more than the art style. The type was all sans serif, with equal weight in all strokes. I knew they were shooting for clean and utilitarian, but to me the effect was amateurish. The nightmare was in reading the heads. Not only was there no contrast in the type, but the spacing was all screwed up. No kerning. Bad leading. No sense of a word as a graphic unit. The

fifties designers put so much space between the letters
within each word that the words themselves weren't distinct. I couldn't tell where one word ended and another
took over, not unless I sat and stared at the ad for a minute or two. I hated fifties design and could spot it from ten
feet away.

The ad I was looking at was typical. The heading said
"Box-Her Some Roses Today" and ran across the top of a
photo of a large foam-based dog's head made out of roses.
The dog, I supposed, was a boxer, his muzzle dark roses,
the flame on his forehead white roses, the rest of his fur
probably pink. Mercifully—to me, at least—the ad had
been black-and-white when I found it. Toward the bottom
right of the floral dog, the designer had inset a small photo
of a woman receiving a long box of roses at her front door.
She could have been June Cleaver or Harriet Nelson, or
any other fifties woman whose profiles seemed identical to
me. The product was roses. I imagined how thrilled the
copy and design team must have been when they came up
with their concept. After all, they were able to get in a box
of roses, a pun, a recipient of roses, and an extremely cre-
ative example of foam design, which was all the rage with
the invention of floral foam.

I couldn't decipher a message here, though, no matter
which way I looked at the ad. My watch registered 2:00. I
could tell I'd be getting very tired soon. Why couldn't I
see it?

I stood and walked to the sink. I turned the water on
cold, dipped my hands into it and splashed some on my
face. George junior's battery-and-candle cache was sitting
beside the sink in my parent's old deco ashtray. I turned it
over on the counter to empty its contents, picked up a lone
green tapered candle from the pile, and returned only it to
the ashtray. I carried them both back to the table. I posi-

tioned the ashtray as if I were going to smoke a cigarette, then anchored the candle between my index and forefingers, as I would have a Vantage.

That's when the phrase jumped out at me. The ad was a one-third-page horizontal and ran across the bottom of a page that was mostly editorial. That's probably why neither Hart nor I noticed the ad this afternoon. It was a casket spray and boldly proclaimed: "When Words Are Not Enough."

I quickly flipped through the other pages looking for all the phrases used on the cards. I found every one of them, although some were much easier to see than others. "Fresh Cut Just for You" was a refrigeration ad, a half-page vertical with a corresponding article about refrigerated jet transport.

The other two phrases were the hard ones. "Flowers Are the Food of Life" wasn't an ad head but, rather, the title of an article about the conversion of a grocery store into a supply shop. The opposite would happen today, I realized.

At first I couldn't find "Broken Hearts Don't Heal" or anything resembling it. When I finally did, the phrase wasn't what I found. After going over all the ads three times and then the articles even more, my eyes were drawn to a small photo accompanying one of the least of the articles. The photo showed a young woman handing the three-dimensional hearts, the ones I was to receive tomorrow, to a tall man. The caption said, "Judy Kiser, one of Charlotte's most noted floral talents, donates 'multiple floral hearts' to Dr. Dan Fitch." I lifted my cookbook close to my eyes. When I did, I could even see the triangular patterns on the carnation hearts. The article's headline said, "Healing Broken Hearts" with the subtitle: "Florist Makes Commitment to Charlotte Memorial." It had been years since Carolinas Medical Center was called Charlotte Memorial Hospital, but from the woman's long, straight suit and small veiled hat, I could tell this was much earlier still.

I wondered what magazine I'd copied this page from. I couldn't imagine a national pub mentioning Charlotte by name in the fifties. Even today, with a promotional budget in the millions, the city still has little name recognition. The rest of these pages had all looked familiar, some more than others, of course. But I couldn't remember this one at all. No ads were on this page either, just this article and several columns of another one. The other one was titled "Elvis Phenomenon Spreading."

I decided this particular sheet of paper wasn't one I'd used on the UFAS booth. I decided the killer had put it in my car for a reason.

I stopped at that point and tapped the candle on the edge of the ashtray. I looked more closely at the page itself and saw that its type ran off its edges. It didn't have magazine margins. How very odd, I thought before I began to understand what I was seeing. This wasn't a magazine page at all. It was a partial *Charlotte Observer* page. I should have recognized the difference more quickly. Only then did I look at the article itself. I was pleased, and only mildly shocked, when I saw the byline of the young Women's Page reporter named Merilee Poole. I recognized Poole as the name of the first of two husbands my Merilee had outlived.

"I'll be damned," I said all alone. I tapped the candle on the edge of the ashtray as if unloading a large ash. I tasted candle wax, and saw my tooth marks on the poor candle's untapered end.

24

I shone the reading light on the floor beside my bed and saw a pile of pale yellow fabric. It was the only queen-size blanket I own. I didn't care that it was a lightweight thermal. Any degree of warmth was better than the numbness I was feeling now. This tingling cold had encased my body like a broken-off advancing iceberg, and I desperately wanted it to stop.

My hands felt on the verge of breaking. After I doubled the blanket and smoothed it to cover my side of the bed, I found an old pair of red mittens inside a matching red ski cap on a shelf in my closet. I took them to bed with me, eased under the doubled thermal, then turned off the reading light and laid it on the bedside table. Wool pills, formed after years of washing, covered the cap's red surface. When I pulled it over my head, it was tight. The mittens had shrunk since the last time I'd worn them, and once they were on my hands, I wondered if these belonged to Joan instead of me. Not that I cared one bit, but the half inch between the mitten and the base of my fingers made me wonder.

Once I was as settled as I was going to get, I listened for Tom. His breathing is loud and rhythmical when he sleeps. In this early morning hour, it wasn't. He moved slightly once, and I heard him clear his throat and then swallow.

For thirty minutes I didn't move. I knew that if sleep were to come at all, it wouldn't be deep in spite of how tired I'd grown. I doubted I'd sleep at all.

"Any revelations?" Tom's voice was thick, but not like when he wakes from sleep.

"Hi," I said in return, but didn't answer him right away. "Any sleep?" I asked him instead.

"Don't think so."

"I think I discovered something," I said.

He didn't say anything then. We both lay still like the lumps we'd become, Tom entombed in his layers of throws and I in my thermal package. A full thirty seconds passed in silence.

"Tell me about it," he finally said, the thickness even heavier now.

So I told him what I'd found in the papers, every tiny detail of it. Even about fifties-design styles and other minutiae I knew would bore him. Normally, he'd tell me to get to my point when I'd digress as I was doing now. He didn't this time. I decided it was because he was tired. He only showed interest when I got to Merilee and her article about the young woman.

"That's got to be forty years ago," he said. "Are you sure it's the same Merilee you know?"

"Yeah. I am. Her maiden name was Gutenberg. She's ancient, Tom."

He chuckled softly. I felt his hand on my stomach.

"Don't leave it there long. It may freeze," I said.

I felt the mattress springs sway as he shifted his body toward mine. He turned on his side to face me. His right forearm now lay where his left hand had and his fingers lay under my breast.

"Let me come under then," he said. The dark turned fuzzy where his head was, his steam escaping when he spoke.

"We need to talk first," I said, although I really didn't want to myself.

"Talk then," he said softly.

"I'm taking the Trooper to breakfast with Merilee. You're going to have to figure a way to get yourself, the kids, and Sally and Hart to the Center. I can't do all that."

"I solved the kids and me already. Jeep's going to pick us up at eight. I'll send him back out for Hart and Sally."

"When did you call Jeep?" I didn't remember him calling.

"Your car phone," he said impatiently. "I'm cold out here. Let me in." He cupped the side of my covered breast and squeezed lightly.

"What makes you think he can get over here?" I wanted Tom's problems to be more difficult than they seemed. Difficult like mine.

"Why do you think we call him Jeep?"

"Because he has one?" This was too easy for Tom.

"Always has. Ever since I've known him." He laid his head on top of my collarbone, his hair touching the edge of my chin. "Anything else?"

To my surprise, I stiffened. Tom was wound tight too. The tension I sensed in his touch wasn't just sexual. Underneath our conversation, we were telling each other something entirely different from the words we used.

"I sent you some coffee in an evidence bag today," I said. "Did it even reach you?"

"Of course it did. Why wouldn't it?" His tone wasn't defensive, but it was close.

"I don't know," I said. "You haven't mentioned it."

"A lot going on," he said, as if I didn't know. "The mayor's wife showing up didn't help any."

"Can't you let that go?" I breathed loudly through my nose. I heard the rhythm of my heart inside my ears.

Neither of us spoke for a minute or two. Tom's hand lay motionless on my chest. He sighed heavily.

"They're testing it for colchicine," he said. "We'll have the results tomorrow. Where did the coffee come from?"

"Joel's booth. I was surprised you hadn't removed it already."

"Why? And foil your chance to tamper with evidence?" His sarcasm cut each word to a point. He continued, "Not even two hours after we decided to investigate. That's when you found it, right?"

"Don't be defensive, Tom. I didn't go looking for it. I was just surprised the booth hadn't been combed. That's all."

I could feel Tom's hand leave my breast and curl into a fist on my breastbone. After thirty seconds, he released it. His fingertips brushed the inside of my breast as he did, sending a tingle across my shoulders. I shivered.

"It's a mess" was all he said, but at least his voice was soft again. "It's over," he added, but I wasn't sure what he meant. The case, our conversation, or maybe even us?

"But we still don't know who's been doing it," I said, hoping he'd fill in the holes in my knowledge.

He was silent. His breathing seemed almost to stop. Then he said, "We have more evidence than you know." I knew there were things he wasn't telling me.

I knew not to ask what it was. I knew he wouldn't tell me.

"Is Curtis still in jail?" I asked instead, deciding to go at it sideways.

"Yes," he offered, and no more.

Did the evidence point to Curtis? I decided it must if Tom was still holding him.

"And Barry Firth?" I asked.

"What about him?" That edge in his voice again.

"Was he okay at the end of the day? Have you had a report?"

I heard him taking a deep breath, almost a sucking sound. "Dammit, Sydney. Stop. We're doing what needs to be done." He didn't really sound angry, just frustrated. He didn't answer my question either.

Tom pulled back from me and propped himself up on his elbow. A wool throw fell between us and scratched the side of my face. He pushed it aside and grabbed the edge of the pink blanket.

"Let's combine all this," he said, then covered the two of us with it. With his right arm free, he picked up a few of the throws and tossed them on top of us randomly.

I felt his knees slide up my thigh, then cross over my pelvic bone. He swung his arm over my chest and grasped my shoulder with his hand. His head came down on my pillow, his nose nudging at my ear for some room. I slid my head over. He eased himself along with me. The heat from his nose warmed my ear.

I turned my head toward his and searched for his mouth with my own. I kissed him so violently that my teeth ached from the pressure. My aggression released the same in Tom, and he buried his mouth into the base of my neck, as if suction pulled him there.

Tom reached up and removed my ski cap. "You won't need this," he said, his hot, hard breath on my face.

Lovemaking isn't always that. Sometimes you make something else. Sometimes you expel your tensions, your poisons, and more. This night it was more.

I could smell faint apples in his hair and idly wondered what shampoo he'd used. I liked the odor of his body better: its pungent oils, the ripeness of his skin, its bursts of heat and life.

He was asleep now, though. His body still enveloped me, warmed me as a blanket would where our bodies met, as close as fleece before shearing. His head lay in the center of my chest; his cheek used my breast as its pillow. Only my shoulders felt the chill in the room. I pulled my hand out from under the covers and smiled to myself. Here I lay naked, but I still wore those horrible mittens. Tom hadn't even mentioned them. I gently removed his forearm from the covers on top of my arm and placed it along the ridge of my shoulder. His warmth sank into my nakedness there.

The deep red of a stormless new day washed the dark windowsill. I hoped it meant we'd have sun.

Tom stirred in his sleep. His lips brushed my breast. He moaned.

Sadness overwhelmed me. I felt tears beginning to form in my eyes. I didn't want to cry, so I willed myself to hold them back. My nostrils stung from the effort; they filled up instead and I thought I would burst. I opened my mouth and gasped for air, then left it open until my breathing slowed. When I was sure I had control again, I took the deepest of breaths and felt my shoulders rise. I watched the top of Tom's head fall while I let my tension go.

"What happened to us yesterday?" I whispered.

* * *

At seven-thirty I left Tom and the kids throwing snowballs in the backyard. Jeep wouldn't come until eight and I had to be at Merilee's by then.

The kids and I had awakened to Tom's organization in full swing. He'd already packed the Trooper, filled it with gas, and brought home a bag full of buttered biscuits with hot drinks for all of us. I sipped the hot chocolate before dressing under the covers.

A shower would have helped my mental state as well as my body, but not the cold shower I had access to. It would have to wait until Savannah. I put on the same silk long johns I'd worn last night, but did bother changing to a fresh black turtleneck. Since today was mostly for driving and the public was gone from the show, I wore heavy gray sweatpants and hooded gray jacket to match. Over my tennis shoes I'd slipped yellow rubber Wellies, just a shade away from the pom-pom on top of my striped wool hat. My red parka completed the ensemble. I was ready for the runway, no doubt.

I found my leather driving gloves in the glove compartment, but they were frozen to the touch. After I started the car, I held each one of them up to the exhaust pipe just so my hands could fit. If I hadn't, I couldn't have driven at all. The strangely curving icicle, which yesterday had been a steering wheel, was just too cold.

The city had frozen its damn magnolias off. Hardly anyone was out as I drove to Merilee's. If I'd had any side roads to maneuver, other than my own, I wouldn't have tried it either. But the city had dispatched its slag trucks early and often. The drive was really not bad, as long as I kept to the middle of the lanes.

I listened to a morning-drive talk show. Six more

inches had fallen on top of what we already had, they said. The temperature was twenty and expected to hold until tomorrow night. By Sunday afternoon we would be back into the low seventies. The talk show duo told snow jokes then, but they weren't very funny. I didn't laugh at one of them. It wasn't my state of mind that kept me from laughing. In fact, I wanted quite desperately to laugh.

Merilee lived in one of Queens Road's finer old homes, a twenty-four-room Georgian with six working fireplaces. Just after Merilee's second husband died, the house was divided into four apartments and Merilee bought one. That was twenty years ago. From the street, it still looked as if one family lived there.

I was grateful today for its circular drive. Merilee's bones were over eighty even if the rest of her wasn't. For all her illusion of youth, I wondered sometimes how she really felt. Still, she protested when I steadied her as we walked from her front door to the car.

On the thirty-minute drive to IHOP, a drive that should have taken ten, she said I wouldn't need to bring her back home. "Just get me to the paper," she said. "Eric bought up all the tire chains in Charlotte. Someone will take me home." Eric was Eric Porter, Merilee's managing editor and a man who relished deadlines more than anyone I knew, except maybe me.

Other than the novelty of the snow, the only thing we talked about during the drive was the news I'd caused in fingering the mayor's wife. Her hit-and-run was now infamous, Merilee said with a girlish giggle. I didn't want to talk about it. Merilee usually gets the conversation she wants, however, and this morning was no exception. I don't think it went quite as she'd hoped it would, though, because the two of us got sidetracked.

"How could you not know who she was, Sydney?" Her

tone reminded me of my mother's when, as a six-year-old, I picked a weed and threw the daffodil away.

"I swear, Merilee, I didn't." Exactly what I'd said to my mother forty years ago.

"Don't you ever watch the local news? Or read my column even? The woman sticks her mug in whenever there's coverage. She thinks she's Barbara Bush, you know. She told me she thought she looked like her." Her enthusiasm had fogged my windows.

"You're fogging the windows. Stop talking so much." I pulled my wool hat off and used it to wipe in front of me.

"Turn the defrost on, child. It's what the dang thing's for." She swiped at her side window with beige wool gloves, leaving what looked like the letter "Y."

"It's on," I said. "It can't handle too much breath at once. Just tone it down a little." I turned my head toward her. "Try talking without all the breath. See." I withheld my demonstration until she finally turned to watch me, at least thirty seconds later. "I'm talking, see? But you don't see a bunch of steam coming out of my mouth."

"What do you do with your breath, Sydney Allen? You *are* alive, aren't you?" She leaned forward so she could look back at me instead of sideways. Her penciled brows flattened. She pulled her thin red lips into a wrinkled orb of surprise.

"It doesn't take a lot of air to talk," I said, stifling a laugh. "Not unless you're being all breathy and dramatic." I grinned at her then and almost slid into a parked and stranded car.

She settled back in her seat and smiled herself. "I'll have to practice keeping more of my breath then. I'm always amazed at what you teach me, child. I didn't realize I was giving it away unnecessarily."

Over all these years of knowing Merilee, I've learned

far more from her than she has from me. Her wisdom does span generations. One thing I've learned, though, I'd never tell her she's taught me: When two strong women get together and talk, no subject's too small to argue over.

I hoped the subject of the mayor's wife was a dead one. If I could keep diverting her, I felt it was. Over breakfast, I'd look at her story about Joel, and I'd show my gratitude for her writing it. It's not that my gratitude wouldn't be genuine. It would. In fact, if you had asked me Wednesday what I wanted most of all, I would have said this story about Joel Fineman. But Wednesday seemed a lifetime ago. For some of us, it was. Today I needed something from Merilee that I feared she wouldn't remember.

IHOP was open, thank God. I knew some places wouldn't be. A patrol car was the lone car in the lot. I patted the pocket of my parka where I'd folded the xeroxed *Observer* page from forty-odd years ago. I turned off the defrost and the lights before shifting to reverse and turning off the car.

By the time I reached her side of the Trooper, Merilee had embarked alone and trudged the few feet to IHOP's door. There are more ways to take a stand, more ways to draw a line than with words.

25

We both ate too much. Between the two of us, we had enough dollar pancakes to bankroll a year of *Woman's Day* diets.

We devoted at least thirty minutes to her "Deathstyle" article while we ate. She was pleased she'd been able to pull it off, to make death design come to life, so to speak. And well she should have been. I can't imagine a more challenging subject for a Lifestyle editor.

Yesterday, even, I'd been fascinated with the topic, but today it sat too close to home. Still, I feigned more interest than I actually had. She'd highlighted the cemetery totem sculptor and the topiarist and played down Joel next to them. The lopsided copy bothered me, but I knew why she'd done it: 'Tis better to help the living. I had to concur. Merilee, in her undercover fashion, had been doing that all her life.

At a point toward the waning of that conversation and with syrup pooling on our plates, I removed the xeroxed page from my pocket. Since I'd folded it in quarters, it could fit in the palm of my hand. I squeezed my fingers over it in a fist, then laid my hand on the table, knuckles down.

Merilee stopped in midsentence and tapped my wrist. "What's in your hand, Sydney Allen?"

"It's something else, Merilee," I said, shaking my head. "You're not through yet. Tell me more about the kind of wood he uses for the totems."

"Bullshit. Totem scrotum, child. You're not interested. Why not tell me what's on your mind?" She looked from my face back to my balled-up hand, then held her own hand out flat, palm facing upward. "Put it here," she commanded. "Right this instant."

"It's not that I'm withholding," I said as I dropped the paper onto her outstretched palm. "I didn't want to interrupt you, Merilee."

She closed her hand around it, then retrieved her pocketbook from the floor. She next lifted her reading glasses from an ornately embroidered case. I watched her closely and couldn't help noticing her hot pink rouge. It matched to a tee her reflective ski jacket.

"Interrupt me? Humph." She adjusted her glasses, pulling them down the ridge of her nose. "What do we have here?" she said as she unfolded the article she'd written so long ago.

I waited nervously as she looked over the whole page, then zeroed in on her story. As she read she sucked the shiny film of a maple syrup spill off her index finger. I stacked our plates in a corner to keep busy then propped my elbows on the table. I sank my jaw onto my hands and watched her some more. Slowly she began to smile.

"Where did you find this?" A dreamy nostalgia flooded her eyes. When I didn't answer, that look gradually disappeared, replaced by vague worry. "Sydney? What are you doing with this old article of mine?"

"How much do you know about the murders at the Center?" I didn't want to have to tell her the whole thing. For the life of me, though, I couldn't remember what I'd said to her already.

"I know someone killed the Mauldin woman, stabbed her." She rolled the tip of her tongue around inside her cheek. "Sorry, but I can't remember her first name."

"Tina," I said. "Joel Fineman was murdered too."

Merilee pointed at her "Deathstyle" story. "*This* Joel Fineman? I thought he had a heart attack." She is rarely shocked, but her mouth didn't close with her question.

"That's what we *all* thought at first," I said. My voice sounded muffled to me, belying the emotion I was trying to suppress. "If we'd known what was happening . . ." I began but was wobbling. "If I'd paid attention right away when I got the same message . . ." I broke off, then tried to begin again. "If I'd looked more closely at the technician in the corner . . ." I started to choke on my own words, but kept talking through the wave of emotion. I coughed, then stopped to take a deep breath. I looked into Merilee's wise eyes. "We thought that too about Joel, but he was poisoned . . . we think. We'll know today for sure."

Merilee looked me over, as if assessing the value of a secondhand purchase. She patted my hand, then held it. "Hold on a minute, Sydney," she whispered. She waved, then whistled for the waiter as she would have for a New York cab. "Two fresh coffees," she said to him while she shoved our plates into his hands. She returned her photos and story to the cardboard folder she'd brought them in.

I blew my nose with a paper napkin and lectured myself to calm down. I kept telling myself I had to or she'd never understand my request. I glanced at the uniformed policeman sitting in the corner booth. I wondered if he knew what was happening at the Center and decided he didn't. He was reading the morning comics. He'd stopped briefly, but only when Merilee whistled.

The waiter left with our plates and immediately returned with our coffee. He nodded at Merilee but not at me, then was gone. Merilee returned the xeroxed page to the table, sipped her black coffee, and motioned me to do the same.

"Want to start at the beginning?" She laid her hand square in the middle of the sheet of paper, looked at it briefly, then back up at me. "How else will I know what to tell you about this?"

I told the events as I'd experienced them. It was the only way I could. Even so, I knew the order of my experience wasn't the order in which things had happened. I'd learned that much from the woman in Suzannah's Flowers yesterday. Whatever happened to all of us this week had been set in motion long ago. How long, I wasn't sure. Forty years? Could it possibly be that long? Why else throw this article in my face?

Like the solid reporter that she was, Merilee stopped me from time to time. In addition to questions about time frame, she asked some of what I'd been wondering too. Why, for instance, didn't the chief close the show after Tina? Why did it take this threat to me to do it? Did Tom believe Curtis Lewis was guilty? If he did, why did he? The confession? Or something else? And, in the face of the bloody message to me, did he still?

When she asked, I wouldn't touch what Tom was thinking. I couldn't. I sidestepped every question about him and his thoughts. Merilee didn't push me further either. I felt I could talk about Curtis, though, and why he'd confessed when not guilty. I gave her the answer I'd given to Tom, although Tom had obviously discounted it.

"One more time, Sydney. I'm not sure I got it."

So I told her again. "He's still practicing. His addiction

is full-blown. Where he's coming from, the two sit side by side: absolute denial and total assumption of guilt. No difference in those two for him, Merilee. Neither reflects his reality. He's trying everything on for salvation. If it fits, whatever it is, he'll wear it."

Her eyes were tiny slits, she was concentrating so hard on my theory.

"His memory is so riddled with potholes of blackouts, the poor guy figures he might have." I waited, giving her a chance to let it sink it.

She frowned. Why couldn't people see the logic in the alcoholic brain?

"I've seen it happen before," I said quickly, before her mind could set. "Last year in a meeting. A wife had accused her husband of cheating. She confronted him right there in the middle of the meeting. All any of us could do was sit there. The poor drunk husband spent thirty minutes denying any and all shenanigans. When the wife clearly rejected his denials, he did a flip and said the opposite. He said he'd slept with everybody in AA at that point. Hell, Merilee, he told her he'd slept with me. The wife believed him then, so he was happy. He wanted forgiveness any way he could get it. Absolution above all else. It's the name of the alcoholic's game."

"So this Curtis is looking for forgiveness from his wife?" Her voice still sounded incredulous.

I nodded but said, "You don't have to believe me. Just tell me why the blood on the ads and scissors was still wet." I touched the piece of paper between us, then looked into her eyes. "Tell me where this came from. Curtis was in jail then. He had been for hours."

She pulled the sheet closer and glanced at it again, although she'd already read it twice. She removed her reading glasses but held them loosely in her hand.

"Are you asking if I remember writing this?"

I nodded.

She shook her head slowly. "No, I don't. It was a long time ago." Merilee gazed down at the paper again, touched the picture with her thumb. "I'm trying to remember this girl here." She bounced her thumb on the woman's face as if doing so would dislodge her memory from the source.

"Maybe it's the doctor," I said. "Do you remember him?"

She looked up at me, her thumb still on the picture. "Vaguely. Those were such different times, Sydney. Charlotte was small then. The number of visible people was few so I ought to know both of them. Yes, I remember the doctor. The girl is familiar too. The name just doesn't ring a bell. I don't remember any florist named Kiser. She certainly wasn't 'noted' either. Florists were prominent in those days. I'm surprised I don't remember."

We sat silently, each thinking separately.

"I believe Dr. Dan Fitch died last year," she said. "Given that your monster has a thing about florists, though, I think the message is in the girl." She put on her glasses again and picked up the sheet.

She was reading it yet again when I said, "It doesn't mention which florist she worked for. Isn't that strange?"

She chuckled, then looked at my confused expression. "I'm telling you. Things were different back then. If a family was prominent and its name was on their business, I would have been chastised for mentioning it. Sort of like explaining to today's reader that Clinton is President whenever you mention his name. Florists were that prominent." Merilee rolled her eyes to the ceiling, then back at me. "Her name alone should tell me enough, but it doesn't. The biggest florist in town in those days was Willys Florists out Central Avenue."

"Central?" Damn.

She nodded quickly, aware that she'd triggered something.

"Where on Central, Merilee?" I reached out, touched her hand on the table. "Do you know Suzannah's, the florist that's out there now? It's the florist who's sending these flowers. Out past Eastway?"

"Across from that scrumptious Vietnamese deli?" she asked, her eyes eager for either closure or spring rolls.

I was excited now too. Some connection just had to be here. I said, "I saw several Vietnamese stores. A restaurant, a grocery store, a—"

"That's it. That's where the deli is. Yeah, I knew there was a florist near that deli. If it's an old brick house, it used to be Willys. They had an acre of greenhouses too."

I finally felt I was moving toward something. I had no idea what it was just yet, but the movement felt good anyway. I felt better. I picked up the sheet of paper.

"We still don't know who she is, though."

Merilee took the check and started to stand up. "You get me to the paper and I'll find out. There's nothing I can't uncover when I'm there."

We fought over the check, but she won that little skirmish too. I stood beside her at the cash register while she paid. I put a dollar into a shoebox with a blurred color snapshot of a young girl with leukemia, then a quarter into a Lions Club candy dispenser. I turned its metal knob and cupped my hand at its mouth. Two large sour balls fell into my hand. I wondered why I'd bought these things.

After we were back in the Trooper, both having maneuvered on our own this time, I gave her the green candy and put the red one in my mouth.

"Where did this come from? Did you *buy* it?"

I sucked and nodded.

"Why on earth?" she asked me. She'd taken it out of its cellophane, though.

"So people will see," I said as confidently as I could.

"That's nice, Sydney, but it's the biggest hard candy I've ever seen." She popped her own and commenced sucking along with me.

"Thanks for breakfast," I said, pushing the massive sour ball between my molars and my cheek. "And for everything else, Merilee. This whole situation's been hell on me. I haven't had anyone I could talk to about it."

"My pleasure, child." Merilee removed the green ball and held it between her thumb and her forefinger for the rest of the drive. "What's happened at the Center is horrendous. I thank God the damn chief finally saw the light. If he hadn't, he'd have had me to answer to if anything were to happen to you."

I smiled and the sour ball rolled around, then settled again at my cheek. "Always my defender, Merilee."

"You don't need my defending, Sydney Allen. You're a big girl with another big girl of your own coming on. And besides, you've got Tom Thurgood defending you now, although he's done a pretty poor job during this mess. Couldn't he make the chief act sooner?"

We had come full circle to that question again. I sighed.

The snow and ice crunched as the Trooper climbed over the tracks of others in the *Charlotte Observer* parking lot.

"Tom tried," I said. "At first, he wanted to keep the show open too. I think he thought they'd catch someone quickly that way."

Merilee was shaking her head. She pushed the window button, letting the window down halfway. She tossed the sour ball onto the snow, then touched the button again. "Sorry, Sydney," she said.

"But he changed his mind quickly," I added. "Very quickly. Tom did want to close it. The chief didn't. Not until now."

She reached up and pulled down the visor. In search of a mirror, I was sure. Merilee always reapplied her lipstick after eating.

"Well, better late than not at all, I say." She opened her pocketbook in search of her elusive lipstick.

"For me, maybe," I said, then hesitated to say what was on my tongue, just waiting there. Then I said it anyway: "Maybe not for Barry Firth."

She looked up for a second, made eye contact with me. "Let's hope not. What does your Tom say?"

"He doesn't say much." I sucked the red sour ball in order to concentrate on something. The stinging had started in my eyes again. I pushed my own window button and turned away from Merilee to throw away my candy too. For both of us, it had been too much. "He hasn't said much throughout the whole thing," I said. I smiled at her then, and when I did, a damn tear dribbled over my lid and onto my cheekbone.

She returned my smile. She didn't make a big deal of my sudden emotion either. Instead, she held two lipsticks up for me to help her choose. "What do you think? Should I go Pop-Up Pink all the way or should I put on the red?"

"The pink," I said quickly, glad she'd asked for my input—no matter what the request. I needed to stop thinking about Tom and me.

She blotted her lips on an IHOP paper napkin she'd lifted for that purpose. Then she turned to me and said, "Savannah will be good for you and Tom. From what I've seen of him, you've got yourself a good man. I know you won't toss him like we did those irritating sour balls." She winked, hugged me, and opened the car door.

I thought, if only she knew. These last two days I'd felt, if not tossed, at least pushed away.

"Can you make it to the door?" I asked, knowing the question would irritate her.

She pulled back from her dismount, the car door still open. "I'm going to pretend you didn't say that, child. Now, where will you be so I can call you about that girl in the picture?"

"We'll leave for Savannah in an hour or two, I guess. Until then, I'll be in one of two booths. Either UFAS or Rhyne Garrett's. They'll take the phones out last."

A smile burst onto on her face. "Rhyne Garrett, the last of the great Garrett floral dynasty. How's that old curmudgeon?"

"He is an old curmudgeon, isn't he? A harmless old curmudgeon. I didn't know you knew him."

She glanced over her shoulder into the parking lot, then back at me. Another employee was backing in, two spaces over. "The Garretts were big at one time. Controlled the flow of floral supplies up and down the East Coast."

Here was more history I wasn't aware of. "You're unbelievable, Merilee. I'm gonna put you in my pocketbook and take you on every new sales call."

Cold air hit the warm air inside the Trooper, and steam formed between the two of us.

"The Garretts are an old Charlotte story. Tell you all about them sometime when we've nothing better to do. Just so you'll know how big they once were, I'll tell you this much. His daddy bought an A&P grocery store to retail supplies. Can you imagine? That was in addition to the wholesale he already controlled. Money and power. Those Garretts had them both." She started to close the door and leave, but hesitated. "For a while anyway," she said quickly, closing it then.

26

The running neon marquee said *Show Canceled. Snow!* and I wondered who'd decided to lie like that.

"It's not a lie. Doesn't say 'Show canceled *because* of snow, just 'Show canceled' and then the separate statement 'Snow!' I thought it was brilliant myself, and I concur completely with the way the city of Charlotte is handling this mess." In less than thirty-six hours, Jerry had turned into Tina Mauldin. He'd spun his insecurity and hesitancy into overbearing confidence.

I'd passed the UFAS booth on my way in and seen Jerry inside it alone. He was sitting at the corner desk and scribbling on a legal pad. Today he'd worn his red tie again, but he'd changed to a kelly green sport jacket and khaki pants. I didn't see a satchel in the booth, so he probably hadn't brought a change of clothes. Obviously, Jerry wasn't going to help in his booth's dismantling. He'd better not ask us, either, because Tina hadn't contracted us for that.

He continued lecturing me, clearly enjoying his new

roll as spokesman. "Neither the city nor UFAS wants anyone to panic over what's happened. We'd like to think FloraGlobal has a future here in Charlotte."

He was even smiling as he said it, the lone dimple in his left cheek set deep and constant now. His brown hair was cropped so close that its natural curl was all but invisible. I wondered when he'd had time to get a haircut.

"Ah, I see," I said, staring into Jerry's lofty little face. "You're looking at a long-term contract with our Queen City?"

"We're talking about one," he said. "Of course, this first FloraGlobal is a big loss to us. Charlotte recognizes its culpability in that loss."

"Culpability?" He was telling me more than he should have. That happens sometimes when the power's so new.

He nodded, only too pleased. "Why yes. The city's security breach caused the loss of life, not to mention a loss of profit."

"Your profit was up front, Jerry." I wondered if he even knew that. "Did your lawyers fly in from Richmond, or did your people hire Charlotte lawyers to do your negotiating?" I tapped my fingers on his desk.

His dimple had faded just a bit when he finally made eye contact. "I don't know who's handling the legal end. I know only what I'm told."

I gazed at him sadly. The edge of his horn-rims cut across his eyes just as they had Tina's. I didn't connect with him for that reason and so many others untold.

"And now you tell others. That's your job." My tone was harsh, I'm afraid.

He nodded slowly, cautiously, almost as if afraid of me. I wouldn't have blamed him if he were. I'd spit those words at him, and I wasn't sure why. Jerry and I had essentially the same jobs. I was a mouthpiece, too, at times.

Sometimes I found my message distasteful, even offensive, as I had delivering Tina's message about Joel. Yet I usually delivered those messages anyway. So what bothered me about the exuberance he showed in his telling? Was it that he believed his own words, and I no longer believed mine? Was I jealous of his innocence that way?

"I'm sorry, Jerry," I said after we'd both fallen silent. "I'm tired. I shouldn't take that out on you."

I saw relief in his eyes but not understanding. He couldn't understand. What he saw, I felt certain, was an aging female advertising type, one close to burnout. Once he put me there, any chance for understanding was gone.

He picked up a corner of his legal pad, then let it drop back to the desk with a thump. "Don't mean to be rude, but I have this press release to write. You'll be interested in what it's about."

I couldn't imagine, but I raised my eyebrows appropriately.

Jerry had a ballpoint pen in his right hand. He motioned with it over my left shoulder. "The bumblebee won the competition." His voice was flat, no exuberance in it at all.

I turned and saw the sign announcing it: INTRODUCING THE UFAS BUMBLEBEE: RUMBLING ALL OVER THE WORLD. An eighteen-by-twenty-four-inch glossy of Larry in bee drag sat under the words. The picture wasn't a very good one.

"Oh, God," I said, not able to hide my surprise. "I know you wanted the hummingbird." I had a hard time turning back to him once I'd seen the poster.

"What can I say? The showgoers voted." He shrugged. "At least it's not that ladybug."

I backed out of the UFAS booth, my emotions mixed. In spite of his corporate enthusiasm, Jerry's job would be hell once the curtain rose on Larry's next act. The typical time span for a public relations job slot is four years. I wasn't giving Jerry more than two at UFAS. I purposely didn't look at our sepia ad panels as I turned and walked away.

It was after nine-thirty and the wide aisle nearly empty. Most show participants were just arriving for what they thought would be their last morning of sales and demonstrations. Since the decision to close had come late last night, they had all dressed for customers. I noticed, though, that most carried duffel bags or overnight cases. The work they thought they'd perform at noon had simply come early. Small groups had gathered at the edges of their fabricated boundaries.

I spoke to several such groups as I passed them and didn't find a person among them who wasn't angry. These were the people who'd lost money because of the show's closing, not UFAS. The labor they'd hired and the transportation they'd arranged weren't scheduled until into the afternoon. The weather's uncertainty and worse-than-anticipated road conditions would have made this day difficult under any circumstances. If UFAS had bothered to call them last night, they could have arranged morning departures. As it was, they were stuck and damn mad about it. Getting a jump on it would be helpful, if they had only known.

I didn't blame them. They had every right to be angry. I said to several of them, "There's someone in a position to help you. The new UFAS public relations executive. He's in the UFAS booth now if you'll go there."

All things considered, I felt no guilt about directing them there. Hell, it was his job. Good practice for Jerry.

I wondered if Jeep had been able to reach Hart and Sally and if they were here yet. Surely the kids and Tom had made it by now. Where would Tom have taken them, though? Tom didn't know who any of my clients were except, of course, for UFAS, so I decided to go back there and ask Jerry. I didn't want to walk the show's length to the Garrett booth if I didn't have to.

Peg stopped me before I could, however.

"Pssst, Syd, come over here," he whispered loudly. He drew his hand over his mouth in an exaggerated pretense of secrecy.

He wore white wool pants that were baggy over his knees and thighs. His shiny black boots hugged everything below his knees like riding boots do when priming their wearer for a hunt. The difference was these boots had fur liners that Peg had flipped over the tops, creating himself cuffs.

"Sable," he said. "You should know I'd never go faux. And these uppers are patent leather, not plastic as that gauche Larry boldly, yet incorrectly, observed this morning."

"Is he here? I want to congratulate him."

Peg rolled his eyes. "That vain man. I left him primping." He cupped his hand to the back of his head, his elbow directed upward. He batted his eyelashes ten inches from my face.

I laughed in spite of how tired and depressed I felt.

"The new UFAS doofus arranged a photo session for the big bee. So he'll spend the day in some studio in town. They're even sending a car for him."

"Good," I said.

"Not good. His head swelled this morning to the size of the rest of him." He shook his head. "No gratitude."

Large corrugated boxes lay open inside his booth. One had an arrangement inside; the rest, flaps open, were waiting to be filled. All had IT'S A CORBEIL! stamped on them in red.

"How did you arrange his tryout with Tina?" I had nothing to lose by asking, I decided.

At first I thought the question offended him somehow. "I simply asked her for it," he said, as if even the memory was somehow beneath him now.

"But you told me you didn't know her, Peg."

"I didn't. Not really. Don't you believe me?" His tone clearly challenged me. He planted reflective legs side by side, almost a military stance. "She called me and wanted something. I merely parlayed her agenda into my friend Larry's financial needs." He had that haughty tone he always has when he's playing with me. He wasn't defensive, though.

"What did she want from you?" I tried to stand as straight as Peg, but I couldn't pull it off. I was simply too tired to keep trying. I slouched instead and held on to the back of his chaise.

"To buy me, Syd dear. Three point five mil was her offer." He looked me in the eyes. "They needed a franchise designer, she said." He laughed. "Can you believe that one?"

Yes I could. UFAS wanted it all while pretending to foster the individual. "I know you didn't sign on," I said, "so how did you get Larry the tryout?"

He smiled, a sheepish sweep across his face. "I told her I would but not yet."

"So you lied to her?" I couldn't smile. He had lied to me too.

"Yes, I lied to her." He briefly surveyed the booth, then returned his gaze to me. "It's how I got this prime spot across from UFAS, and it's how I got Larry his chance at the big time. In case you're interested, I'm not proud of what I did."

"I'm not your judge, Peg."

All of a sudden my exhaustion was too great to ignore. I asked Peg if he'd mind my sitting on his chaise while he packed. "Just for a minute," I promised, and I shared with him some details of my sleep-deprived night.

His face reflected his horror when I told him about the xeroxed pages. "You found them stabbed where? And they were bloody?"

"I thought you would have known that part," I said. "It's why the show has closed."

"Not the fluffy white stuff?" He held both arms in the air and wiggled all nine fingers as he lowered his arms. Peg had a way of teasing even when he didn't mean to.

"No. It was the threat to me yesterday. Hart and I found it right after you and Larry left."

He shook his head. "I'm sorry, doll. I really, really am sorry." It was the first time I'd ever heard pure sincerity from Peg. No edge to the words, no setup to turn those words on me, no undercurrent of sarcasm waiting to spill over.

When I thanked him for his caring, he became embarrassed. He squatted and pinched the phone cord from its temporary outlet and began wrapping the cord around the antique phone.

"How much do you know about Charlotte's floral history, Peg?"

"Some," he said, relieved the emotion was over. "Try me."

"Okay. What does the name Judy Kiser mean to you? She was a floral designer in the late fifties. She was young-looking then so she's probably still around."

He shook his head while I described her. Finally, he said, "Nothing. Never heard of her. Should I?"

"I guess not. What about the Garrett family?"

"Rhyne Garrett? Your client?"

"His family," I said, "way back. Do you remember their buying a grocery store and converting it to a retail supply store?"

His eyes finally showed recognition. "Yeah, an old A&P. It didn't work out, though."

Why hadn't I bothered with the article about that last night? It would have taken me two minutes to read. And I knew it was important even then. It was the basis for Barry Firth's arrangement, so I knew it was important.

"The building sat idle for a couple of years, then went back to being a grocery store. Still is, I think. Harris Teeter this time, though." He laughed ironically. "One of those big mother stores with the monster floral departments."

"Is it out Central?"

He scratched his head. "No, not Harris Teeter. It's the one near Cotswold, I think." He stood close to the chaise, bent over me. "Why all these questions, Syd?"

"I don't even know," I said. "Not really. Just old newspaper clips that copied along with the ads. I thought they were somehow connected, but right now they don't seem to be."

"Well, good," he said lightly. He was weaving the telephone cord in and out of itself so it wouldn't unravel after being packed. He leaned over the box with the arrangement in it, pushed back its gilded leaves, and eased the phone down onto a bottom lined in Styrofoam peanuts. I loved to watch him work, even doing something simple like packing. Peg was meticulous about everything he did.

I was thinking about getting up, going to ask Jerry about Tom and the kids, when I saw my son skip past Peg's booth.

"George junior. Hold up!" I cried, and he did.

27

George junior told me they'd been here "forever." After closer consideration, he shortened it a bit: forty-five minutes, maybe an hour. Joan was in the Garrett booth awaiting his return with two Cokes. The way George junior told it, both kids had been indentured to Rhyne Garrett as cleanup crew. Tom had left as soon as they arrived.

"What do you mean by 'left'?" I asked him as we walked.

"Some cops came to the booth to get him. He left us with Jeep and Mr. Garrett."

"Do you remember what those cops said to Tom?"

"They wanted him to look at Firth, they said." He popped his can of Coke and sipped the brown liquid that pooled beside the mouth opening. We slowed while he sipped.

"You sure they didn't say 'look for Firth' instead of 'at Firth'?"

George junior shrugged. "When can we leave for Savannah?"

I looked at my watch. It was after ten. "Before noon, for sure," I said.

"Why not now?" Normally, his voice would have sounded whiny saying words such as these. It didn't today, and I wondered if the change was permanent, if my baby was growing up.

"Because our clients might need some direction," I said. "Allen Teague planned their booths. We're the best ones to decide how to take them apart."

"Does that include washing the tables and vacuuming?" His tone was about as sarcastic as George junior can be, which isn't very.

"If it helps us get out of here quicker, yes it does." I watched for his reaction from the corner of my eye. He seemed to actually give my words some thought. I continued to watch him. Casually, without him knowing. His head was level with mine now, both of us at five eight, an inch and some portion shorter than his sister. Last time I'd noticed, I could see over the top of his head. I also saw his face fuzz differently. It had transformed. Or was it this garish Center light? The tiny strands were facial hair now, not fuzz. I hated to say this, but my little boy needed a shave.

Rhyne Garrett's four director's chairs were in use: Rhyne himself sorting paperwork in one; Jeep, just sitting in another; Joan, a paperback facedown on her lap and a bag of store-bought popcorn unopened beside her; and now George junior. I pulled a utility stool to the edge of their loose configuration. George junior handed his sister her can of Coke.

"How many is that for you two?" I asked Joan.

She made eye contact with Jeep. They both grinned, he less so.

Jeep answered, "We drove through Hardee's on the way in. The boy and girl got drinks."

"Hardee's? For more food? Didn't Tom tell you they'd already had breakfast?" As I said it I remembered I'd just had my second breakfast with Merilee.

Jeep was looking at me, but he didn't answer. Tom probably told him I'd gone out to breakfast myself so who was I to bitch. In fact, I was sure Tom must have told him since it was why Tom asked Jeep for help in the first place. He was still staring at me. Embarrassed, I looked away.

Rhyne was smiling as he leafed through his paperwork. "Good show, Sydney," he said, and raised his eyes toward mine. He then smiled directly at me. "A very good show." He held up a stack of yellow papers two inches thick.

"Are those orders, Rhyne?" If they were, it was highly unusual to get that many at a show. Shows are mostly for making contacts, not actually selling.

"Not just orders. Big orders, thanks to you and Hart. I tell you, Sydney, he's a fine fellow. A fine, fine fellow." Rhyne turned toward Jeep. "Do you know Sydney's art man, Hart Johnson?"

Jeep shook his head, didn't look interested.

"Brilliant technical artist." He pointed to the panels surrounding us. "This is his work. Look at the detail he put into that pick machine," he said, leaning toward one of the still-erect panels.

Jeep still didn't look interested.

I nodded toward the pick machine panel and asked Rhyne if he was going to throw them away, as he'd originally planned, or keep them for future shows.

He feigned shock at the very thought of pitching the art. "Keep them, of course," he said. He played off Jeep's presence again, looked at him and said, "These flimsy little walls cost me a much as a college education."

"Community college, two years," I said to Jeep. "He's probably made ten times that already." I shook my head.

Why the two of us were competing for Jeep's favor, I didn't know. Clearly, Jeep couldn't have cared less.

I suddenly realized Hart and Sally weren't here, yet Jeep was. "Jeep," I said, "I thought you were going to pick up Hart. My other employee too."

"I sent a man," he said. "Should be here shortly."

"Tom thought you—"

"Tom doesn't need to know everything. He tried programming my whole morning." He shook his head.

I heard Sally's voice. I looked down the long hallway and saw the two of them approaching us. Hart was wearing the same navy coat he'd worn yesterday. He wore a new scarf, a red one. Sally wore blue jeans, brown hiking boots, and a purple microfleece jacket that she'd already unzipped. Under it, she wore a plaid flannel shirt and, under that, a silk turtleneck.

I looked back at Jeep. "Can you or one of your men take them home when they're through working? Tom and I will be off to Savannah shortly."

He thought about it a minute. While he did, I noticed his eyes. They looked glazed over, filmy almost, the way a sick dog's eyes get. Seeing them made me realize they'd looked this way yesterday, too, only not as bad as today. I decided he was in pain. I knew some pain medicines made eyes look like that. I'd seen addicts whose eyes looked like that too.

"If Tom says to do it, it'll get done," he said.

I thought that was an odd answer. What was he telling me? That he didn't believe Tom and I were going to Savannah? That he'd do it for Tom but not for me? But he wasn't even agreeing to do it at all, just that "it'll get done." It sounded like one of those department things, which I knew to really be ego things. After all, Jeep was head of security, not just in it. Perhaps I'd offended him by asking. I'd need to remember to ask Tom to find them a ride.

I sent Sally to Peg's booth to ask if she could help with anything and told her to check on Jerry in UFAS too. "UFAS hasn't paid us to help," I told her, "but make sure he's packing up the plywood panels with padding between them. If he doesn't the surfaces will scratch. Tell him that."

After three hearty rounds of handshakes with Rhyne, all initiated by Rhyne, Hart set about dismantling the poles that gave us our boundaries.

Rhyne leaned over to me then and whispered, "You ought to give your fellow a bonus for this good work."

How magnanimous of Rhyne, I thought. "I will," I said, "if you'll give me the money to give him."

Rhyne shook his head, looked at Jeep again and uttered something unintelligible.

I noticed Jeep's hands were clutching the wooden arms of his chair. Unmistakable pain showed in the furrows of his brow. I asked him if he was all right. He nodded slowly that he was.

Rhyne said, "I'm leaving now, if you have everything under control." He'd returned the sales receipts to a brown plastic portable file cabinet and picked it up by its handle.

"Hart and Sally can handle it," I said. "I'm leaving soon too."

Rhyne pulled his heavy herringbone wool coat off the metal tree and, with his free hand, swung it over his shoulder. He nodded at Jeep. "Nice seeing you again, old buddy," he said, then turned to leave.

"You two know each other?" That surprised me. How different could two lives have been?

Rhyne turned back toward us. He smiled, first at me, then Jeep. "We go way back, don't we, Jeep old boy?"

Jeep nodded slowly, a kind expression on his face. "About as far back as two old guys can go, I guess."

Rhyne then turned to me and said, "Jeep Ford and I grew up together."

"Neighbors?"

"In the fifties, everybody in Charlotte was your neighbor. In those days, you knew everybody and everybody knew you. Not that way anymore. Not in this town anyway." He turned from me again and started to walk away.

"I almost forgot something," I said. "Did your family have a retail distribution outlet in a grocery store at one time? An old A&P?"

His back was to me when I asked him that question. He stopped moving abruptly, but he didn't turn around. He said, "That A&P wasn't old. It was almost new when Father bought it."

"Oh, thank God," I said. "I've been thinking that wasn't yours—"

He interrupted me, his back still all I could see. "*What* wasn't mine, Sydney?"

"The store. I read about it. Actually only the headline. I saw an article from an old *Observer*. The day after your father bought it, I guess."

"That would be June twelfth, then. Nineteen hundred fifty-seven."

"Damn, Rhyne, what a memory. I can't remember—"

"I'm leaving now," he said, cutting me off again. "Good day again, Jeep." He hadn't turned around once during that whole exchange.

I watched him for a while as he walked toward the front of the skeletal show. I was trying to understand what I'd said to upset him so. It didn't make sense to me,

Rhyne's reaction to my knowing that history. I knew he had a lot of pride, though; I'd seen it always in him. I supposed he was private, too, and a family history that had broken to pieces wasn't small-talk fodder for him. By the time I turned around to Jeep, I was ashamed I hadn't been more sensitive.

He appeared to agree with me. "Why'd you do that to him?" he said. "You should have read that article you have. The Garretts lost just about everything when that store failed. Rhyne's slowly built the damn thing back, but, God, you should have had the decency to think about that." His sick, pasty face glowed red now.

I didn't feel a minor lapse of sensitivity warranted this much vehemence on Jeep's part. What I thought I was experiencing was something more.

I said, "Jeep, you really don't like me, do you?"

He stared at me, his face still red.

"What have I done to you for you to dislike me so? Is it Tom? Huh? Are you jealous, Jeep? Is that what this is all about? I've taken your buddy?"

"It has nothing to do with Tom," he said. He looked away from me then.

"What then?" I was mad now too.

"I thought you had more to you, that's all." He looked back at me. "Tom's always saying how sensitive you are, how smart you are. He says you're perceptive." He laughed, although the sound of it wasn't pleasant, like the sound of an old car on downshift. "I don't dislike you. I just don't see your value."

"Have you seen that article about Rhyne's family, Jeep? Did Tom bring it in and show it to you?" At that moment I didn't know whom I trusted less, Tom or Jeep.

He'd taken a stoical position now, no expression on his face at all. He did look into my eyes, though, when he answered me that he hadn't. "Tom didn't bring it in. He didn't show it to me if he did." Then he added, almost to himself, "I don't need to read it. I remember it."

"How do you know I have it then?" I had moved off my stool and walked over toward him and the kids. Both kids fidgeted. I knew our tones were making them nervous, although I wouldn't allow myself to look into their eyes.

"You just said you had the article." His eyes met George junior's. "Didn't she, son?"

"No, I didn't. I said I'd seen the article. I could have seen it anywhere. That doesn't mean I have it."

His glare was unwavering, then he sighed heavily and winced in pain. "Splitting hairs. You're splitting hairs, Sydney." Then he grabbed his thigh at his knee and squeezed tightly. "Damn leg."

In spite of my anger, I felt sorry for him. The pain was obviously deep. I stooped and put my hand on his chair, afraid to touch him if he didn't want me to. "Can I get you some medicine, Jeep? Is it your arthritis?"

I watched the pain wash over him in two more waves, then subside. The kids hadn't said a word throughout. I glanced over at them now. They were watching Jeep too, a painful empathy in their eyes.

"I have some pills in my coat pocket," he said, still with some effort. "If I can get two or three in me, I'll be like new in a couple of minutes. Flat sends this pain away."

I supposed that was why sometimes Jeep couldn't walk at all and other times he didn't even appear to have a problem. Joan had jumped up and run to the khaki all-weather coat hanging on the tree with the other ones. She handed me a bottle and handed Jeep her half-empty Coke can. Instinctively, I looked at the prescription label. I don't know why I did. It was probably the mother in me. The pill was Ativan. I'd heard of it and knew it was strong. The prescription called for one to two for pain every four hours. The prescribing doctor was the only thing odd about the bottle. He was an oncologist whose office was just down the street from Allen Teague. I knew that he specialized in bone cancer. Damn. Jeep had been lying to everyone. He had bone cancer, not arthritis.

He saw me reading the bottle. When I handed him the two pills, our eyes locked. He nodded for me to give him a third and I did. He cupped his hand around the pills, threw his head back and dropped them in. He drank only enough to swallow once and handed the can to Joan.

"Tom thinks it's bad arthritis," I said.

"Everybody does," he said, his voice straining now. "Doctors did too for a year. Hell. Maybe I had that too. Called it gouty arthritis. Shoved other pills at me for that."

Colchicine. I knew doctors prescribed colchicine for gout. I tried to touch his hand. He recoiled, though, when I did, and it surprised me. I decided he had reason to be bitter. I thought about Tom and was overcome with sadness for him. He truly loved this man. No matter what Jeep felt about me, I knew he loved Tom in return.

He must have seen it in my eyes. "Don't tell him," he said. "Promise me that."

I nodded.

"Go on now. I'll be like new in a minute."

I nodded again and turned away, not knowing how I felt about any of what had just happened. Both Joan and George junior were staring at me, waiting for me to do or say something to relieve the tension we all felt. The bag of popcorn had fallen onto the floor beside Joan. I picked it up and whispered to them both, "How about some popcorn?" If it wasn't exactly comforting, it was the best I could do under the circumstances.

Actually, those simple words were enough for them to smile. George junior took the bag from me and began to rip at its seams.

Jeep asked what time it was.

"You took them just a minute ago. Give them a couple more minutes to start working." Of course, I thought, he wanted to know when his pain would go away.

"No," he said urgently. "The time. The exact time."

I told him what my watch said: Ten forty-five. "I'm always a few minutes fast," I added.

George junior said softly, "Want a piece of popcorn, Jeep?"

From the utility stool where'd I perched in Rhyne Garrett's booth, I could see the bank of doors leading to the boneyard and onto the loading docks. If I'd thought I could get away with it, I would have parked there today as I did yesterday. But I knew I couldn't. If that underground roadway weren't packed with long-haul trucks already, it would be within the hour. Even the show participants caught in the early closing were expecting to pack up come noon. Their trucks would be backed up and waiting before then.

One of those doors opened while I was looking in that direction. Tom and two uniformed policemen entered what was left of the FloraGlobal Show. Every booth was in some stage of dismantling: metal poles and bars clanging as they were separated, carpet tubes here and there, looking like thin rolls of wheat in a fall field. The three men were talking as they walked. Tom was doing most of it, something I've noticed he does when he's working. He doesn't talk so much when he's not. The other two were taking notes, occasionally adding something to what Tom was saying. They seemed to be heading toward us.

I sipped some coffee I'd found one booth over and waited, still wondering about Barry Firth. Joan and George junior had left with Jeep to get yet another snack in the coffee shop. By the time we hit the road, just when Tom and I would want lunch, the kids would be sugar-logged and cranky. I was willing to bet on it; it had happened just like this that often.

Jeep had been right about his miracle pill. Within five minutes he was up and walking as if nothing was even wrong. He had acted more civil to me, too, although I could sense animosity still.

Hart had ripped apart some discarded cartons and was reassembling them as frames for his foam core. The nails he'd driven had split the thin wood, so he'd just plugged in the glue gun and was waiting for it to get hot. Sally and he had moved all furniture off the carpet, and she was rolling it up. Someone turned on a power drill just as Tom and his men walked up to me. Although it was loud, its grinding was intermittent. I felt it, though, each time it was turned on, its vibrations pulsating from the power outlet, along the cement floor, and up my stool to my legs.

"Are you close to finishing?" I asked Tom, then said good morning to the two men with him.

Tom nodded. "Details" was all he said. His men looked at him.

I was tired of letting it go at that. So I said, "What kind of details? Barry Firth?"

Tom nodded again. I looked in his eyes to see what the nod meant. What I saw there completely bowled me over. Guilt. As a mother and daughter, I can spot it from ten miles. I'd never seen it in Tom Turgood's eyes before. I couldn't believe I was seeing it now.

28

"Is he dead?"

"I'm so damn sorry." His eyes were steady on mine, but his voice was thick.

I looked beyond him toward the boneyard doors. "Back there?"

"A shipping box. He'd been cut up bad."

So it was Barry's blood on the papers. I closed my eyes and thought about yesterday, Hart and I passing through the boneyard when we did, Barry already dead or dying in a damned floral shipment box. So many people passing through there.

"What happened, dammit? Where was all his protection?"

"They were with him most of the afternoon. You know that." His voice was a monotone.

I began shaking my head. "No. They weren't with him. Barry's dead. That's what I know." I continued shaking my head. "No," I said again. Then I stopped, peered into his eyes, and pointed my finger at him. "Where was his protection?"

"They were pulled," he whispered, and reached to touch my elbow.

I stepped back. "What?" The word fell out of me in a rush of lost air. I didn't want to look in his eyes. I didn't want to hear any more.

He cleared thick mucus from his throat. I watched the cartilage in his neck move when he swallowed. "After Lewis confessed," he said evenly. "That's when they were pulled."

Someone turned the drill on then, driving its rumblings into me and up my spine. I began to slip off the stool.

Tom's hand steadied me. "You okay?"

"No," I said dully. "Should I be?" I turned away from him.

I noticed the other two policemen were walking around in our general area, not standing with us anymore. One of them had gone over and looked behind the still-assembled divider panel in a booth across the aisle. The other was standing in the wide hallway. He was slowly, methodically turning around, his eyes like a pair of periscopes surfacing. They were looking for someone or something.

Tom noticed Sally still struggling with the carpet. "When did Jeep bring your employees in?"

"He didn't. He sent an underling," I said sarcastically.

I checked my watch again. It was eleven forty-five already.

I followed the one policeman's eyes, the policeman who was standing in the aisle. I could barely see it coming then. About fifty yards down, half the length of a football field, a man approached with flowers. At first, they looked only red. At twenty-five yards, they began to take form. A few yards later, as he angled his gait toward our corner of the floor, I knew they were for me. All I saw, though, were mounds of bright red carnations, not the hearts they'd formed.

Tom quickly moved between me and the poor delivery man. Never before had I heard him so angry. "Get the hell out of here," he screamed. "Don't you have any sense? It's over. Over, you hear? Get out! Get out! Get out!"

The deliveryman looked afraid, but he kept walking.

The two cops grabbed the man by his elbows and turned him sharply around. When they did, the arrangement fell out of his hands to the hard cement floor. A half-dozen red carnations flopped down around the still form and a lone white one tumbled to my feet.

"Look what you did to her flowers, you fools," the man said loudly.

"Get him out of here," Tom repeated, although not as angrily.

The policemen secured him again and walked toward the show's entrance. Around us, people seemed only mildly interested. They were too busy trying to get out of here themselves, to get back home or back to work before the week was lost entirely.

Hart had put down his glue gun, though. He'd been sitting with his legs crossed, exaggerated like a yoga position. He stood without uncrossing them, the outsides of his feet taking his weight. I can't describe the expression on his face as he stared at Tom. It wasn't the anger I was feeling. It wasn't as bold as that. His face spoke more to a great disappointment, a letdown of major proportions.

He stepped around the overturned flowers and stood between Tom and me, facing me, his back to Tom. Hart didn't say a word; he simply hugged me tightly. I resisted the hot salty tears fighting to escape my eyes. It was almost as if Hart's embrace was squeezing them up and out of me like juice being pressed from a lemon.

I looked down at the arrangement. It seemed so innocuous lying there. Its green foam was exposed like the panties of a comatose woman thrown from a car wreck. The plastic cardholder had broken off and lay in two pieces next to it. The envelope had skidded a foot or so away. I couldn't help myself. I had to see the words. I bent down and picked it up.

"No, Sydney. Why?" Tom said. He tried to guide my elbow away.

I pulled it from his grasp. "I have to."

I opened it and stared at the words awhile. "Broken Hearts Don't Heal." I said it to myself over and over.

I said to Hart, "None of the ads said these words. Neither did the articles." I stared into his eyes. "Could the killer be talking about himself? Do you think that's possible?"

Hart shrugged and turned his focus to Tom.

"No," I said. "I asked you. I didn't ask Tom."

"Hart doesn't know anything about it, Sydney," Tom said. "Why are you asking him?"

Hart turned back to me. He touched my arm. "I just knew you were upset."

I would have given anything in the world, at that moment, to talk to anyone other than Tom Thurgood. I had to ask him one question, though. I looked into his eyes, eyes I used to consider my refuge from the evils I saw elsewhere. Eyes I'd thought reflected a pure soul. Here was a man I would have trusted with my life. In fact, I had trusted him and, because of that trust, I was in a position I wouldn't wish on my worst enemy.

"Tom," I began, wondering if he'd lie to me now, "do they have results from those mugs I sent you?"

His head nodded slowly as he spoke. "Colchicine like you thought."

My mind went immediately to three or four people. Any one of them could have easily gotten colchicine. Most of the people at the show could have gotten their hands on it, in fact.

Hart said, "Knowing that doesn't help you much with *these* people, does it?" He would have been right if I hadn't focused in on just a few of them now.

But Tom and I were staring at each other, not listening to Hart at all. Tom seemed very nervous to me. And deflated at the same time. If I hadn't been so damn mad at him, I might have been concerned.

I said, "What about the fingerprints? Any on the second mug?"

He nodded. Very slowly.

"The old florists' promo mug?"

He continued to nod although he said nothing. What did he want me to do? Pull it out of him?

That's when the phone rang and everything started falling into place. It startled all of us. I turned toward the sound of the ring and saw Sally answering it. She listened for a few seconds, said something herself, then motioned for me to come there. When I walked to the phone, both Hart and Tom did too.

"Found your girl," Merilee said right away. "I knew I would once I got to our archives. How are things going down there?"

"Not too good, Merilee," I said. I watched Tom's face the entire time I stayed on the line. His eyes were focused on me. Like maybe he was expecting some answers too. I remember thinking I wasn't going to tell him what I found out. Hart and Sally stood around too, although Sally had no expectation of anything. How could she, unless Hart had shared with her what he knew?

"Oh my God, Sydney," Merilee said when I told her about Barry. I'd forgotten she knew him from his days at the paper. "The poor boy didn't ever harm a flea. I didn't know he'd come out of the closet."

"Did you know he was gay for sure?"

"Oh, yes. Barry told me that when I'd known him just a short time. When he was leaving his wife, if I remember correctly." People always told Merilee things they didn't share with the rest of us. Here was another example. "He didn't want anyone to know, though. I guess he changed his mind."

"He didn't change his mind." I looked straight at Tom when I said, "He wasn't killed because he was gay. The police were wrong about that."

She was silent for a few seconds while I continued to stare hard at Tom. Tom's stare at me never wavered either. He still appeared nervous.

"Damn," she said. "Poor Barry."

"The woman in the picture," I said, although I felt guilty after hitting her with the news about Barry.

"Ah, yes. The girl. Here's what I found out. Judy Kiser was divorced with no kids when she died in 1980. I found an article about her death in addition to the obituary. The poor girl jumped to her death from a bridge overpass. Looks like it was one of those hours long standoffs with psychologists and ministers. Nobody could talk her out of it. Not even her brother."

I felt like I needed something to write this all down on. I asked Merilee to hold on while I located a pen and pad. Both Hart and Sally were looking for my pocketbook and client idea pad before I could even ask them. Sally returned with it. I uncapped my pen and returned to the phone.

"Okay, I'm back," I said. "You still there?" I wrote down the woman's name, and beside it wrote *1980—suicide*.

I stood there with my pen poised.

Merilee laughed, then said, "I know why I didn't remember the name Kiser now. I knew there weren't any Kiser florists, remember? Turns out Kiser was her married name. I knew there weren't more than one or two florists prominent enough to mention in those days."

"What was the big one? Willys? Wasn't that the name?" I noticed Tom shifting his stance as I said that name. His eyes didn't change, however.

"Yes, it was Willys all right. The girl was one of them, but she and her husband owned it when that picture was taken in 1958. She'd taken over for her parents that year. They'd run it since the thirties. Willys Florists had been around since the mid-eighteen hundreds. Old, old Charlotte institution."

I interrupted her. "Not any longer, they aren't. Was Willys Florists out Central? Is that a fact?"

"Yes, Sydney Allen, that's a fact." She laughed. "You're starting to sound all legal like your daddy and your brother."

"Sorry, Merilee. I didn't mean to. I'm just trying to sort the facts here from the fiction. I'm afraid I've been getting a little of both until now." I took a deep breath. "So, Judy Kiser was Judy Willys at birth," I said, and started to write that on my pad.

"No, no, no," she said. "I was getting to that. She was Judy Ford. Her mother was a Willys. She married a Ford, but the mother had inherited the business. I even remember the Ford kids. They were good kids, hard-working kids. Judy worked in the shop, if I remember correctly. Her brother was the delivery boy."

"The brother's name?"

"You know, I've been sitting here trying to remember. The paper said she was survived by her brother Albert, but that's not the name I remember. Seems he had a nickname. Yes, yes he did. I remember now. When he turned sixteen and started driving all over town, his daddy converted an old Willys Panel for him to drive. Outfitted it with a cooler even."

"What's a Willys Panel?" I wished Merilee would get to the point.

"You don't know a Willys?" She laughed. "Well, I forget you're not my age sometimes, Sydney Allen. A Willys was the first Jeep. Came out of World War II. It was the rage everywhere. That was going to be their trademark, you know. Jeep Willys and all. So the boy got called Jeep. I never knew his name was Albert. I don't think anyone did. Wonder if he's still saddled with it."

"Yes, he's still saddled with it," I said to her while I stared at Tom. I told her I had to get off, I'd call her later.

It had all come together with that phone call, but I knew I'd suspected Jeep before then. I'd suspected other people, too, though. The formerly invisible Jerry who'd wanted Tina's job so badly. I thought he might have been willing to kill her for it. And for a few moments I'd suspected Rhyne Garrett. He'd resented what Tina represented as well, and he was old enough for those ads to hold special meaning. When I witnessed the anger he still harbored from his family's past, his guilt emerged as a real possibility. I was relieved it wasn't Peg. For all his bitching about the state of the industry, I knew he would never be affected. Not personally anyway. His disagreements with the Tinas and the Barrys were philosophical and his shedding of Joel as his lover wasn't that big a deal. Yet he'd told me himself that he worked with colchicine, and that fact had worried me. Poor Curtis Lewis was the only suspect who didn't have the ready access. He just happened to be at the wrong place, on the Center's steps, when Jeep needed a credit card and a knife.

I understood Tom's actions then. Understanding and accepting aren't synonymous, though. Maybe they should be, but they're not. Not when his actions, or lack of them, came close to killing me and had, in fact, killed Barry Firth.

Tom's expression had changed toward the end of my talk with Merilee. There was a finality about it and a dread. It was as if he'd heard exactly what I'd heard.

Hart said, "Was that important?" It must have shown on my face.

I didn't answer him. I was still looking at Tom.

"You knew" is what I said to Tom.

"I suspected," he said. "I had no facts."

"You do now, though. Don't you? They're Jeep's fingerprints on that mug, aren't they?"

"Even that wouldn't have been enough," he said. "We have him on tape drinking coffee with Joel Fineman." He looked down at the ground.

"You what? How long have you had that tape?"

"Since yesterday morning. He admitted drinking coffee with him. Said Fineman was an old friend. Until the colchicine showed up this morning, we didn't have a case against him." He stopped then, took a deep breath, looked at both Hart and Sally and finally back at me. Only then did he release the breath he'd taken. "Sydney, it's important you understand this. I know how you must feel." He reached out to me.

I couldn't stand hearing him. I wasn't willing at all to hear him, in fact. I cared about only one thing at that moment: that Tom or his men arrest Jeep Ford. Instinctively, I backed up. I held both hands up to make him stop.

"No, you don't. You don't know how I feel." I stepped farther back so that Sally and Hart were almost between Tom and me. "Why hasn't he been arrested?"

Tom stepped forward, but Sally and Hart moved together slightly, sheltering me from him. His face crumpled. I think he realized, for the first time, what his blind loyalty to Jeep could cost him personally.

"The three of us," he began, then stopped and looked around for the two officers who'd come with him. It was almost as if he'd forgotten they'd left. "We thought he was picking up your employees. Sydney, as long as he was a suspect I'd never have left him alone with you or the kids. We were going to wait for him here." His head dropped. A piece of his hair fell over his forehead like it always has. Only I didn't find it endearing this time. He searched my eyes for something I couldn't give. "Sydney . . . this is the hardest thing I've ever had to do." His eyes were moist. When I didn't respond, he sighed heavily. He turned around slightly and surveyed what he could see of the rapidly emptying exhibit hall. "Do you know where he's gone?"

I thought about it and then I remembered.

"Oh God no!" I screamed. "He's with the children!"

29

I took the stairs two at a time getting to the Center's upper level. Sally, Hart, and Tom were all behind me. Tom kept asking me where he'd taken them. I wouldn't answer, but Sally finally told him. When she did, he overtook me and ran ahead.

The College Street Café perches on a mezzanine level of the Center, visible from both the College Street and Stonewall Street entrances. I saw Joan and George junior immediately. They were sitting in a booth toward the front, near the College Street entrance. Tom had already reached them, was talking to them when Sally, Hart, and I got there.

Joan said, "What's wrong, Mom?" I suppose it was pretty obvious.

"Where's Jeep?" I said.

George junior looked from Tom to me. "Is Jeep sick again?"

Tom answered for me. It made me angry that he did. "Nothing's wrong, Joan," he said. "Nothing for you to be concerned about anyway. And no, George, Jeep isn't sick. He just limps sometimes."

George junior wasn't buying those words. His eyes said he didn't believe Tom. He knew Jeep was sick, very sick. He'd seen how sick himself. "Mom, is that true?" he said.

Joan started to answer. Her tone was upbeat. She said, "Of course it's true. Tom wouldn't—"

I cut her off. My kids weren't babies anymore. I could no longer shield them from truth—no matter how ugly. I said, "You know he's sick, George junior. But something else you need to know: Jeep's mind is sick too. He's done some very bad things. That's why Tom needs to find him."

I finally looked at Tom's profile as he gazed down at Joan and George junior. While I was still staring at it, I said to the kids, "Tom needs to stop him from hurting anyone else."

My daughter's face, normally so animated, appeared to freeze. Her mouth had been open when I said those few words. She didn't close it for thirty seconds.

I told myself I'd done the right thing. I'd been lied to in the name of protection, and it hadn't caused anything but harm. I was tired of doing that same injustice to my kids.

"Where did he go?" I asked them again.

George junior was eating a chopped pork barbecue sandwich. He almost knocked it to the floor when he placed both hands on the table and hit the side of the plate. Tom caught the plate just as it slid to the table's edge. George junior then pulled himself up so he could slide his knees under his body for more height. His eyes were on the Stonewall Street door. He pointed there.

"He went out that door, Mom. He put a twenty-dollar bill on the table, then got up and said there was something he had to do."

"He said not to tell anybody." Joan sounded angry, but

not at Jeep. Her anger was directed at her brother. And probably at me too. I'd said some things she'd just as soon not hear.

Tom said, "How long ago?" I couldn't help noticing he asked Joan instead of her brother.

"About ten minutes ago," she said, her voice still showing shades of disgust. At Joan's age, snitching was probably only slightly less offensive than murder.

I turned to Sally and Hart. "He's a sick man so he couldn't have gone very far. Will you two stay until I get back?"

"He wasn't limping anymore at all," George junior said. "He took more of his pain pills."

Tom had already started running toward Stonewall. I looked beyond him as I tried in vain to catch up. All I could see was the solid white plain that Charlotte had become. Every bit of it a wasteland, every bit of it frozen.

The twenty-degree air hit me hard as I opened the glass door. Tom was crossing Stonewall by then. I was afraid I'd lose sight of him right away since he was so much faster. I started for the steps, but stopped short. They looked like a frozen waterfall. Sand was spread on the ones closest to railings so I held on and, oh so slowly, walked down that way. It still took me a few minutes. I wondered the whole time how Tom had maneuvered them so quickly.

Traffic was one impediment I didn't have to worry about. I heard one truck roar, but I didn't see it. It was downshifting as it entered the Center's underground roadway. There was no other traffic on Stonewall.

Tom was in the parking lot across the street. He was standing beside an old red Jeep with oversized all-weather tires. The car had on its hardtop rather than the canvas convertible type I'm used to seeing. He was rubbing the navy sleeve of his sweatshirt against the frosted windows, trying to clear them enough to see inside. Neither of us had on our coats. Jeep didn't either, if I remembered right. I could picture his khaki coat on the metal tree in the booth.

The friendly redheaded attendant came over to see if he could help us.

Tom told him he was looking for the car's owner. "Seen a policeman about sixty? In uniform. A little overweight. He would have come from the Center."

The attendant was grinning, the gap in his front teeth as prominent as it had been Wednesday night. "Yeah, yeah," he said quite pleasantly. "Nice man. He tipped me a twenty and I hadn't even done anything for him."

"When?" Tom's tone was urgent.

The young man didn't recognize Tom's impatience for what it was. Perhaps he interpreted it as eagerness. At any rate, he saw that simple question as an invitation to talk about the man who'd been so uncommonly nice to him. "He tried to give me sixty but I wasn't taking that. I said, who are you? That Gates guy or somebody?" He stopped and laughed.

Tom screamed at him then. "I want to know how long ago, dammit. Now! Tell me how long ago!"

The poor guy closed his mouth, then swallowed hard. "Well, not more than five, at most ten, minutes ago. I'm sorry if I—"

Tom cut him off again. "Where? Where is he? Did you see where he went?"

The attendant turned around slowly. I remember he was wearing a baby blue wool cap with a wool strap under his chin like babies' caps have. The snap on his strap must have broken because he'd tied it in a bow to keep it secure. As he turned he was looking in all possibilities of direction, all 360 degrees. When he'd turned completely past me, I noticed the baby blue bow under his jaw. At that moment he reminded me of a doll I'd owned when I was a child. I couldn't get it out of my head. It's strange what I remember.

"You must have seen him walk off," Tom was saying. "He gave you the damn money. Surely he didn't vanish."

"No, sir, I didn't see where the man went." He lowered his eyes to the ground in front of his feet and added, "Guess I was too busy looking at the twenty?"

"Go on then," Tom said. He'd made the attendant feel guilty about Jeep's disappearance, something he had nothing to do with.

"Go where, Tom? It's his lot, not yours." I didn't care how bad Tom felt. He shouldn't have made the attendant share in his guilt.

The redhead retreated to his booth. He even lowered his glass window and the paper shade behind it to sit in cold darkness. As long as that boy lives, I thought, he will never understand what happened between them that day.

Tom and I just stood there then. Neither of us had spoken to the other, with the exception of my defending the redhead. Tom continued to turn and think.

I listened for the snow's quiet power. In its silence I heard something more. A rhythmical whooshing, like the surges of big trucks on a highway somewhere. My eyes followed that sound to Morehead Street two short blocks away and its bridge passing over Charlotte's inner-city beltway. I knew then that's where Jeep had gone.

"I think I know where he went," I said to Tom. "I hope I'm wrong."

He watched me for a second, then turned toward the west as I had.

"Jeep's dying, Tom," I said, even though I'd promised I

wouldn't. "He'd just as soon end it today, I think. Maybe that's what it's all been about. His sister's honor before he joins her." I was groping for something that might make sense, no matter how flawed the reasoning might end up being.

Tom didn't look in my eyes, although I was looking in his. I really tried to connect with him as we stood there. It would be the last time I would.

"He's not terminal," Tom said, allowing his anger to show.

"Yes, he is. You don't know everything. He has bone cancer. A little honesty here might be good for everyone—especially Jeep."

I watched a stream of tears begin to flow down Tom's cheeks. There was nothing I could do to make his sorrow go away. He needed to feel it. I didn't want to feel sorry for him, but I did.

He hadn't made the connection with the overpass, but I didn't want to tell him that too. "How did his sister die?" I said, hoping it would be enough.

"I just know she killed herself," he said softly. "I don't know how, only that Jeep couldn't talk her out of it. The experience shattered him. I never understood how much." His tears tracked the lines in his worried face. He brushed them away with the same shirtsleeve he'd used on Jeep's frosted window. "God, where is he?"

"Maybe the Morehead bridge," I said, and hoped my instincts were off this time.

I'd like to say we ran to the overpass, but we didn't. We couldn't. We trudged, at best. All the angles were gone, angles you never think matter. Like the right angle of a curb, the pitch of a mound of dirt, the dip to a drain grate. The snow had flat-lined them all or softened them so that their discovery through my Wellies was unexpected. Nothing had been cleared or sanded where we walked. Not the sidewalks, nor the closed parking lot one block over. We both slid and fell. Neither of us stopped to help the other at those times. We were making our ways separately to the bridge. There was nothing left for either of us to say.

The I-277 overpass at Morehead Street runs sixty-five to seventy feet, not very long as bridges go. Along its outer perimeters are pedestrian walkways protected by waist-high concrete railings. Atop the outside railings is an iron bar running horizontally the whole way across. In all the years I've lived in Charlotte, I've never seen anyone walk on these walkways. They're used primarily for what Jeep was about to do: jumping to one's death down on 277. I knew of three who'd done it successfully and one whose attempt failed.

A utility worker had noticed him first. He'd pulled his truck off the road beside the overpass and was standing beside it. He told us Jeep demanded he stop there.

"He said he'd jump if I came closer so I haven't." He spoke to Tom: "I think he's a police officer. He has on a uniform."

Tom thanked the man. "Yes, he's one of ours," he said. I knew he'd chosen those words purposely.

Jeep had placed himself squarely in the middle of the side of the bridge. He was leaning away from the outside railing, his hands firmly holding the iron bar on top. Except for his hands and feet, no part of him even touched. He was arched, sort of like a bow when pulled back or a diver on the verge of a dive. I closed my eyes when I first saw him there. He was ready, and I knew it.

Tom called out to him. Said he was coming. The utility worker and I stayed where we were.

When Tom was fifteen feet from him, I heard Jeep yell, warning him not to come closer. Tom stopped right there.

Then they talked. From where we were, though, I couldn't hear anything that was said. I'm glad I couldn't. Some talk shouldn't be heard. Once, I saw Tom wipe a tear away. Jeep never budged.

Someone must have reported the drama. Sirens began in the distance and moved closer with each passing second. I wondered who'd called, instinctively looked around for an office window in view. No building looked close enough to Tom, not with an angle to see this anyway. Then I heard noise from below the bridge. I walked to the sloping guardrail to look down. At least ten cars had pulled off the beltway, their drivers and passengers outside now. They were watching the scene as if it were a movie. Some were yelling at him. Horrible things. One called him selfish. One told him, "Come on and jump." I saw a woman holding a car phone too and assumed she'd called 911.

I walked back to where I'd stood before and noticed Tom had worked himself to within five feet of Jeep. For him, that's an arm extended. At the same time, emergency vehicles began to arrive. They were gathering down on the beltway, not one of them up with us. I saw eight cruisers in all. I wondered if that bothered Jeep, his peers being brought in on this. They stopped traffic quickly in both directions, although the spectacle itself had slowed much of it already. I saw the detective who called himself Shep Scott get out of one of the cars. I saw Ollie and another reporter I knew setting up cameras on top of their van. A fire truck waited where Jeep couldn't see it on the other side of the overpass. If he changed his mind and needed a ladder, they had one.

Then Tom turned toward us and motioned for me to come. I froze. I didn't want to be part of that. To this day, I don't know how I felt about what was happening. A part of me wanted him to die out there. A part of me felt he should.

Tom turned again, frantic this time. He screamed my name.

The utility worker gently pushed the small of my back.

Within a few feet of Tom and less than ten feet from Jeep, I stopped.

"Sydney's here," Tom said. His tone was what he'd use with a child.

"A riddle," Jeep said. He sounded high, disconnected, floating. It could have been the Ativan. He'd had four, five, or more in the last hour.

"What steals into your heart at night and, while you're dreaming, whisks your dreams away and, with them, the heart that houses them?"

I didn't understand what he was talking about, but how could I tell him that? When I didn't say anything, Tom glared, nodded furiously.

"What, Jeep?" I said weakly.

"What comes to you unbidden, cuts the cord of birth and wags you over the universe till, wagging so, you think you dance?"

I swallowed with difficulty. "What?" I said again. "What does, Jeep?"

"Come on, Sydney. You think you dance. You know. I know you know."

Tom stared at me. What did he want me to say?

I shook my head. I didn't know what either of them wanted me to say.

"You know now, don't you, Sydney? You know."

Tom mouthed for me to say yes.

So I did.

Tom was nodding his head at me, thanking me in his way for helping him, when Jeep jumped.

30

The snow did melt that Sunday. We had flooding on Kings Drive and some of the other low-lying streets. The temperature set a record, in fact, at seventy-six degrees. That's one of the downsides to living in Charlotte: these drastic fluctuations. It happens in both spring and fall, four months out of twelve. So I never feel prepared.

I'm told there was still standing water at Jeep Ford's funeral the Tuesday after. I was at work so I wouldn't know. On East Boulevard we had some melting still, but nothing like standing water. Rhyne Garrett was at the funeral, though, and he told me about the water problem.

Rhyne was by the office yesterday. He's been here a lot recently because of the new silk line. It's going to be a big line, a big investment, and understandably he's a little nervous about it all. He's delighted with the plans Hart has drawn up for it, however.

Hart's stepped up around here. And it's not just the Garrett business. He seems to understand the need for income all of a sudden. That correlation he's never seen, the direct line from work to food he's always disavowed. He sees it all now. He's handling most of the silk line without me. I just sit here and wait for questions. He's good about asking when he needs to and just as good about knowing when he doesn't need to.

Rhyne and I have talked about Jeep only once—the afternoon of the funeral. I didn't want to hear what he had to say because he started by making excuses for him.

"Look what you're doing here," I said. "You can't make excuses for murder."

"That's not what I'm doing," he insisted.

"What then?"

"About how he was before. I wanted you to know. I think you would have liked him, in fact."

When I didn't stop him, he talked. I knew some of it already from Merilee, but it did Rhyne good to talk so I let him. They'd known each other since toddlers, that knowing that's always been there. Jeep's great gift to the friendship was his loyalty, he said. "Once Jeep decided you were his friend, he would have done whatever he had in his power for you. I think it's the loyalty that sent him over."

It sounded like more excuses to me. I told him so.

"I'm not making them. I told you that. Whys don't justify a killing, but they sure can shed light on it. Jeep would've cut his arm off for that sister. She married a bad one and that just made old Jeep all the more loyal."

"Stop it, Rhyne. I'm telling you I'm not interested."

"Let me finish now. He didn't marry because of Judy. Some people might think that made Jeep a little odd, but I knew where it came from. It was the loyalty. See, he wasn't going to let her go just like that. When Willys closed after all those years, Judy had nowhere to turn. Except to Jeep. The girl thought she'd destroyed the family name when she lost the business. Jeep couldn't convince her otherwise."

"So Jeep decided to kill the people whom he deemed were to blame." I knew I was sounding sarcastic.

"Jeep was always there for her."

"Of course." I clipped the words. I wanted him to stop. Rhyne sighed.

"Look. I know he was the best friend a man can have. Now you're telling me he was the best brother a woman can have. I stipulate to both those. I just like to add the rest when Jeep's name comes up. He murdered a florist he'd known for thirty years and a woman who'd never even met him. And, when those weren't enough, he picked up some scissors and slaughtered a poor grocers' mouthpiece. That's all Barry Firth was, after all. A talking head. He made no decisions for the grocers. Just like me, Rhyne. I don't make decisions for you or for any of my clients. Yet I was next on his list. Goddamn, Rhyne. The man was killing symbols."

The reason we've never discussed Jeep again is what he said next. Merilee didn't believe me when I told her. He said, "Jeep meant well."

That was that.

Actually, I have another theory about what Jeep meant by all the evil he did. I give him more credit than the others. I think he intended that show to stop at the start. I think he was calling bluffs. He'd been threatening Tina and Barry for a year. Probably Joel, too, although, of course, we'll never know that for sure. Like an elaborate game of chicken, only nobody flinched when the time came. So then he turned to me. I'd studied the way the industry had changed. He knew it because he'd heard me talk. He knew I'd used old ads for the UFAS booth. He thought I'd get the connection. He thought somewhere along the way I'd say, "Hey, everybody. Somebody's telling us something here. Let's close this show and find out." He wanted the show to fail and the participants in it to fail and the alliances being formed to fall through. He wanted to save his sister, even though she'd been dead for years. What gave him the nerve for any of that was his own imminent death.

I don't think he ever imagined it would go so far. After the first murder, after Joel, I'm sure that he thought we'd find out. We might have, too, if the florist had been able to get her hands on the flowers Jeep stipulated. When she couldn't, the whole plan was backed up and he had to kill both Joel and Tina on the same day.

What kept us from seeing was something no one would have anticipated. It was something so simple. It was Curtis Lewis and his hatred of gays. If Curtis hadn't hated gays, Jeep might have gained our focus. We would have asked our whys with more probing. We might have read the ads and articles. We would have seen the growing concentration of industry in the hands of a few. And, when we saw it, we might have commented on it. And Jeep hoped we'd have said it was bad. Jeep hoped we'd have understood.

But nobody saw anything like that because Curtis Lewis hated gays. We went with assumptions instead of questions. At least, some of us did. The ones who should have known not to, in fact. If there's anything that'll get a question unanswered, it's to go with the assumption instead of the why.

Like I said, that's just my theory. I have a couple of others too.

Something Tom said then keeps circling my mind. He said it wouldn't make any sense when it was over. I remember him saying it clearly. Of course, nobody expects of his good friend what Tom got from Jeep. That part, I am sure, leaves him numb. I'm also sure he's confused, just as I am. I don't know, though, because I haven't seen him.

I found out something else that afternoon Jeep died. Tom told me he hadn't shown that tape to his chief when he found it. He thought there'd be no need to, he said. Didn't want anybody, and he did mean anybody, making assumptions about his friend. I walked away at that point. Everything I know about it now I know only secondhand. The result, though, is that Tom's been put on leave.

I don't know what to say about Tom Thurgood. He's called me, but I can't talk to him. I know that he's hurting, but I can't. He isn't who I thought he was, and I can't handle that. Not now anyway.

I'm having a hard time handling lots of things these days. Thank goodness business has been slow. I haven't made a sales call in weeks. There's an ebb and flow to the advertising game. Maybe the tide's going out. I don't worry, though. It will come back.

I'm not sleeping well and that hasn't helped. It's the nightmares. Not the nightmares I would have expected. Not Jeep out there on the bridge. I dream about his riddles instead, about what they might mean. In my dreams, a dense shadow approaches. I know it has come for my heart. I run from it. I hide. I confront it sometimes. Always, it evaporates before my eyes. Sometimes I think I know what it is. Could it be bitterness? It does fit. Bitterness ate away at Jeep as surely as his cancer did. Maybe that's too logical though. I know Jeep wasn't following logic. Was his second question the same riddle or a new one? What comes "unbidden" and "wags you" until "you think you dance"? In my dreams, I twirl and twirl and twirl on the surface of a ball. I am dizzy from the turning. I think the answer to the second riddle is insanity. Maybe it's the answer to everything.

I'm thinking a change might help. A trip. The kids and I are going to Savannah for Easter next week. We never got there the weekend we were going for the tournament.

George junior has asked me to drop his "junior." I told him I thought I could do that. I know I can try. I was worried about him and his sister just after the Jeep thing happened. Especially his sister. I shouldn't have been. Not really. They are so much stronger than I let them be. Sometimes I'm amazed how much stronger.

In the end, I told Joan and George everything. About the murders. About Tom's refusal to see what was happening. Even about how close my own murder might have been. They now know everything I do about Albert "Jeep" Ford. They know how he lived and they know how he died that day on the Morehead Street bridge. They understand that he was a man who broke in two and, when he did, picked up his bad self and left the good to memories long dead. They don't hate him. They do hate what he did. They do hate that he killed. And for killing himself too. They even hate that.

I'm still sorting out how I feel. I'm not sure what I hate and why. Nothing's quite that simple anymore. I wish it were.